"Stevie, you're all wet."

Two huge blue eyes stared back up at David. There was evidently no ready response for such a charge. The little tyke continued to suck his thumb and look limpidly at him.

David glanced at his watch. Eight-fifty-four. He must be getting old to be totally wiped out so early. He sighed. "You need a complete overhaul, kiddo. And it's past your bedtime. Your mom needs to give you a bath, clean diapers and pajamas."

David stopped and thought about that for a moment. Annie was out in the kitchen putting away dishes and scrubbing kettles. She ran this race around the obstacle course of the campground and motherhood every day. It probably made her more tired than anything *he* could claim.

Thinking about Annie exhausted, trying to bathe five overtired children, twisted something painful inside his chest.

"Come on, Stevie," David said as he lugged the little one toward the stairs. "You, too, Amy. Let's round up the rest of the gang and get the bath brigade started."

Dear Reader,

Welcome to Silhouette **Special Edition**...welcome to romance. Each month Silhouette **Special Edition** publishes six novels with you in mind—stories of love and life, tales that you can identify with—as well as dream about.

This Valentine's Day month has plenty in store for you. THAT SPECIAL WOMAN!, Silhouette **Special Edition**'s new series that salutes women, features a warm, wonderful story about Clare Gilroy and bad-boy hero Reed Tonasket. Don't miss their romance in *Hasty Wedding* by Debbie Macomber.

THAT SPECIAL WOMAN! is a selection each month that pays tribute to women—to us. The heroine is a friend, a wife, a mother—a striver, a nurturer, a pursuer of goals—she's the best in every woman. And it takes a very special man to win that special woman!

Also in store for you this month is the first book in the series FAMILY FOUND by Gina Ferris. This book, *Full of Grace,* brings together Michelle Trent and Tony D'Allessandro in a search for a family lost... and now found.

Rounding out this month are books from other favorite writers: Christine Rimmer, Maggi Charles, Pat Warren and Terry Essig (with her first Silhouette Special Edition).

I hope that you enjoy this book and all the stories to come. Happy St. Valentine's Day!

Sincerely,

Tara Gavin
Senior Editor

TERRY ESSIG

FATHER OF THE BROOD

Silhouette®

SPECIAL EDITION®

Published by Silhouette Books New York

America's Publisher of Contemporary Romance

For my children, who drove me over the edge and into a fantasy world long ago. But it was a great trip and I've met an awful lot of interesting characters in that other world. I love you all.

SILHOUETTE BOOKS
300 East 42nd St., New York, N.Y. 10017

FATHER OF THE BROOD

Copyright © 1993 by Terry Parent Essig

All rights reserved. Except for use in any review, the reproduction or utilization of this work in whole or in part in any form by any electronic, mechanical or other means, now known or hereafter invented, including xerography, photocopying and recording, or in any information storage or retrieval system, is forbidden without the permission of the publisher, Silhouette Books, 300 E. 42nd St., New York, N.Y. 10017

ISBN: 0-373-09796-4

First Silhouette Books printing February 1993

All the characters in this book have no existence outside the imagination of the author and have no relation whatsoever to anyone bearing the same name or names. They are not even distantly inspired by any individual known or unknown to the author, and all incidents are pure invention.

®: Trademark used under license and registered in the United States Patent and Trademark Office and in other countries.

Printed in the U.S.A.

Books by Terry Essig

Silhouette Special Edition

Father of the Brood #796

Silhouette Romance

House Calls #552
The Wedding March #662
Fearless Father #725

TERRY ESSIG

lives in northern Indiana. She has six children attending five different schools, playing four different musical instruments and participating in at least three sports at any given time. They are Scouts, Young Astronauts and Earth Crusaders. Thirty-six first cousins drop by. Terry finds it all...inspirational, she guesses.

Prologue

"Why in God's name does every contract we have with Glenn Data Processing turn into such a complete nightmare?" David Kennedy leaned back in his chair, removed his glasses and rubbed his eyes. "Honest to God, doesn't Victor Glenn have anything better to do with his time than argue over every comma and every dot over every *i?*"

"No, he doesn't. You know that by now. When his wife died, he tried to get his daughter to move her family back from Wisconsin and in with him, but it didn't work. You remember Annie, don't you? She used to work here. Annie had gone back to nature and wanted nothing to do with the business world ever again," his second in command, Mary Ellen McGee, responded.

"Man, that was years ago. You'd have thought he'd come out of his funk by now. The man needs to get a life," David stated baldly, slipping his glasses back on and blinking tiredly. "He needs to reconcile with the daughter. She's been gone at least ten years. There must be a couple of kids by now. Old Vic needs some other interests in life besides driving me crazy. A couple of grandkids'd do nicely as a diversion.''

"Actually, I never completely lost contact with Annie. She's got five children and was widowed last year. Her husband was killed in a hunting accident, she said last time I talked to her.''

"Really? That's rough.'' David bounced the eraser end of his pencil against the highly polished surface of his desktop. It left little round smudge marks. He ought to stop, but he was restless and not ready to go back to the fine print on the contract yet. "I can't even begin to imagine dealing with five kids by myself. Vic ought to get up there and help her out," David commented idly as he flipped through the remainder of the contract to see how many pages were left to go through.

Mary Ellen eyed David thoughtfully. "You're right, of course. A reconciliation is exactly what's needed. But how in the world would you go about pulling one off? They're both stubborn as can be.''

"Hell if I know," David admitted as he leaned back and stretched so far behind himself his hands hit the picture window behind his desk. He yawned.

Mary Ellen leaned forward and circled a couple of figures on the page in front of her. "These numbers don't look right.''

David sat up and looked at the page. "How'd I miss that? They don't look right, do they? I tell you, Mary Ellen, when this is all over I'm taking some time off. I need a break.''

Mary Ellen looked at him in surprise. "Really? In the three years you've been branch manager, you've yet to take a vacation. Where will you go?''

He shrugged. "I don't know. Someplace. Maybe I'll try camping.''

"Camping! Are you serious? You've never struck me as the outdoorsy type."

"Hell, I'm not talking Canadian wilderness—just something peaceful and civilized. Rustic, but with a working toilet, you know?" David had no intention of giving up the past several centuries worth of progress toward human comfort. Nature was okay in its place, and as far as he was concerned that place was right next to a hot shower. "I'm not even thinking of going too far. Maybe an established campground in Wisconsin or possibly the Michigan peninsula. Something simple like that."

Mary Ellen eyed him consideringly. "I know just the place. Right over the Illinois–Wisconsin border. It'd only take about an hour and a half from here. Clean, secluded, but with all the amenities. Central toilets, showers and a laundry facility. Even has a small camp store in case you've forgotten anything."

David didn't trust the expression on Mary Ellen's face. He'd seen it before and it always seemed to precede trouble. "Hey, wait," he said, slightly alarmed. "I'm not sure I actually want to do this. I'm just feeling restless. It will probably all pass over by tomorrow, so let's not do anything rash." He nodded at the contract in front of him. "How about if you go get the figures we need to check this. I want to finish it up today."

Mary Ellen rose. "Yes, they're on my desk. I'll get them." She paused with her hand on the doorknob. "But this is a great idea, David. You just leave everything to me. I'll write out the directions and—"

"You're no more a camper than I am. How do you know about this place?"

Mary Ellen shrugged David's suspicious question away. "Oh, you know. Friend of a friend kind of thing."

Her eyes gleamed with hidden humor as she studied David, making him even more ill at ease.

"Just forget about it, okay? I—"

"No, no. I think I even know somebody who'd lend you a tent and the other camping gear you'd need. I'll call him and get you all set up. Not to worry, David, you're in good hands."

She left before he could protest further, leaving him to wonder why the push for camping from Mary Ellen. Something was wrong with this picture.

Chapter One

The sun was going down again.

Even though Annie Glenn Cronin had steered away from the windows since shortly after lunch, the lengthening shadows in the living room kept her informed of the day's passage. She kept her face averted from the room's failing source of light as she swept through the front room, busying herself by picking up toys. Somehow, though, her feet carried her unwilling body over to the window and she braced herself on the sill as she stared out, gaging the sun's retreat. The golden orb's low autumn trajectory had it momentarily hung up, caught in the branches of the gnarled old trees in the small apple orchard guarding her campground's entrance. Too heavy for the branches to support for long, she knew the sun would soon finish its retreat, taking all the light with it.

A brief chill took her as she thought about the time of year. October's calendar position was one of working its way toward the winter solstice. Tonight's time of darkness would be longer still than last night's. Last night's had lasted an eternity.

She sighed as she watched the sun sink. "Maybe tonight won't be too bad," she said in an attempt to comfort herself. She knew she should turn away, busy herself. The coming night could well bring a return of the receding anxiety attacks and sense of hopelessness she was beginning to work herself out of. Of course, if she sat here and brooded, she'd have herself all worked up into a tizzy while she still had a bit of friendly daylight left. "Buck up," she directed and surveyed the room around her. Activity always proved a distraction. "Pick up the rest of the toys," she told herself. "And stop thinking. Thinking just gets you into trouble."

But her body was still propped on locked elbows in the window frame when the car turned into her driveway from the main road. Surprised, she leaned farther forward. It was not a car she recognized and she wasn't expecting any more campers. Her few hunters with reservations had already all checked in.

As her small clapboard-and-Wisconsin-stone house balanced on the crest of a small knoll and the season had cleared the apple trees out by the road of most of their leaves, Annie was able to watch the car's progress. It wound through the small overaged orchard slowly, in all likelihood as a concession to the rutted condition of the lengthy driveway, she acknowledged. The car bounced and Annie vowed that new stones for the potholed drive would be one of her first investments—just as soon as there was a little money to spare. As the car bobbed closer, color became distinguishable. Green. It was a forest-green . . . Mercedes. Her eyes widened. Now she was positive it was no one she knew and equally doubtful it was a last-minute camper looking for a spot. To her knowledge, not many Mercedes owners were into freezing their expensively clothed backsides camping in late October.

Annie left the window, snatched up the small granny-square afghan she used to protect the back of the living room sofa and threw it around her shoulders like a shawl. Opening the front door, she stepped out and waited on the stoop for the stranger to arrive and identify himself.

The car rattled to a stop not far from the front door. A tall, tawny-haired man in unfaded blue jeans and either a new or—God forbid!—an ironed flannel shirt climbed out and peered a bit uncertainly over the top of the car, studying her through glasses framed in thin black wire.

"Hello. Are you the owner?" he questioned tentatively. "Your campground was recommended by a friend. I'd like to rent a spot for a few nights."

Suddenly the man paused, peering over the car's hood more intently.

"Annie? Is it you?" Damn, unless David missed his guess, that was Victor Glenn's back-to-nature, used-to-work-at-WCN daughter on the stoop in front of him. He took off his glasses and tucked them onto the dash as his eyes narrowed. Mary Ellen had set him up, he realized. Pure and simple, that's what she'd done. He'd wring her neck when he got back.

Annie studied the man before her. He'd called her by name. First name at that. She hated it when that happened. It meant she'd met the person at some time or another and should at least have a vague recollection. Her poor memory for names and faces was one of her biggest trials. She never knew if she should try to fake it, hoping she would pull a name out of her brain before she gave the game away, or risk insulting someone by admitting she hadn't a clue who they were. She gnawed her lip for a moment, debating. It couldn't be anybody from the grocery, the library, the school or the church that she just wasn't recognizing out of context—not driving a Mercedes. Her noncommittal, "Yes, it's me," was a stall.

The wind whipped the calf-length skirts of her loose-fitting prairie jumper and white eyelet underskirt around her legs as she stood on the stoop. Her head was as high as her five-foot-two frame could hoist it, her cheeks were reddened by the wind and embarrassment at the stranger's intense scrutiny. She just knew she should know him.

Annie felt the recently blooming bud of her long-sought peace of mind curl back in on itself. This man, this Mr. With a Face and Body Like This You Ought to Remember My Name would not be an easy or restful acquaintance. She knew that fact as surely as she didn't know his name.

The man came around the car to the bottom of the steps. Although the stairs remained between them, his masculinity crowded her, made her want to take a step back. She did not allow herself to do so. For heaven's sake, she was a widow and the mother of five. She should be above being affected by blatant masculinity.

He spoke.

She shivered.

"Annie, you may not remember me, but—"

Annie leaned forward, caught by a certain husky tone in his voice. It jogged something. "David?" she questioned. "David from Worldwide Computing?"

"Why, yes."

A puff of elation brought a grin with it. Maybe she wasn't that far gone, after all. Then Annie Cronin, widowed mother of five, thought about the time she'd known David. Before the children, before the campground, before her marriage. It had been a simpler time, if she'd only known it, when her biggest problem had been trying to fit her artsy-crafty personality into a tailored gray wool business suit. She'd tried, for her parents' sake, to fit into their world, but the floppy neck bow on the cranberry silk shirt she'd used to set off that gray wool suit had done its best to strangle her and she'd ended up casting it aside at the first opportunity. While she'd never be sorry she'd had the children, in retrospect, changing blouses would have been a heck of a lot easier.

A lot of feelings she'd thought long buried welled up and her eyes grew moist as she gave into those emotions. Gathering up her skirt, she flew down the stairs and threw herself into the arms of those simpler times.

"Oh, David, it's so good to see you," she exclaimed when he staggered at the impact, but managed to hang on to his balance as well as her. She was mortified to find herself crushing his shirt and stepped back a bit, still smiling up at him a bit inanely.

David laughed a little uncertainly, wondering if his brief hiatus from Victor Glenn's multifootnoted contracts might be getting off to a less than auspicious start.

However, he was not the type who could turn around and just walk out on a lady in tears, even though it did seem an odd greeting from someone trying to build up a customer base. "Hell, Annie, if I'd known I was going to get a welcome like this, I'd have tried camping a long time ago," he said.

Annie smiled mistily, pleased that she'd controlled the tear ducts she'd considered hyperactive most of the past year. She hugged him again. "I'm just glad you're here now." Annie stood there, luxuriating in simply being held in someone's arms. She imagined David was wondering why she was so glad to see him. After all, they'd been co-workers at the same firm for a brief two years and even that small connection had ended years before. They'd never dated or anything, they'd just occupied the same office space during the same time frame.

How could she begin to explain the relief in allowing herself to be weak for even the short period of a hug? To let someone else hold her up, just for a moment. Although, come to think of it . . . "David, what are you doing here?"

"I just told you, I want to try camping."

"In October?" she asked, sounding mystified.

David looked over her head, off into the distance to the pink-and-orange sunset and the black silhouetted trees of the state park that took up behind Annie's home. There was no way of knowing if she kept up with her family's business. He picked his words carefully. "I couldn't get away until just now, and things at work were . . . getting to me. Sometime in the next year or so, I'll probably be transferred, maybe have to move." He shrugged. "I thought I'd try and squeeze some vacation time in while I could." David didn't know why the need to get away had been so strong. It never had been before. He only knew he had to shake it out of his system before the next step in his career plan began to unfold. New positions within the company demanded total concentration.

That old familiar sensation of cobwebbed brain-itis had asserted its presence and she shook her head to clear out any web spinners. David had been the mail-room clerk. They had no problem scheduling vacations. Come to think of it, how could a mail clerk afford a Mercedes? Things were just not clicking into place here.

"Annie, let's finish this discussion inside," he suggested. "You're starting to shiver. Now that the sun's down, it's too cool for you out here. Where's the camp office? Inside the house?"

He would have to remind her that the sun had set.

David turned and began steering her toward the front door. It seemed to sense their approach and, catching the same breeze that swirled Annie's skirt, slammed shut in their faces. Annie heard the lock click into place.

She looked at it and sighed. One more opportunity to show what a featherbrain she'd become. Well, she'd risen to the first occasion, she'd remembered his name. She'd rise to this one, as well.

"Annie?"

"Hmm?"

"The door blew shut."

"Uh-huh. I can see that."

His arm rode her waist. She seemed almost frail with the wind buffeting her as he guided her safely to the top step. "Do you, um, have your keys in your pocket?"

Annie found herself patting the hip area of her denim jumper, even though she knew they weren't there. "No, I don't guess I do."

David spoke as though feeling his way through a mine field. "Okay, do you maybe have one hidden outside, like under the doormat or in a flowerpot?"

Annie racked her brain, once more trying to remember where she'd tucked the key hidden for these occasions. Nothing came. "Yes," she finally admitted. "I did hide one out here." She shrugged. "In fact, I did such a good job I haven't been able to find it ever since. But don't worry," she went on, determined to put a good face on her mental aberration. "This has happened several times since I hid the spare key. After the first time, I started leaving the living room window closest to the door unlocked. All I have to do is jimmy it up and climb through."

"Annie, this is nuts," David informed her through gritted teeth as he supported her on his shoulders a few moments later while she worked on the window. His conscience was insisting on helping her back into her house before getting on with his vacation—he wondered how to tactfully inquire if there was another campground nearby—and he didn't like holding her ankles while she balanced on his shoulders. They felt slim and smooth. His hands easily encircled them. They felt . . . good. Too good.

Hell, he'd driven all the way up into Wisconsin at the tail end of a long workday to get away from Victor Glenn and his ilk. If he wasn't so tired, he'd turn right around. He got the distinct impression spending his well-deserved time off with Vic's daughter would not be particularly restive. She aroused protective feelings in him he'd thought buried with his frail mother.

Annie was well aware oddball things consistently happened to her. He didn't have to rub it in with snide comments about her being nuts. "Yes, well, welcome to Annie's resident funny farm and campground," she told him as she finally hoisted herself through the opening. She leaned over and rubbed her ankles in an attempt to dispel the warmth David's touch had generated before she turned and curtsied. "Ta-da! There, now go back over by the door. I'll get it from inside. In fact, I'll get the back door, as well."

"Annie, how often have you had to climb through your windows?" he asked once she'd unlocked the door and he was safely in the living room.

"Oh, just a few times," she hastily assured him. "Only once last week, in fact. Here, sit down." She swung her afghan shawl off her shoulders and patted it into place on the back of the sofa she indicated to him. The dimensions of the living room were small. This was the first time it seemed claustrophobic. "I usually register people in my office at the camp store, but I think I have some forms here, too."

"Oh. Good." *Get them and let me out of here.* Vic's daughter. Hell's bells. He'd kill Mary Ellen. Covertly he studied Annie. She was a lot better looking than Vic; she must have taken after her mother. He sat and breathed in her essence from the shawl. He squirmed, trying to escape the affecting aroma as he glanced around the room.

Annie tried to see it through his eyes. The older home had no entrance foyer. Instead, the front door opened directly into the living room. David appeared to be uncomfortable on her yellow-and-blue floral sofa. Once upon a time, it had been a good piece, but was now past its prime. David's constant shifting as though in search of a comfortable position attested to that fact.

The sofa ran against the one long unbroken wall in the room, the one that ran opposite the front door and windows. In an effort to protect the sofa's arms from sticky little fingers, she'd placed yellow Turkish hand towels on the two ends that matched the color she'd chosen for the walls. To tell the truth, David didn't look that out of place. His flannel shirt was decidedly rumpled now and his hair was windblown. He looked good.

Annie absently lowered herself into the yellow-and-blue plaid armchair she'd angled by the sofa and noticed the walls needed a coat of paint. She hadn't realized—it must be eight years . . .

"Annie? The registration papers?"

"Hmm? Oh, sorry, David. I'll get them." She rose and went into the dining room, trying to ignore the odd look he gave her.

He could hear drawers being pulled open.

"Tell me about yourself," she requested as she came back and handed him the form and a pen. She sank into the chair and, after slipping off her loafers, drew her feet up under her in the chair seat.

"Not much to tell." He squinted as he filled out his name and home address without the glasses he'd left in the car. "Finally finished up my degree after six years of night school and I've been steadily working my way up ever since. I became branch manager almost a year ago."

David had worked his way from mail-room clerk to branch manager since she'd left the firm? My gosh, he must be proud of that kind of accomplishment, and with justification. He'd achieved so much during the years she'd spent working herself into a hole. A definite twinge of jealousy poked her.

It was bittersweet for Annie to be reminded of how she'd walked away from everything David had fought for. She was now the one struggling. "It sounds like you have a lot to be proud of," she commented softly.

"Yeah," he admitted. "I guess I've done okay." Then before he could really think his next words through, he said, "I'd have liked for my mom to know I'd made it, though. She died before I had the chance to pay her back for the double and triple shifts she put in trying to keep a roof over our heads." There was something about Annie that brought his mother's plight to mind. He found himself leaning forward in Annie's worn armchair, contemplating his hands. He felt awkward at opening up so unexpectedly. "Well, here's the form." He passed it to her and then, to fill in the silence as she perused it, asked, "So how've you been? You enjoying life in the country?" Suddenly he remembered Mary Ellen's comment on her husband's death. He flushed at his tactlessness. "I heard about your husband," he admitted. "That's rough. I guess things have been hard for you?"

Rough? Hard? She mulled the words over. They seemed rather anemic adjectives. She massaged her forehead. "Yes, it's been—difficult." Another anemic word. "You hear about people shooting each other in the woods, but it never happens to someone you know. Certainly not to your own husband."

Uneasily David looked around. Life must have indeed been difficult for her the past year. The home's furnishings told him there wasn't much money available. No wonder memories of his mother had been popping in and out of his head.

"Do you want to talk about it, Annie? I'm not in any great hurry. It's already dark. There's no rush before I try to set up my tent." He was getting sucked in, by her looks, by her circumstances. He didn't like it, but was there any option? None that allowed for him to live with himself afterward.

She pressed her lips tightly together to prevent their momentary trembling, shaking her head. "What's to talk about?" she asked. "I sometimes wonder myself how things reached the point they're at now." She wondered a lot. One little decision made years ago and, boom, here she was.

"Tell me about Craig," David directed gently, hoping it was the right tack to take. The lady needed to talk. He didn't want to listen, but he was old enough to make a difference here, and he hadn't been when his own mother had literally worked herself to death. Restlessly he shifted on the sofa. He was bright enough, and honest enough, to know it wasn't just the helplessness he'd felt then that made him want to help Annie. She was a damn sexy lady. Her vulnerability only added to the aura. Vic's daughter turned him on. If her mind was anything like Vic's, it was a convoluted mess. Damn. He had no time for this right now. His career was paramount. Well, he had some time, a few days. He could handle it for that long. He went back to trying to draw her out. "Craig must have been something special to get an up-and-coming young executive like yourself to leave everything behind."

Annie bent forward in her chair and touched two fingers to each temple. Thinking back made her head hurt. "I hated that life, David. In retrospect, I think Craig represented my ticket out."

"What?"

Annie leaned back and rested her head on the chair back. Closing her eyes, she tiredly quoted a remembered grammar school English maxim. "Good, better, best. Never let it rest, until the good becomes the better and the better becomes the best."

David was having trouble following her chain of thought. "What's that supposed to mean?"

She opened her eyes and gave him a baleful look. "It means I was treading water as fast as I could, but I was still drowning. I couldn't be what they wanted me to be. I couldn't be a 'best' in their world and being 'good' wasn't enough. My mother was never able to get pregnant again. I was it. I was supposed to get some work experience at WCN, rise up the ladder a bit and then go to my dad's firm where I would eventually take over. The place would have gone under in a month with me at the reins."

Still puzzled—and a bit angry that someone would voluntarily walk away from an opportunity he would have killed for—David said, "You're exaggerating."

"Okay, so maybe it would have taken *two* months," she admitted. "But the Peter Principle was definitely at work. I was rapidly rising to my own personal level of incompetence. In way over my head by the time I left. My father refused to see I didn't have either his drive or his business brilliance. He just wouldn't listen."

Sounded like Vic, all right. David got up and paced off the short length of the room. "Annie, I admit I was pretty involved in my own problems back then, what with working days and attending school at night, but are you sure—"

"David, the only reason I got that last promotion was because my father's firm was such a big customer for WCN. Ted, the old branch manager, was many things, but stupid wasn't one of them."

He came back to her chair and stood in front of her. "Maybe you need to cut yourself some slack here, Annie. Maybe you could have done it." As far as he was concerned, she *should* have done it. If you had enough money to live comfortably and a stable job that provided a steady income, everything else would follow. David had vowed long ago that he would never again have to struggle to put food on the table or pay his rent.

Annie shrugged. "Maybe. I don't think so, but maybe. The thing was, I didn't *want* to do it. I hated all those dry numbers and figures. I hated computer programming. My gosh, misplace a lousy comma, mispunch a character, and the whole program is tied up in knots it would take a month of Sundays to unravel."

David had to grin. "You got me there. I hate the programming part, too." He sat back on the sofa and propped one foot on its opposing knee. Letting that one foot bob up and down energetically, he asked, "Admittedly this is none of my business, but are you saying you were just ripe for the picking when Craig showed up?"

Annie briefly thought about that, just as she had many times in the past. "No, no. Well, partially," she decided. "But certainly there was more to it than that." She tried to put feelings from years ago into perspective and then into words. "There was something in him that touched something in me." She struggled with her position in the chair while she struggled with her words. "We were, um, kindred spirits almost, you know?"

David captured his foot and held it still with his hand. "No, I'm sorry. I guess I don't."

How to explain it better. She drew her legs back underneath her until she sat Indian style in the wingback and drummed her fingers on her knees. "I had wanted to be an art major in college."

He looked surprised. "Did anybody at work know that?"

She shook her head. "No, what was the point in wallowing in lost dreams? My parents insisted on marketing, with minors in business and computer science. I didn't have the strength to stand up to them." She was still annoyed with herself for that. "Craig wanted to write poetry, maybe try a novel at some point."

David made a disgusted sound, then looked stricken. "God, I'm sorry. That was uncalled for. I love the business world and I haven't got an artsy bone in my body. It's kind of hard for me to relate—but go ahead. I won't interrupt again."

"I understand," she said graciously. Heck, it was the typical response from someone of David's bent. Translated that noise meant writing poetry is nice, but it doesn't put food on the table. She'd heard it before. Too bad it still hurt.

David lifted his head. "Sounds like the back half of the house is being invaded. Do you need to go check it out?"

Annie listened momentarily. "It's just the kids. They're fine." She called out, "Hey, you guys, I just mopped up the floor. Take your shoes off at the back door if they're muddy and wash up. I'm going to start dinner in a few minutes."

"Aw, Mom" came a chorus. "You mean it's not ready yet?"

What time was it? She glanced at her wrist and remembered her watch had died a few days before. It was hard to tell time by a freckle count. She sure hoped David didn't think she was trying. "No, it's not ready yet. But soon. I promise."

There were a lot of "aws" and "gee whizzes" that made her feel negligent.

"I guess I ought to get going." David rose.

She got her legs out from under her and stood, too, placing a hand on his arm. "No, don't go yet, David, stay for supper. It'll take a while to get your campsite set up and you'll be starving by then." She told herself the offer was because it was pleasant having another adult around to talk to. Surely it had nothing to do with the heady male scent tinged with the odors of autumn that clung to David and now perfumed the previously innocuous living room. She took a second look around to make sure she recognized her surroundings. She called to the back of the house, "Everybody wash up. Check your backpacks for homework, do a job or practice the piano. You've got about twenty minutes.''

Her attention had never left David. Now she stood in front of him and drank in the quiet strength she'd never noticed ten years before. Of course, they hadn't known each other much past first names then, either. Maybe the strength and purpose had been there all along. But they'd each been set on their own paths at the time, on different levels in the company's hierarchy. Studying him now, she felt a nagging sense that she'd been the loser when they hadn't become more than nodding acquaintances as co-workers.

David glanced at his wrist and she noticed a little resentfully he had a watch strapped to his arm.

"You're down to about seventeen or eighteen minutes to get dinner ready," he said while searching his pockets for his keys. "I'll get out of your way if you would just point me in the right direction."

"I wasn't just being polite. Stay," she requested softly. "Come meet the kids."

"But their dinner—"

"We'll talk while I make it. If you're good, I'll let you stir the pot." Her kids would have gone for that in a minute. She thought of them and the turns her life had taken the past ten years. A sense of melancholy wrapped around her shoulders as snugly as the afghan she'd used for a shawl earlier. Her eyes began to fill and she wiped at them before tears began to roll.

David noticed and felt the noose tighten. A boy was helpless in a situation like this; a man was not. "Don't cry, Annie," he implored. "I can't think how an extra mouth to feed could be anything but a trial, but if it'll make you feel better I'll stay." And love it. Oh, damn.

"It won't be anything fancy," she warned, pleased with the solid feel of him by her side. Not that she couldn't make it on her own—she'd proven that, hadn't she? No, it was just nice. It was just a feeling, but she thoroughly suspected that even with this soft side he was showing her, he was probably a heck of a branch manager.

He sounded distressed. "Whatever it is will be fine, and certainly not worth any tears. I'm not fussy." He'd learned not to be. There was a lot of peanut butter and jelly in his history.

"Oh, don't worry about the waterworks." She sniffled, gesturing helplessly. "This happens to me a lot lately."

David did not appear convinced, but stepped closer and put his arms around her in a universal comforting gesture.

Annie Glenn Cronin, financially struggling widowed mother of five, felt glands she'd thought atrophied long ago suddenly switch on at David's touch and flood her with a ton of troublemaking hormones. Even allowing for her faulty memory, she didn't think she'd ever felt such an instant jolt, not even during the first few years with Craig....

Chapter Two

This couldn't be happening to her. She was finally getting the last few pieces of the jigsaw puzzle that was her psyche picked up and put back into place and didn't need this. But David's flannel shirt was as red as the forbidden fruit in the garden of Eden and, Lord help her, she'd taken Eve for her confirmation name.

Tears came faster.

David pulled her closer and patted her back in a useless gesture meant to comfort.

His new proximity made Annie aware of a new fact. Lord, sexual frustration *now*? After everything she'd been through? Had the past ten years taught her nothing?

She cried harder.

David's patting picked up speed. Whatever was wrong with Annie, she didn't need a virtual stranger coming on to her. He tried to direct her head onto his shoulder, determined to offer nothing but a bit of comfort, but the height differential was too great. He finally swung her up into his arms and sat down on the sofa.

It had grown dark while they'd talked, but neither had thought to turn on a light. Now a young voice reached across the dusky room. "Mom, whose car is out in front? We get another camper this la— Who's that?"

It was more effective than a bucket of cold water. Annie's troublesome glands immediately reatrophied and her tears turned off. She sat up. "Casey? Is that you? Hi, honey, come on in." She watched her eight-year-old carrot-topped daughter come into the room, and cringed when Casey planted herself on widely spaced feet a goodly distance from the sofa and eyed David with disfavor.

"Mom, we studied this in school. Don't you remember when I showed you the stuff? He's a stranger. When a stranger asks you to do something like sit on his lap, you're supposed to say 'no' very loud and run tell somebody."

Annie managed to shape her water-logged face into a trembly smile. "And that's just what I would have done, only David's not a stranger. I know him from a long time ago, before you were even born."

That seemed to impress her daughter. "Really? Does he know our secret password and everything?"

"Oh, yes. He knows all about Sandy Supercilious." She emphasized the phrase to be sure David would pick it up.

"Sandy was a friend of mine," David put in and tried to look sincere.

"Wow. Cool. But still, why are you sitting on his lap?"

Annie tried to think. Why was she on David's lap? Let's see, she'd been thinking of those early sweet times with Craig before the children had started coming. Before she'd discovered that Craig had been unwilling to mature into an adult and be a father. She'd found herself always with one more child than she'd given birth to and no partner.

She'd gotten a bit weepy and then David had put his arm around her and her body had started to hum in the most astounding way.

No, no, she couldn't tell Casey she suddenly realized she needed a man. That wouldn't do.

"Your mother was feeling sad," David announced to the child.

Annie looked at him in grateful surprise while her daughter appeared doubtful.

"Hasn't your mom ever comforted you on her lap when you were down in the dumps?"

"Yes..."

"Well, sometimes grown-ups get sad and need comforting, too. That's what I was doing, comforting her."

"Oh." Casey walked over to the sofa and put her hand on Annie's thigh in a sweet, natural gesture. "Are you still sad, Mom?"

Annie held back a sniffle. "Ah, maybe a little bit, honey, but I'll be fine in just a second."

Casey nodded her head sagely. "Okay, that's good." Then the thin waif whose head gleamed orange even in the dim light informed David, "Sometimes Mom misses Dad. He's been gone almost a whole year now, you know."

"Yes, I only recently found that out."

"He was a lot of fun," she told David matter-of-factly. "Really good at hide-and-seek. We were all sad when the angels took him, but Mom was the most saddest of all."

Annie pushed her hair back off her forehead and glanced at David to see how he was taking her daughter's candid appraisal of Annie's psychological state. It was impossible to tell. His features appeared carefully schooled. She tried to interrupt, "Uh, Casey, honey—"

Casey leaned toward David in an earnest manner. "Dad used to write her poems."

That seemed to interest him, Annie noticed.

"Is that so?" he asked.

"Oh, yes. Well, I mean, he wrote all of us poems, but ours were silly and made us laugh. Mom's were long and mushy. She used to kiss him on the forehead and her eyes would water bad when he'd read one to her."

Annie stood and self-consciously adjusted her skirts. "Okay, that's enough now, honey. Let's all go out to the kitchen and get dinner going. You can set the table."

Craig had written her poems. They'd been sweet and had made her smile. It was impossible not to love Craig when he'd tried so hard to please in the only way he knew how. He'd given her five beautiful children. In the end, she'd loved him in the same way she'd loved them.

Annie led the way back to the kitchen. David watched the subtle sway of her hips as she walked in front of him. She couldn't be doing it on purpose. Her attention seemed centered on her conversation with Casey. Annie reached to flip an errant lock of her daughter's hair back over her shoulder and laughed at Casey's description of a kid named Stevie's antics.

Annie couldn't be doing it on purpose.

But that slight swish that seemed an unconscious yet integral part of her walk had her skirts flirting shamelessly with her calves and his heart trying to force-feed his entire blood supply through his temple arteries.

It was damned unfair, that's what it was. A man should have more control over his own body. Hell, it had never been a problem before. Maybe he was secretly a masochist. He'd have to be crazy to even *think* in terms of a relationship with a mother of five. Just imagine being father to a brood like that. Hell, kids were kids. The best of them were as unpredictable as a fireworks factory. Put five of them under the same roof and God only knew...

Annie turned around to welcome David into the kitchen and toss a few supper choices out for debate just as David touched his fingers to his temples and began massaging them. "Here we are. Now your choices are—David? Have you got a headache?"

David straightened and dropped his hands immediately. "What? No. I'm fine. Just fine."

"I can get you some aspirin, if you need it."

He doubted aspirin would cure this particular ailment. A lobotomy might be more helpful. "Really, I'm fine." He took in his surroundings. Annie's kitchen was antiquated and cramped. The stove didn't appear to be a woodburner and the refrigerator had no place for an ice block, but neither was much further along the evolutionary line of appliances than those early prototypes. An old Formica table surrounded by a whole bunch of chairs crowded the only open area in the room. It was the exact antithesis of the spacious, ultramodern cooking center in his own home.

Five little bodies took up the rest of the floor space and five sets of wide blue eyes had him as the center of their unblinking focus. "Uh, hi, guys," David said weakly.

There was no response, not even from Casey, the one he'd already met. He cleared his throat. "Well, I assume this crew belongs to you, Annie. And Casey was right, they do all look hungry." Actually, they looked accusatory and hostile at his intrusion. Probably blamed him for the lateness of their dinner hour. The faster he got out of there, the better for all concerned. "What can I do to help get dinner on the table? I wouldn't want these guys reduced to eating the table legs." Or his, either.

"David—"

"Yes! I mean, yes?"

Annie looked at him oddly.

He returned it, with interest. How could anyone willingly live like this? She'd *chosen* this. She probably hadn't had a minute to herself in the ten years since he'd last seen her. For sure, he couldn't have lived like that.

The undeniable attraction he felt for this back-to-basics country queen was the final blow. He felt both beset and put upon without knowing why.

Annie put her hands on the shoulders of a blond boy the same height as the red-haired Casey. "This is my son, Mark."

David manfully shook Mark's hand, finding it more difficult than that first overture handshake with a new client. He did know enough, however, to talk directly to the children instead of over their heads at Annie. "Are you two twins?" he asked Mark as he gestured toward Casey.

"Nah, we're not twins, but we'll be the same age in a couple of weeks."

"Uh-huh." David took his hand back and straightened upright again, rocking on his heels slightly while he tried to puzzle that one out.

"They're ten and a half months apart," Annie explained with a smile. "For a whole month and a half every year they're the same age. Mark's about to be eight, and six weeks later Casey will turn nine."

"Ah." David nodded wisely.

"And this is Amy, that's Billy." Like a magician with a trick run amuck, Annie pulled another child from behind her skirt. "And this is my main man, Steve."

Her "main man" Steve was all of two and a half feet tall.

Exhibiting more bravery than he'd known he possessed, David shook hands with each and every one of the brood.

"Hello" and "How's it going?" comprised the extent of David's conversational capabilities with the eight-and-under set. When that was exhausted he cast about for something else.

"So. How about if I . . . set the table?"

"That's *our* job," three children informed him simultaneously and sanctimoniously.

"Okay. All right. I'll . . . help your mother instead."

The children looked doubtful, but kept silent. David assumed they were leaving it up to Annie to tell him to butt out of the family dinner-hour ritual.

But she didn't. Instead, by some kind of democratic process David was totally unfamiliar with, a menu was decided upon and David was assigned tasks. He spooned applesauce onto plates. He ladled some kind of creamed tuna mixture made from canned soup, canned tuna and peas over varying-sized hillocks of rice.

"Let's say grace," Annie suggested once plates were full and everyone was seated around the old Formica table. Immediately all hands were folded and every chin was tucked down to chest level. "Amy, it's your turn to lead."

And she did.

"Bless us, oh Lohd, and these thy gifts, which we ah about to weceive from Chwist, Ouw Lohd, amen."

"Amen."

"Amen."

"Amen, amen, amen. Let's eat."

"Mark," Annie said, drawing the name out like a warning.

"Well, I'm hungry!"

"We all are. However, I expect you to behave."

Mark seemed disgruntled, but refrained from inhaling his food. David was impressed with the relative civility of the dinner table. It might not have made the Drake Hotel in Chicago's Loop list of best-mannered guests, but neither did it degenerate to the bedlam he'd expected.

By the end of dinner, the kids had grown friendlier and he was almost relaxed.

"That was delicious," he declared.

"I don't know about delicious," Annie returned. "But it's filling, hot and relatively nutritious."

"Just what I meant to say," David said, feeling magnanimous. In retrospect, dinner with the eight-and-under set and old Vic's runaway daughter hadn't been bad at all. Especially since Annie seemed to have whatever had upset her back under control. She'd smiled and laughed throughout the meal. "I'll help you clean up and then I've really got to get down to the site and get things set up. I've never done this before, so it might take a little extra time, especially in the dark."

Annie was shocked. He'd never set up a tent before? Hadn't he been a Scout? It was pitch-dark out there and October evenings were cool, verging on cold. When he'd said he was going to try camping, she'd assumed he'd had *some* experience. But it turned out he was a total novice. Good Lord. She rose and grabbed plates, stacking them haphazardly. In the manner of a woman who, once introduced to motherhood, becomes the universal mother quite capable of transferring motherly worries onto anyone coming into her hemisphere of influence, Annie immediately came up with a whole list of things that could go wrong. "What kind of tent did you bring with you, David? Has your sleeping bag got a decent rating for these cold nights? Do you have enough propane for your lantern? Sometimes those gauze mantles can be hard to get on right, then the lantern's almost impossible to light. Maybe I better—"

"Annie! Annie, stop." David was already standing. He reached over and took the precarious pile of dishes away from her before somebody's uneaten applesauce could dribble on the floor. The linoleum already had a light sprinkling of leftover rice. "I'll be fine. How hard can it be?"

"Well, I can think of a couple of things—"

Using his free hand, he set a finger against her lips, quieting her. "I'll be fine. I'm an intelligent male, I'll figure it out."

Annie jerked her head back, away from the finger that had burned her lips. How had he done that? She tried to focus on his hand. It didn't work. She licked her lips. "Just because you're a man—"

Watching her did him in. This time he kissed her to quiet her. Stupid. He felt the buzz.

She felt the buzz.

The kids went nuts over such a delicious display of disgusting adult behavior.

"That is so gross."

"Ooo, I think I'm gonna be sick."

"Does that mean they awe getting mawwied? Is David gonna be ouw new daddy?"

The buzz, at least for David, short-circuited. It rang through his body now like the bell for a five-alarm fire. He dragged his lips away and apologized gravely. "I beg your pardon, Annie. I never should have done that, especially in front of the children." Hellfire and damnation. Him, the new daddy of five little ones? He'd either have to be a candidate for sainthood or the funny farm. For sure it wasn't the former, and he hoped like hell to avoid the latter. No, when—*if*—he ever married, it would be to somebody who could spare a few minutes for him. He deposited the dishes in his hand next to the sink and returned the few feet to the table, snatching the remaining plates off the Formica top.

Annie watched him and felt decidedly dazed. She touched her lips with two fingers. If the last hour and a half with David had taught her anything, it was that the woman in her wasn't dead. She squinted, trying to focus on David, studying him intently. "David, don't bother. I can do that. It's all right." She'd always assumed her roles as widow and devoted mother of five fatherless children were both permanent and inseparable.

Maybe not. Huh. How about that? Of course, David was all wrong for her. Kind, certainly, but she sensed his uneasiness with the children. And anyone who'd worked as hard as he must have to go from mail-room clerk to branch manager had to be pretty intent on the fast track. That wasn't for her. But the kiss gave her hope as much as it surprised her. Maybe, someday, there'd be someone.

She settled the drain plug into the sink and started the water, squirting a stream of detergent in as she did so.

"Okay, David, you're on a sandbox site just down the dirt road that goes by the front of the camp store. The number is on a marker in front of each site. I've only got a few other campers right now, since it's so late in the season. They're in pop-ups farther down in the part that has electrical service. They won't bother you." She walked him to the front door after setting the dishes into the foaming sink and turning the tap off. "If you need anything, just come back and knock, don't use the bell. I'm putting the kids to bed fairly soon, but I'm, ah, a light sleeper. I'll hear your knock."

Annie sent the children upstairs to start the tub and get their clothes off while she walked David to the front door. He made his escape just as one naked little body hurtled down the stairs and streaked through the living room in hot pursuit of another naked little body.

"Hey, hey, what's going on here?" his hostess questioned while arranging her expression in as severe lines as was probably possible for her. "You know you're not supposed to chase each other on the stairs. One of you might get hurt."

He noticed she said nothing about running around the place in the nude.

The one who's arm she'd grabbed—David's glance dropped, a boy so it must be Billy—replied breathlessly and rapidly. "Amy'th the one, Mom. I wath doing what you thaid, but her thaid 'whooee' to me." He pointed to the giggling smallfry half-hidden behind the dining room entrance doorway. "Her did that to me. Now I have to get her." Amy shrieked in happy horror and took off again.

Billy tried to follow, but Annie maintained her grip on his forearm.

David let himself out the front door with a final good-night wave he doubted Annie saw. He breathed deeply, taking in the essence of nighttime October. Fall had a distinctive smell to it, one he hadn't taken the time to enjoy in a long time. His pace quickened and gravel crunched under his shoes as he reached the driveway and his car. He was going to enjoy these two weeks; it would be kind of a time out of time.

He scratched around the door handle with the tip of his key, realizing how dark it had gotten. He had difficulty finding the key's slot. Glancing up, he noticed the moon and most of its attendant stars had disappeared behind clouds. The few remaining pinpoints of white provided little natural light, and as he glanced around he realized that other than Annie's front porch light, there was no artificial illumination.

He finally got the door open and slid into the front seat. He started the engine, then leaned over the steering wheel as he drove slowly down the rutted lane in search of his spot. Country dark was dark indeed. Inky dark. A heavy blackness that saturated the air and fought with the car's headlights, allowing only a reluctant path of light directly in front of him.

Twenty-five, twenty-six...there it was. Twenty-seven. He swung into his site and turned off the engine. Momentarily remaining in position behind the wheel, he stared through the windshield. In the light of his lowbeams, he could see the rough-hewn beams that really did form what looked like a giant sandbox. He hadn't questioned the term, not wanting to appear ignorant in front of Annie, but even a neophyte outdoorsman such as himself could see he was supposed to pitch his tent on the oversized sandbox. It was the only remotely level spot anywhere on the campsite.

See? This entire procedure was just a process of using your head, applying a little deductive reasoning and logic.

He got out of the car with a sense of renewed enthusiasm. This would be fun. A time of getting back in touch with himself and nature. A learning experience. Educational. The eerie darkness would not creep him out. City boy that he was, he would learn to love it for its very difference.

"Now what have we got here?" he asked himself as he popped open the trunk and began riffling through its contents. He hefted a large canvas sack out and propped it against the rear of the car. "That's the tent. Mary Ellen's friend, Hank, said it was a piece of cake to put up, so that should be no problem." He removed a smaller sack. "Tent stakes, I think. Um, lantern. Duffel bag with clean jeans and stuff, sleeping bag. What's this? Oh, yeah, I remember throwing that in. And here's the cooler and the box with dry goods." He slammed the trunk back down and glanced around with anticipation.

"Here goes nothing," he murmured and began dragging, lifting and toting his collection of camping necessities over to the wooden picnic table he noticed sulking between the oversized sandbox and the fire ring. The table groaned with each addition and David hoped it would wait to collapse until the camper after him occupied the site.

"Okay, first things first." He stared at the picnic table full of supplies. "I guess that means the tent." Hesitantly he placed a hand on the large canvas bag holding his shelter for the next thirteen nights. "I need to see. If I work fast, the car's battery should be okay. It would take too long to figure out the lantern now." He leaned inside the car window and pulled the headlight knob, thereby illuminating the sandbox.

"*Now* the tent." He hefted the canvas sack off the table and lugged it to the middle of the site, dumping it out onto the ground there. He kicked it with his foot. There was nothing there but tan canvas. Where were the poles? "Must be wrapped up in the middle of the thing," he assured himself and began to unfold the large packet as rapidly as possible.

"Damn it," he cursed when he found nothing. He tried to think. "Okay, not to worry. They're here somewhere. Maybe they're with the stakes."

He hurried back to the picnic table, knowing the stake bag was too small but needing to check, anyway.

"All right, don't panic. This kind of thing must happen to people all the time," he assured himself after sifting through the stake bag, supply box, and searching the perimeter of the trunk and his back seat two more times. He sat on his front bumper. "This is simply another case requiring logic and deductive reasoning." Of course, there was always the possibility Mary Ellen's friend had been instructed to leave them out, accidentally on purpose. It just might be Mary Ellen's way of forcing him to stay in Annie's house tonight. She'd known what time he was leaving. His eyes narrowed. Well, she wouldn't get away with it.

He crossed his legs and put his head into his hand while he thought. The car bobbed lightly underneath him.

Nothing brilliant came.

He crossed his legs in the opposite direction and switched hands cupping his chin. The car bobbed again. "I wonder if Annie's got something in her camp store I could use?"

He examined that idea. It was a possibility. One that he would reconsider when he had exhausted all others. The evening's earlier events left him with the odd notion he'd had a narrow escape. A chill took him. Imagine anyone in this day and age having five children. He had one friend with three, but that was only because his wife had complained that her two sons left him with a lot of baseball partners and nobody to keep her company shopping. After their third son was born, she'd given up, as well.

Of course, Annie's kids were cute. Imagine little Amy teasing her brother with a catcalled "whooee" when he'd undressed. David smiled involuntarily at the memory. They were funny all right, but it was more the sheer numbers involved. There was such a thing as too much of a good thing.

David was twenty-eight years old. Plenty old enough to recognize male-female chemistry when he felt it brewing. He sighed in disgust, his rear still planted on the car's front bumper as he admitted in all those twenty-eight years he'd never felt such a strong or inappropriate chemical bond.

No, he would not bother Annie or take the chance of waking her brood once she got them down unless it became absolutely necessary. "Frankly," he muttered as he stood and stretched, "I'll sleep in the car before I get that hard up."

He lowered his arms and squinted thoughtfully once more in the direction of his still-two-dimensional tent. It desperately needed a third dimension if it was to be of any use to him. There was no overhanging tree limb to hang it from. "Too bad, rope I've got." He stepped up onto the sandbox and kicked at the canvas experimentally. "Sticks could work."

"For what?"

David jumped. He whirled around. "Annie! What are you doing here?"

"After I got the kids down, I went out on the porch to enjoy the peace and quiet for a moment. I noticed it was clouding over."

David glanced up. "Yeah, I noticed that, too. It sure is dark without the moon, isn't it?"

Yes, it was dark. Without the haze of city lights, the stars and the moon were ten times brighter in the country night sky. These starless, moonless nights really got to her since she'd been alone. She tried not to dwell on it. "I was thinking more in terms of the rain."

"Rain?"

"Yeah, as in the precipitation that will probably begin falling from the sky within the hour. Since I was the one who delayed you, I wanted to make sure you were set up okay before it came."

Besides, it was something to do to hurry the night hours along.

David was unsure if his heart was beating overtime from the surprise of Annie's unexpected ghostlike appearance or the thrill seeing her seemed to precipitate. He found neither reason particularly acceptable. The first didn't seem terribly macho and the second he'd already declared self-destructive.

"I'm fine," he told her. "Just fine."

Annie glanced around doubtfully. If this was all he'd accomplished so far, things were not going well. Maybe he was one of those men who couldn't ask for help. "I don't mind lending a hand," she offered. Besides, it would delay going back to the silence of the dark house. "I told Casey where I was going. If they need anything, she'll come get me."

David checked the sky once more. The few stars visible when he'd left Annie's had been systematically blotted out until not a pinpoint of light remained. He sighed. Either path he chose here would not be in his best interest. "Okay. I was going to try and find some long sticks to use for tent poles. Evidently my friend forgot to include them. Although I suppose," he admitted reluctantly, "I might have left them behind when I loaded the car. Either way, I'm in something of a bind."

Chapter Three

Annie studied the amorphous mass of canvas on the sandbox site. Yes, he was in a bind. For one thing, as nearly as she could tell, he had the tent's only egress positioned to open into a tree. Now, how to point that out to a delicate male ego.

"So," she said, "uh, what's the plan? With two of us working, maybe we can get you set up before the rain comes."

She held her breath. A lot of the men who came into the campground were experienced and needed no extra guidance, but those who weren't almost invariably refused to admit it. She'd often thought she could make her fortune selling admission tickets to some of the camp setups she'd witnessed. From the little she remembered from ten years ago and the facts she'd gleaned during dinner coupled with—what? A general aura of competency?—she knew David was used to being good at what he did. Camping, unfortunately, was not among those skills. But would he admit it?

David surprised her.

"To tell you the truth, I give up. I haven't got the foggiest idea what to do right now," he said. "I'm not sure even having the poles would be all that helpful." He looked at the flat canvas in defeat. "I thought if I found long sticks, maybe I could jam them into the seams where the poles are supposed to go. What do you think?"

She felt like a duck hunter in an arcade alley. "I don't think you could find sticks the length you need that would be straight enough to suit your purpose." Ping. "If they were thin and able to slide into the seam, they wouldn't be strong enough to support the tent." Ping. "And some of the poles have to be joined with an elbow where the tent curves. You can't do that with sticks."

David nodded glumly. Sometimes getting away from it all was more hassle than it was worth. "Then I guess I'll throw this stuff all back into the trunk and sleep in the car tonight. I'll go into town tomorrow and see what I can pick up." He reached for the cooler, resigned to an uncomfortable night scrunched in the back seat.

"Why don't you come up to the house and sleep on the sofa?" Annie bit her lip after the words came out. It was against her personal rules to invite the campers to stay in the house. After marrying Craig, she'd decided she wasn't a particularly good judge of personality. And while David didn't worry her in terms of being a rapist or murderer, she was very much afraid of the feelings he generated in her. Uncomfortable feelings. Supposed to be long-dead feelings.

David dismissed her offer. "No. It wouldn't be right. It might scare the kids to find me there in the morning."

What a relief. What a disappointment. "Well, if you won't come to the house, we'll just have to get this tent up.

Now, if you're interested, a year or so ago I witnessed a rather creative woman who, in between bellowing at her three sons for using their tent poles for light sabers and her husband for not stopping them, built a stick tepee thing over the tent and then tied the tent up to that with rope.''

"I've got rope."

"Well?"

He thought out loud. "You could use thick sticks that way that would really support the thing."

Annie scratched the toe of her shoe in the dirt. He liked it. She could tell he did. She felt like a creative genius.

"Let's do it."

It took half an hour, but they managed to lash together a lopsided wooden superstructure shaped more or less like a tepee. Eyeing it critically, Annie felt it leaned more to the *less* than the *more*. But they were able to hang the tent from it without it collapsing.

"It looks silly," David decided as he studied it.

"Hey, whatever works . . ."

"People will laugh."

"What people? There's hardly anybody else here and they're total strangers to you."

David straightened his shoulders. "Right. Can't worry about the opinion of people I'll never see again." He unzipped the opening and tied the flap back. "I'll throw the supplies inside and then we can sit and talk. I've got some pop and chips here someplace."

"We can't eat in there," Annie immediately protested. "And you can't store food in the tent, either."

"Why not?" David asked, pausing with a box he'd just picked up from the picnic table. "There aren't any bears or things around here."

"No, there aren't any bears, but there are raccoons. Nocturnal raccoons. Raccoons that will come right into the tent while you're asleep if they smell food, and they've got great noses. It wouldn't take more than a few crumbs or an empty candy wrapper to alert them."

That stopped him in his tracks. "Really?" He wouldn't object to Annie sneaking in while he was asleep—providing she'd hired a sitter—but he didn't particularly care for the idea of a four-legged companion slipping into his sleeping bag with him. "Well, I'll put it back in the car. We'll sit out here and munch."

"It's starting to mist." Annie had to bite back a smile as David lifted his frustrated face to the sky. She'd been unable to stay in the silent house when she knew David was right down the road, but she also knew she really shouldn't remain. The elements appeared to be looking after her tonight. They, too, realized she should get back to the house before the odd attraction she felt could develop into something she was unable to handle.

David had no idea why he wanted Annie to stay. She was a good-looking woman, but he'd met others he wouldn't work this hard to convince. No, it was nothing tangible, it was just *there*. "Okay, we'll sit in the car." He opened the door and ushered her in before she could come up with another excuse.

He reached over the seat and took a bag of chips and a six-pack of cola from the box on the rear seat. "Here, open two of these." He handed her the pop and tore open the top of the chips bag, placing it on the seat between them. "Never let it be said I don't entertain in style."

Annie gave up and relaxed against the car seat back. So she'd leave in a few minutes. If the kids needed her, Casey knew where she was. If she was feeling especially urgent or it started raining too hard for her to run between the drops, Casey could get her with the beeper Annie always carried when she went out to the campground.

She took a sip of cola and decided to savor her brief getaway. She reached into the bag and took the biggest chip she could find. She never got the big, unbroken chips. It wasn't worth the fight. She leaned over and peeked into the bag and took out three folded-over potato chips. Those curled up ones were the real prize in any bag. These were unbroken, as well. She held them in her hand for a moment, enjoying the fact that nobody was at her elbow clamoring for these perfect specimens. She held one up, examining it closely before she brought it to her lips and bit into it. "Umm," she murmured. "This is wonderful."

David rested back against the car door and watched the production Annie made out of eating a potato chip. While the way she picked and chose her chips gave him pause as to Annie's mental condition—he'd never known anyone who didn't just blindly reach in and grab a handful—the almost sensual enjoyment she displayed while eating that potato chip had to be one of the more erotic things he'd ever witnessed.

He licked his lips, sure he could taste the salt glistening on hers. He cleared his throat. "You, uh-hmm, you like potato chips, do you?" He swallowed along with her as she polished off that first one.

Annie looked over, suddenly embarrassed. She must seem like an idiot drooling over a potato chip like this. For heaven's sake, they weren't even *hers*. Maybe David liked the curled ones and she'd just hogged them. "Here, David, take these. I'm used to eating the broken ones, so it doesn't really matter. I noticed some in there that were cooked almost brown. I like those, too."

David had no idea what she was talking about. He only knew he'd upset her, which had not been his intention at all. "Hey, it's okay. You can have the curly ones and any other special ones you want. It's my pleasure." Believe him, it was his pleasure. He was dying to watch her eat another.

"It's just that these are so perfect and the kids always scramble for them and—"

David took one of her perfect folded over ones and put it to her lips. She had no choice but to bite. He ate the other half, watching her solemnly as he chewed. "You're right. This is the best chip I ever ate."

Annie almost cried. "Oh, David, this is stupid. You must think I'm an idiot. I've been surrounded by children too long. I don't know how to be with a man anymore."

"No, you don't," David agreed.

Annie hung her head, humiliated.

"It's refreshing, though," David mused thoughtfully. "You're not all over me, not into word games. I suppose you have to learn patience dealing with kids all day, but you didn't even laugh when I couldn't put the tent up. I've enjoyed myself. You're easy to be with." He didn't have to like it, but it was God's own truth.

She looked back up.

"I didn't thank you for helping me out, did I?" he murmured as he lowered his head and, against his better judgment, decided to kiss her.

Annie watched his mouth come down. If she'd had time to hyperventilate, she would have, but instead she hastily ran her tongue around her lips, checking for potato chip crumbs.

David groaned at the action. He could be in serious trouble here, and it seemed to him he could be doing a better job of fighting this thing.

"You're lethal," he panted when they finally had to stop or pass out.

Annie sat back and looked at him oddly. "Funny. It's never been that way before. I assumed it was you. For example that breathlessness—what was that?"

His laughter burst through. This whole thing really wasn't funny, and there he sat laughing like a demented lunatic. "Oh, Annie, how you can be so sweet and naive with the father you've got, I don't know, but here you are. And your kiss, Lord, it packs a punch worthy of a marine."

"How do you know my dad?"

"The branch has several contracts going with his company right now." So she didn't keep up much with her dad's business. Somehow that didn't surprise him.

"Oh. I don't kiss like a marine."

"I didn't say you did." He brushed her lips lightly again to forestall her next comment and still felt as if he'd been walloped. "I'm taking you home," he informed her. "I think I'm overtired. It's been a very long day."

He drove her down the path back to her own front door, delivering her inside as though it had been a real date. "Maybe I'll see you tomorrow," he said, turning back into the still-light mist and his car.

"The kids would love it," Annie said as she stood in the glow of the open front door. The lighting gave her an ethereal otherworldly appearance. "They really took to you."

As he trotted back to the car, David groaned, both in annoyance with his body's reaction to the vision she presented in the doorway and the reminder of those five active children. "Yes, well, let's see what the day brings, why don't we?" Who knew? Maybe there'd be an emergency at work and he'd be called back in.

He waved once more before sliding into the front seat of the car and starting the engine. He waited there in the driveway until Annie closed the door and had had enough time to properly lock up. Slowly he put the car into reverse and performed a three-point turn in front of the house.

The rain began picking up as he bounced down the lane back to his campsite. He pulled in, popped the trunk and grabbed his sleeping bag, pillow and the duffel bag stuffed with clean clothing. Then he raced into his tepee tent and deposited the stuff on the ground. He lit one flashlight and used its light to hang the other one from the ceiling.

Standing in the center of the tepee tent, David looked around. There was nothing else to do. The lighting wasn't good enough to read by and, in any event, his glasses were still on the car's dash. It would be difficult to do any serious camp organizing in the rain and there was certainly not much to organize in the tent. Annie had made him put all the food items back in the car.

He glanced at his wrist. Ten-thirty. Ten-thirty on a Friday night and there was nothing to do except stand around in a godforsaken tent that barely cleared the top of his head and would probably collapse on him at the earliest opportunity.

David pulled the tent flap back and stared gloomily out into the humid darkness. He was a self-made, successful businessman in the prime of his life. Women called *him* for dates. Well, every now and then they did, he amended honestly.

So what the hell was he doing out in the middle of nowhere fighting a strong attraction to a widow with five kids who had "taken" to him? And not only that—he was being held hostage in a canvas bubble by a lot of weeping clouds steadily getting sadder instead of pulling themselves together and blowing away. He was beset on all sides by melancholia. Even the weather was depressing.

"What am I doing here?" he questioned the darkness.

"Where is the map of the campground Annie gave me?"

"What is the meaning of life? Hell." He turned away from the opening of the tent. He pulled a poncho out of his duffel bag and slipped it over his head before stalking out to meet the rain man-to-man. Opening the trunk of the car again, he yanked a paper cup from its protective film of plastic tubing and set it out on the picnic table. Then he went a short distance out into the woods.

When he returned, there was just enough water in the bottom of the cup to dampen his toothbrush. Feeling only marginally more civilized, David decided it was time to retire for the night—before another opportunity for vacation-time fun presented itself.

A sense of clamminess permeated the tent. David himself felt cold and damp after his trek into the woods. He put a hand up on the ceiling and shook it a bit, trying to dislodge any rain that might be pooling up there. He watched in horror as the tent began to leak from the spot he'd touched, suddenly remembering Hank's warning about not touching the inside of a canvas tent should it rain as it would ruin the surface tension and the water would be conducted inside instead of down the outside.

"Hell," he muttered, flipping his sleeping bag open on the other side of the small tent. The tent had no floor and the ground looked hard. This whole idea he'd had about camping basically stunk.

He shrugged. Too late to worry about it now. He'd pack up and leave in the morning if the night got too bad. "What the heck, if the cowboys could do it, so can I."

Several hours later, he wasn't so sure. Cowboys must have been a different breed. The earth underneath him radiated cold. It seeped up through his sleeping bag no matter how tightly he curled up. Rain continued to come down, mostly outside the tent but partly inside, as well. It was starting to roll in under the tent flaps. His sleeping bag would soon be getting wet. He watched morbidly as the water inched closer.

"Should have brought the camp cot Hank offered. I could have squeezed it in the car somewhere. Then I'd be up off the ground and none of this would matter. But, no, macho man Dave has to rough it." He shivered and watched in resignation as the water crept nearer yet. *Go sleep in the car,* he directed himself. *It's got to be more comfortable than this.*

He sat up, determined to squirm out of the imprisoning sleeping bag and make a run for the car.

Somebody else in the tent, he was sure it wasn't him, shrieked.

"What! Who's there?"

A meek, little voice reached across the darkness. "David, is that you?"

Who the devil else would it be? It was his damn tent, wasn't it? The question was, who was sharing it with him? "Yes, it's David. Who are you?"

"It's me."

Oh, of course. How foolish of him. He should have figured that out right away. Me. "Me who? Who is me?"

"Casey. Who did you think?"

Would she like a list of all the possibilities that had sprung to mind with her apparition? She sounded incredulous that he didn't recognize her immediately. "Casey, what are you doing up at—" he glanced at the watch on his wrist "—one in the morning? What are you doing *out* at one in the morning?"

She spoke, much nearer at hand now. "I came to talk to you. I brought Mark with me 'cause it's dark and Mom says we can't go out by ourselves after dark."

David struggled with his sleeping bag, trying to free his body. "I think she meant after dinner, not the middle of the night. Why aren't you sleeping, honeybun?"

"I woke up 'cause I had to go to the bathroom."

"Yes, but you don't have to use the camp facilities. You've got one in the house. I saw it earlier."

"Well, of course there's one in the house. I already used it," Casey informed him.

"Me, too," Mark piped in.

"Couldn't you go back to sleep?" he asked. "Does your Mom know you've left the house?" They were both crouched close now, as though seeking safety and warmth. He wanted to reach out and hold them, pull them onto his lap, but he was afraid of frightening them. Something was wrong, though.

"I was goin' back to bed," Casey admitted. "But I noticed Mom's bed was empty when I passed her room."

"Are you sure?" David didn't know what to make of that. Where could Annie be? He knew she'd made it inside the door. He'd waited to make sure before he'd left. Had she taken a tumble and was even now lying unconscious somewhere in the house? Maybe he should go take a look. He remembered the trauma of finding his own mother hurt and dying. Casey and Mark didn't need that. They'd been forced to face enough this past year. He began struggling with the sleeping bag again. He'd protect the little ones. He'd take care of Annie. He'd—

"Then I noticed a downstairs light was on."

David's hands stilled. Had the poor kid already found her? "Yeah?"

He felt more than saw the nod next to him. "Yeah. Sometimes you can tell because the dark downstairs isn't dark enough, you know?"

"Yeah, I know. Sometimes you can just tell."

"So I went downstairs and Mom was in the living room all curled up on the sofa with her feet right up on the sofa the way we're never supposed to and her arms all wrapped tight around her knees."

"Really?" He didn't know what else to say.

"She only does that when she's feeling sad," Mark contributed.

David accepted his analysis. The description of Annie huddled by herself into a corner of the sofa fit someone who was upset. "Did she, uh, say what she was sad about?"

"Oh, I didn't talk to her," Casey assured him.

"Uh-huh."

"I used to try sometimes. But she always says not to worry, that she's fine. But she's *not* fine," the child declared fiercely. "Not since Daddy went with the angels."

David's heart bled for the children kneeling next to him. Kids needed to think their parents were invincible. David knew. Eight was too young for the illusion to be shattered.

"At least she wasn't crying."

"She wasn't?"

"No. Sometimes she does, though, when she's really sad. I remember a couple of times before Dad went to the angels, even."

Was that a fact? Annie hadn't been happy with Craig?

"I know things aren't right without Daddy here, but I try to be as good as I can, and so does Mark. Really."

"I believe you, honey," David quickly assured her.

"But she *still* gets sad like this. And she doesn't eat right."

"She doesn't?"

"No. Miss Kelley says you hafta eat something out of all the food groups every day, but Mom says her stomach gets upset easily lately and she'd get sick if she ate so much." Casey put a hand out and touched David's shoulder. "We're afraid she's gonna die, too."

Mark nodded solemnly in agreement.

Oh, my God. David gulped. This was getting very heavy-duty here. He didn't quite know what to do. What if he said the wrong thing? "Listen, kids—"

The little girl put her hand out, touching his shoulder. The weight of her hand had all the substance of a butterfly's caress.

"She laughed when you were over for dinner." The little girl paused dramatically. "And she ate all her food without gettin' sick."

She'd kept down potato chips and cola, too, for that matter, he thought. "Casey, you and Mark go jump into the car. Your mother's probably looking all over for you. I'll drive you to the house and make sure you get back in."

Casey jumped up and Mark immediately followed suit. She leaned to brush off her knees. "Ugh, David, it's all *wet* in here. Where's your ground cloth?"

David was busily squirming out of his sleeping bag, bent on getting free, determined to check on Annie. "My what?"

"Your ground cloth."

"I don't think I have one of those," he answered absently. "What's it for?"

"The ground, what else?"

Her intonation wasn't rude, merely puzzled.

"Excuse me," David apologized gravely. "I wasn't thinking. It's for the ground. Where?"

"Why, in here. You're supposed to put a ground cloth under your tent even if your tent has a bottom. It's a big long word, in-something, but it means keep the cold out."

"Insulation?" Ah there. Free at last. He stood.

"Yeah, that's it."

"Good idea. Wish I'd known about it earlier. You two ready to make a run for it?"

"Yes, but David?"

"What is it, honey?" He stood at the tent opening, staring out. No doubt about it, they were going to get wet. The kids'd get sick and Annie would really have her hands full.

"Maybe you better bring your sleeping bag. It's all wet on the bottom side. Mom can put it in the dryer for you."

"Casey, you're full of good ideas tonight. I'll do that. Now, ready, set, go!" He sent the children racing to the car while he wadded up his sleeping bag and followed more slowly.

The living room light was still on when his car approached the front of Annie's home. It was the only light visible in the house, so he assumed she had yet to discover

Casey's and Mark's disappearance. Rather than worry Annie now that the adventure was over, he sent the twosome around the back with instructions to sneak upstairs as quietly as possible. He went to the front door and knocked softly. He did not have to try terribly hard to look pathetic.

He gave a little wave when she looked out the small pane of glass inset into the door. "Annie," he greeted her when she swung the door open. "I'm all wet."

Her eyes widened as she took in his bedraggled appearance. "You certainly are. What happened?" Good grief, she'd only left him a few hours ago. How could he have gotten so wet so quickly? His current condition only underlined what she'd suspected since he'd first appeared. He was a businessman, not an outdoorsman. Given a few more years, the boardroom would be his oyster, not the great out of doors.

David stood just inside the front door and slipped off his shoes. He stood there in his soggy socks and shrugged out of the slicker he'd thrown over his clothes on his way out of the tent. Water dripped from his hair and ran in small rivulets down his forehead and cheeks. Some caught on the corner of his self-disparaging grin. He wiped his face clean with his forearm. "What happened? That tent my office manager's friend lent me leaks. In case that's not enough, the rain came in under the sides of the thing for added good measure. On top of all that, the ground was wet, cold and hard to try and sleep on."

"Didn't you lay a ground cloth?"

"I didn't know I was supposed to."

Annie was horrified. It was all her fault. She'd assumed David would finish setting up camp after she left. She'd had no idea he'd thought he was done at that point. She should have checked. He was new to camping. How would he know about ground cloths? She should have double-checked. He was on one of her campsites, that made him her responsibility. She should have triple-checked. She'd fallen down on the job. Again. "David, I'm so sorry. I—"

"Hey," he interrupted, "I'm not a child. I thought this was going to be a snap and didn't plan well enough. It was my responsibility to see I had what I needed. Don't you dare try to take on my mistakes along with everything else you've got on your delicate little shoulders."

Annie's tongue froze mid mea culpa. Had she heard right? David considered the whole thing his own fault? He wasn't mad at her? Craig had expected her to take care of him, had gotten angry when she'd slipped up. David seemed disgusted, but it was directed at himself. Her brows knotted over her eyes in puzzlement.

David slipped out of his wet socks and asked, "Got a radiator I could sit on for a few minutes? I'm frozen."

"The heat's not on yet. I try to wait a little later in the season. How about a hot shower while we run your things through the dryer? Say, isn't that the same pair of jeans and flannel shirt you had on earlier?" She hustled him into the living room, sat him on the sofa and threw the afghan over his shoulders.

"Yeah, why?"

"You must have frozen out there. I should have told you—"

David reached up and pulled her down beside him, hoping Casey trusted him to find out what was wrong with Annie and had indeed gone back to bed and was not watching from some darkened corner. "Never mind the self-incriminations, it's obvious I should have questioned Hank more carefully on the do's and don'ts of camping. Tell me now."

Mothers are good at guilt. Every childish misstep taken a mother is sure is the direct result of a flaw in her mothering. Annie knew that, but still found it hard to let David accept responsibility for his actions. She tried to just state the facts. "You should never sleep in the same clothes you wore during the day."

"Why not?" David asked, sounding interested, not angry. "I only had them on a couple of hours."

"Even if they feel dry to the touch, they're slightly damp with perspiration. On a night like tonight, your things were more than slightly damp, too. If you wear them to bed, they won't hold your body heat as effectively and you'll be cold."

"That, I was."

"Dry clothes are a much more effective insulator."

"I'll have to remember that. Annie, what are you doing sitting down here in the middle of the night?"

Annie stopped adjusting the afghan over his broad shoulders and stared at him, nonplussed. She'd rather discuss camping. "Just . . . sitting," she told him.

"After five children ran you ragged all day? Why aren't you upstairs sleeping?"

"Sometimes I have a little . . . trouble getting to sleep."

"Why?"

"I just do, that's all."

David put his arm around her and guided her head to his shoulder. "Come on, tell Uncle Dave all about it." He did not want to be there, snuggling on an old camelback sofa with a woman entirely too dangerous for his peace of mind. But Casey's fearful confession hit a much too identifiable chord in David. In the ten minutes they'd shared in the half-up, half-down tepee tent, the little girl had found a niche in David's heart and taken up permanent residence. Something was wrong with this family. He suspected Craig had not left much money, his bequest probably being more along the lines of twice the number of chores for Annie now he was gone.

Annie was trying to cope with five times the number of mouths to feed his own mother had attempted. Unlike fifteen years ago, he had the maturity and the means to ensure a different outcome now. Walking away was no longer an option. Not while Casey still worried and Mark tagged after her all over the campground.

"It's embarrassing."

"Come on." She felt good in his arms. Too good. He had to make an effort to concentrate on her words instead of his body's reactions to her closeness.

"It's got to do with you," she warned, then gave in. "Okay, this will sound stupid, but all my life I've struggled to find my spot in life. But every time I turn around, I feel like I've let down womankind."

David was amazed. "How do you figure that?"

"You know, all the legions of women both back in history and now who've done what they could to overcome sexual prejudices and open doors for the rest of us."

"Uh-huh. And how, exactly, did you manage to let half of the human population down so badly?"

"Don't you laugh at me."

"I'm not. I just don't see you doing anything other than minding your own business, raising your family as best you can. There's certainly nothing there that should offend the sisterhood."

"Women and minorities are locked out of upper-management positions by what's called a glass ceiling."

"I've heard of it."

"My father planned to turn his company over to me when he retired. I could have pulled a lot of women through that hole in the ceiling."

"It wasn't right for you," David protested.

"No, and so I left. All I've ever wanted was a simple life-style surrounded by my husband and children."

Sounded like a contradiction in terms to him, but who was he to judge? "What's wrong with that?"

"I should have been able to have both. Other women have children and hold a job. Even the half I chose didn't work out. I thought Craig was perfect. We both wanted the same things.''

''And?''

''I was wrong,'' she admitted starkly. ''It was a terrible mismatch. When he died, I decided it was time to become independent and strong, to stand on my own two feet—at least in my own sphere.''

''Sounds good so far.''

''It's not working. My life is falling down around my ears. I can't sleep, Casey's upset about my not eating properly...''

That he knew.

''Craig left me temporarily broke, and sitting at the dinner table tonight, all I could think about was how nice it was to have someone solid and sturdy like you around. You and I don't even have the surface similarities Craig and I shared, but I wanted to lean on you. Oh, God, I shouldn't be saying things like that to you. Whatever will you think?''

David would have laughed at her horrified expression, only he was busy being horrified himself. The idea of the two of them together was one of those terrifying, fascinating ideas that could lead to a lot of trouble...or a lot of bliss.

Chapter Four

Annie sat with her back to a gnarled apple tree late the following afternoon, watching the kids gather up the last of the season's apples. Shading her eyes with one hand, she checked on her two oldest children who were swinging like monkeys from the lower branches. From her position, the twisted branches of the trees in the orchard appeared to be scratching the underbellies of the cotton-stuffed cumulus clouds drifting past. "You two be careful," she called out, more by habit than any real need to exercise caution. The branches were low enough and the ground leaf cover thick enough that it was doubtful a fall would do much damage to their pliable young bodies.

"We're being careful, Mom, don't worry," Casey sang back.

"Yeah, Mom, no sweat," her seven-year-old son, Mark, seconded.

Annie shook her head in exasperation, then drowsed lazily back against the tree's rough bark. The late-afternoon sun warmed her and she waved a buzzing yellow jacket off. "Billy, we won't have any apples left for applesauce if you keep throwing them and making Amy play go-fetch."

"But, Mom, Amy'th bein' a dog. She gotth to fetch *thomething.*"

"Not the apples," Annie responded firmly. "They go in the wagon to be pulled back up to the house." She watched for a few moments to make sure her directive was being followed and then closed her eyes. She hadn't seen David all day. She hadn't completely scared him away because the tepee tent still drooped listlessly from its ropes on site twenty-seven. It disgusted her that she'd kept an eye open, watching for him most of the day.

Soon it would be dark. She wasn't looking forward to it, but wasn't dreading it, either. When things had started getting bad the night before, David had shown up. He'd come to get in out of the wet and cold, but he'd stayed and talked to her for more than an hour, until she'd been through the worst of whatever mental hobgoblins it was that insisted on attacking her late at night. She'd been able to sleep after that.

Her head dipped and she smiled at the apples in her lap. He'd slept on her sofa. When she'd come downstairs this morning, he'd been half on and half off the couch and soundly sawing logs. She doubted a man of David's age would appreciate it, but he'd looked very cute.

She glanced up, checking the tree containing her two eldest. "Mark, I told you to be careful."

"I am."

"Then be more careful."

"Aw, Mom."

"You heard me."

He'd looked so young sleeping there. It made her wonder how much older she was. A couple of years, at least. Eons, if how old you felt counted. She was aware no man in his right mind would take on a crazy mother of five. But David—staid, steady, beautiful David—could certainly make a depressed, worn out, maternal type dream again.

Which just went to show you, Annie told herself, just how cantankerous your subconscious could get when your psyche was under the weather. Imagine, her, the flower child born too late, attracted to conservative, business-suited David.

Idly she wondered where David had gone. He'd left the house around nine, shortly after he'd awakened. His car had headed out of the campground around ten. She'd been inexcusably relieved to see the lopsided tent structure still there when she'd made her garbage run around the sites. "Come on, kids. The wagon is just about full. Let's pull it up to the house and get the applesauce started."

It was impossible not to wonder where he'd gone or when he'd be back. A silent reminder that it was none of her business went unheeded. Maybe he'd gone to town to see about tent poles? If so, he'd have quickly drawn a blank. There was no camp supply store in town. So where was he?

"This is stupid," she muttered.

"What is, Mom?"

"Nothing."

"But you said—"

"I was just talking to myself. Can you give the rear of the wagon a shove, honey?"

Forget him, she advised herself. Think of him as just another camper. You should know by now that a business suit, be it equipped with either pants or a skirt, makes you break out in hives. Stop torturing yourself over something that can never be.

She picked up little Stevie and let him ride herd on the apples. "Hang on, Stevie, here we go."

She bent to pick up the wagon's handle and dropped it on her foot when she jerked back up at the sound of flying gravel.

Grabbing her foot, she hopped to keep her balance while she massaged her toes. "Ouch, damn." And hallelujah!

There was a green Mercedes in the driveway.

David was back.

Annie put her foot down and stepped on it gingerly.

The car pulled up next to them and David rolled the driver's window down. "Hi, Annie. Hi, kids."

Her children all chorused excitedly, "Hi, David. We missed the school bus this morning. Mom said the sight of you sleeping on the sofa distracted her. She had to drive us and we were late. It was great."

"Sounds terrific," David returned and wondered what he'd done in his sleep that had distracted Annie to the point she'd forgotten to send the kids out the door. Seemed to him a mother of five would look forward to the peace and quiet a school day would provide. It would be counterproductive not to watch the clock. Then he noticed that Annie was turning an intriguing shade of red right there in front of him.

"You want to sleep over tonight, too?" Casey questioned earnestly. "Maybe we can miss the bus again."

"I don't think so, honey," David said gently, keeping pace with the small group with his car. He hoped the campsite had dried out enough to be usable. He'd bought a plastic dropcloth at a paint store in the nearby small town. Hopefully, it would work for a ground cloth. He'd also gotten a slab of foam rubber for further insulation and cushioning under his sleeping bag. "I picked up a couple of things for you guys while I was in town," he told the kids.

David looked good, Annie thought as she fought to control her blush. Last night's damp flannel shirt had disappeared and the elbow resting on his open car window was now clad in a soft woolen plaid with what looked like a real suede oval elbow patch. The interior of the car was dark compared to the bright sunlight on the driveway, but the collar of David's shirt appeared to be suede, as well.

"David, why don't you drive ahead to the house. We'll meet you there," she suggested, needing a few moments to practice some pulse-controlled biofeedback techniques she'd read about. Time to instruct some loudmouthed children on appropriate and inappropriate family disclosures would also be nice.

"Oh, right. I could hurt one of the kids driving next to them like this, couldn't I? I'm sorry, Annie, I wasn't thinking. Hold on to them until I'm out of the way. Is everybody clear?"

Annie gathered the children by the side of the road and waved David on, embarrassed herself. She hadn't even thought of the danger presented by the car traveling so close to the moving column of children. She would have to be extremely vigilant for however long David intended to stay. She must not become distracted in a dangerous way.

"Okay, kids, it's safe now. Let's get this wagon rolling."

She was suddenly eager to get to the house. David would be waiting there. "Come on, we'll skip. I know, let's race."

"All the apples will fall out of the wagon if we go too fast."

"Oh. You're right. Well, then, we'll walk, but let's walk fast and not dawdle along the way, okay?"

"Okay. Mark, push. Mom, Mark's not pushing."

"I am, too. You're not pulling."

"Mom, Mark says I'm not pulling, but I am. He's not pushing...."

For once, Annie was oblivious to her children's bickering. Her mind was centered on David.

So were her children's.

Amy wondered out loud, "I bet he bwought us a pwesent."

Annie keyed in on that announcement. "Don't you dare ask him, Amy. That wouldn't be polite."

"I only said maybe."

"And I said not to ask about it." Her four-year-old wore a disgruntled expression, but didn't push the issue.

"I hope him got me a Ninja Turtle. I pray for one every night," Billy chimed in.

Annie rolled her eyes and let it drop. Reasoning with Amy was tough enough, arguing with a three-year-old was an exercise in futility.

"Get on one side of the wagon, Billy. If any apples start to tumble out, you catch them before they hit the ground."

Yellow jackets caught wind of their cargo and Annie was kept busy waving them away before they took exception to the fruit's removal. It would be just her luck to get stung and spend her time with David covered in baking-soda plasters.

It seemed an eternity, but finally they had reached their objective and Annie found herself grinning rather inanely as the children surrounded David. He had the solid look of a fort, albeit one currently under siege.

David gathered his newfound popularity centered around missing the school bus, but he had little idea on how to capitalize on his gains. He swung three-year-old Billy up into his arms, which left Amy looking sad. He tried to pick her up, but had to set Billy down to do it. Billy didn't care for that, but had trouble being heard over the complaints of Stevie who sat as king of the apple hills with arms stretched up.

"All right, you guys. Leave David alone. He can't carry all three of you at once," Annie commanded.

"No, no. It's all right. I'll just, uh…" David shifted Amy onto one side and managed to work Stevie into the crook of his free arm. "There." He looked doubtfully at Billy.

Annie had to give him points for trying.

"Bill, let's see, you—you climb up on this and hop on my back. How's that?" The feat accomplished, he grinned at Annie.

He listed as badly as one of the apple trees under a heavy load of snow. She grinned back.

He wobbled, but caught himself. "I hope I'm not intruding."

She dismissed that. "No, of course not."

"I realized last night and again today while I was in town that I am not cut out to do nothing."

"Really?"

"Yes. I figure as long as I'm here, I could help get the house ready for winter. You know, put up the storms and stuff like that."

"But this is your vacation, David. And I was going to start working on them tomorrow, so don't worry about it."

Wrestling with both his conscience and his libido for almost twenty-four hours had exhausted David. He was not in the mood to argue. "I'll take care of it. It'll be a good change from desk work. You can pay me back by feeding me dinner. That stupid little camp stove Hank lent me is for the birds. Took half an hour this morning to heat enough water for a cup of instant coffee." He couldn't believe what he was saying. His head was about to be ripped off his body and he was doomed to permanent curvature of the spine and he had just arranged for more of the torture. How did parents cope with this full-time? At last he could go home to the relative sanity of the office at the end of this so-called vacation. Poor Annie was stuck. "I've got a few things in the car for you."

Annie felt the stab of Amy's stubby little elbow.

"Ith it a turtle figure?" Billy asked eagerly.

David appeared nonplussed. "Uh, no. It's some fresh fruit and vegetables from a produce stand I passed down the road and meat for the freezer to replace some of the food I ate. I thought it would be good for you. Full of vitamins and protein and stuff like that."

Annie stared hard at Amy and bit back a smile at the disappointed sighs of resignation she heard. She told him softly, "It wasn't necessary to do that, David. The little bit of food you got last night wasn't that big of a deal. But I appreciate the gesture. And don't worry about the kids, either. What they need for healthy little bodies is exactly what you brought. Ninja Turtles and candy amount to a quick bribe, but don't last for the long haul. Someday they'll understand that your choices were right." She wondered if he understood any of what she was trying to say, but didn't think she could explain it any better. Maybe you had to live it to get it, she thought. Craig's poems were what she'd *thought* she needed, but they'd been just the trappings of romance. What she'd really needed was someone there beside her, pitching in with her. Craig never had. She shook off a bit of melancholy and said more loudly, "Mark and Casey will help you with the bags, David. The little ones and I are going to get these apples inside."

Annie got bags from the kitchen pantry, and Amy and Billy, aided by an occasionally successful bull's-eye from Stevie, transferred apples from the wagon to the sacks. Annie toted the filled bags inside.

The time consumed by all the carting and carrying brought an autumn sunset followed by an inky darkness that made the bright kitchen seem all the warmer by comparison. It was already six o'clock and dinner needed to be produced.

David cleared his throat, startling her. She turned back from her perusal of the open refrigerator. "I'm trying to think of something I can make for a quick supper. We've been outside since the older two got off the school bus. As soon as they stop moving long enough to think about it, they're all going to realize how hungry they are. What about spaghetti? We can add the ground chuck you brought.''

''I really meant it about getting the storms up for you, Annie. We'll work together on it tomorrow. Right now, though, I need to check on my sleeping bag. Is it still on the clothesline out back? I hope it dried out all right.''

''Shoot. Yes, it's still there. I forgot to bring it in.'' God, nitwit-itis strikes again. David probably thought she was a complete idiot the way she'd been operating since he got here.

''Annie, the sleeping bag belongs to me. I'm the one who slept without a ground cloth in the rain. I'm the one who should check on it and deal with it. Stop trying to assume responsibility for the world. You've got enough on your plate with just this small piece of the universe.'' He gestured around him.

She saw what he meant as she looked around at squabbling children, bags of apples leaning like the Tower of Pisa and a wall clock ticking inexorably on, determined as usual to show she couldn't get dinner on the table at a decent hour. But she was used to shouldering guilt. It was a mother's job, wasn't it? She felt guilty for every slipup her children made, every late meal, the condition of the campground, the inner cities, the states, the country, the continent and the world. The past few nights she'd been up worrying about the proliferation of nuclear warheads, for crying out loud. If one went off someplace, it would no doubt be her fault, too.

''Okay, David, I'll try. You bring in your bag, I'm going to get dinner on the table. Before seven o'clock.''

Annie set a pot of water on the stove and walked over to the window and placed her palm on the glass, wanting to touch the darkness, make peace with it again. ''He'll only be here two weeks," she murmured to the blackness held at bay by the glass. "What would be so bad about letting him help a bit? There will be plenty of time to make up for it once he's gone." An eternity of time. She sighed and set herself to buttering a loaf of French bread.

"Annie?"

"Hmm?"

"By any chance, did the kids play, oh, I don't know, soldiers and Indians, or house, or possibly have a pretend campout today?"

Annie had a bad feeling about this particular line of questioning. "No, Billy and Amy put on a play for Stevie while I folded laundry in the basement, but that was about all. Why do you ask?"

"What was the play about?"

"I don't know."

"It wath about a beeyootiful butterfly who got thtuck coming out of hith cocoon."

"Oh." David looked down at Billy, the supplier of this helpful bit of information. "The butterfly had a hard time getting out, huh?"

"Yeth, he was thtuck."

"Bill, old buddy, what did you and Amy use for the cocoon?"

"Oh, no."

David took in Annie's wide eyes. "Oh, yes," he responded grimly. "And the butterfly's struggle must have taken place in a mud puddle. The sleeping bag is not only wet again, it's now filthy."

"David, I'm so sorry."

"Forget it." He sighed. "I'll do the cold water wash cycle thing you showed me this morning and try again. The thing is, I'm going to have to use your living room sofa again tonight. Is that all right, or would you rather I tried to find a hotel someplace?"

Annie appeared startled. "No, no. Of course you'll stay here. For heaven's sake. There's no hotel for miles."

Naturally there wouldn't be, David thought. Hell. He *wanted* to help Annie. Truly he did. He just wanted to do it from a distance. If he could have at least stayed at his own campsite, there would have been a chance of maintaining an emotional space.

Giving in to the inexplicable attraction he felt would be akin to shooting himself in the foot. And it would hurt Annie, as well. Any gardening book he'd ever perused spoke of the poor probability of successfully transplanting delicate wildflowers and Annie was about as delicate as they came. She'd curl up and die in Northstream, while he couldn't conduct business from anyplace else. No, there could be nothing between him and this beautiful woman even if she wasn't the mother of five, not to mention Vic Glenn's daughter.

Morosely he watched as Annie drained the pot of noodles.

"Anything I can do to help?"

"Uh, no, I can't think of anything. Casey, are you sure you washed the lettuce carefully?"

"Sure, I'm sure. I don't know how this little spot of dirt got here. Probably blew off of Mark's yucky clothes."

"It did not. Mom, did you hear what she said? I bet it came off of her. You know, last night she only *said* she'd taken a bath, but really all she did was use a washcloth on the back of her neck where you feel to see if we're clean."

"That's a lie."

Annie peered uneasily at David, wondering what he was making of her dear, sweet children's behavior. "All right, you two, that's enough. Casey, I think the lettuce needs one more rinse. Mark, finish setting the table and call the little ones downstairs. Make sure they wash their hands. I think we've all got a little dirt from the apple orchard clinging to us."

Casey stuck her tongue out as Mark went by to retrieve his siblings.

"Mom—"

"Just go get the other three, Mark." That way the bedlam would be more than doubled, she realized with a sigh. "Casey, I saw that. You owe your brother an apology."

"He owes one to me," her daughter insisted defiantly. "He promised he wouldn't tell."

"In other words, you really did go to bed last night without washing."

"Well—"

"Never mind." Annie used a sideways glance to see how David was taking all this. He appeared oblivious to the bickering. "David, do you have any brothers or sisters?"

"No." He denied any such possibility. "Not a one."

And he sounded extremely grateful for that fact. Annie took the pot of bubbling sauce and dumped it over the noodles in their bowl.

"Annie? What's this?"

Annie was pulling two loaves of French bread wrapped in tin foil from the oven. "What's what?"

"This pile of metallic things here on the counter. They weren't here earlier."

"Oh, Casey and Billy have allergies. We have to have electronic air cleaners put on the furnace. When the pollen count gets real high, I close up the house and let the filters go to work."

"I see. What are they doing on the kitchen countertop?" he questioned carefully.

"They need washing every now and then. Zapping and frying all those little airborne things builds up a bunch of ash, you know," Annie responded, wishing he'd let the subject drop. She placed the bowl of spaghetti and unwrapped bread on the table. "There. Come sit down and forget the filters for now."

He did as he was asked. Dinner was served, and by the time it was over, David had a slightly green tint to his face. It might have been the lighting, but Annie suspected it had more to do with motion sickness from sitting at the same table with her children. There were occasions, she had to admit, when eating dinner with them made one feel like part owner in a jack-in-the-box factory. The children had continued to pop up during the meal no matter how hard she tried to keep their lids on. There were trips to the bathroom, trips for napkins, trips for the sponge and to return the same to the sink. Salt was required, as was grated cheese and then more milk to replace the spills sopped up by the sponges.

She'd remembered grace, and to impress David that while they might act heathenish upon occasion they were at least versatile heathens, they'd sung the Johnny Appleseed version. It had only served to remind her of the apples waiting to be made into sauce. Unfortunately she had no countertop work space until she could remember how the air filters went back into the furnace. Furthermore, darkness had crept in on the campground once again, and if she wasn't careful she was going to give herself an anxiety attack. David would be a lot more than green after witnessing one of those.

Procrastination sometimes worked well.

"Listen up, everybody, I've got a great idea. Let's get the table cleared and the food put away. We'll have a Go Fish tournament until it's time for bed. I'll even make some popcorn."

Her darling cherubs were having none of it. "I thought we were going to make applesauce," Mark complained. "That's why Casey and me climbed the trees."

"We can do that any old time, honey. I thought since we had company, we'd do something special for a change."

David hastened to urge her, "Listen, Annie, don't upset the uh, applecart just for me."

Annie wrinkled her nose at him.

He flushed. "Yeah, I know, that was bad. But go ahead and make the sauce. Otherwise the kids will be disappointed."

"They'll adjust."

"Mom, you promised."

"Yeah, Mom, you did."

"Oh, all right." Annie scowled. "Everybody rinse your dishes and stick them in the dishwasher. Casey, you help Stevie. Mark, make sure Amy and Billy get theirs into the right slots. I'll clear off the counters so we have some elbow room for working." She stalked over to the countertop and frowned at the metal gridwork rectangles piled there. She picked up the top one, turning it slowly in her hands, searching for some kind of directional marking.

David joined her there as she carefully checked the third piece in the pile.

"Here, Annie, why don't you let me take care of this? The kids are ready to get started. You go work with them. Just tell me what to do."

Annie tried to think. Was this the third or fourth stupid thing she'd done in David's presence? Maybe it was the fifth. "David," she admitted. "If I knew what to do, I'd have done it myself."

He gave her a blank look. "What?"

"I can't remember how to put them back in."

"You've never done this before? Where are the directions?"

"The directions are imprecise, to say the least. The electronic cleaner component goes in with this arrow going the same direction as the airflow. The prefilter goes in front of it."

David nodded. "Okay, that sounds pretty straightforward."

"Nowhere in any of the myriad diagrams does it give a clue as to which way the air in the furnace is flowing."

David frowned now, too. "Oh."

"Yeah, oh."

"And, yes, I've done this before. The first two times I called and had them explain it over the phone."

"That was a good idea," David encouraged.

"I had an even better idea the third time and wrote it down in the margins of the manual."

David picked up a silver block and turned it in his hands, inspecting it. "Did you lose the manual?"

"No, I did not lose the manual, it's right here. However, I scribbled it in so quickly that now I find I can't read my handwriting."

David held the manual out at arm's length. "Even without my glasses I believe I see the problem."

"David?"

"Hmm?"

"You are not to laugh. This isn't funny."

He cleared his throat.

She doubted he had any spaghetti caught in his throat, although it did sound as though he was choking on something.

"I can see it isn't."

Annie began stacking furnace components. She placed the manual on the top and hefted the heap into her arms. "I refuse to call them a fourth time. Start the kids washing the apples. I'll be back when you see me."

"Oh, now wait a minute, Annie. I don't know how to make applesauce and I don't relate well to anything under five feet tall. I haven't a clue what to do here." Damn. He'd

wanted to do some work around the house and grounds for
her. Something helpful but safely removed from the mayhem Annie seemed to specialize in creating, and that included the kids. Shoot. Glancing around the room, he
realized he was surrounded by pint-size faces, every one of
which peered up at him hopefully. Life-is-not-to-be-taken-
lightly Casey included.

And there was Annie, peering at him over the mountain
of metal frames. He'd walk across coals for her, he realized. Digging in his heels and getting all stubborn would
only intensify the burn. "Oh, go ahead. I'll cope."

Her quick flashing smile would likely be all the thanks
he'd get.

It took Annie a full half hour of listening to various tun-
nels formed of metal sheeting to figure out the direction of
the air flow. This time she took a blue crayon and wrote directly on the pipe the cleaner was connected to: THIS IS AN
AIR INTAKE. AIR IS GOING THIS WAY. And she drew an arrow.

She double-checked it, making sure it was legible, nodded her satisfaction and stuck the crayon back in her pocket.

"Hah! There, I did it. By myself I did it." She flicked on
the power to the unit and listened in satisfaction to the faint
crackling noise of microscopic particles being incinerated as
they crossed the electric field she'd created. Gathering her
skirt up in one hand, she bounded lightly up the steps, in a
rush to tell David of her success.

"David," she gushed as she entered the kitchen. "Guess
what? I figured it out." The words tumbled out as happily
as a clear-watered brook bubbled over stones in its river-
bed. Her excitement quickly dried up as she took in the
condition of the kitchen. She closed her eyes, convinced the
depression that had played havoc with her brain had now
affected her sight. She opened them again. There was no

denying the visual evidence in front of her. While the kitchen had been outdated and laid out inefficiently, its crimes were not such as to merit the extent of this punishment.

She entered the room. Her prairie skirt and white eyelet underskirt swirled around her legs as she pirouetted slowly, taking in the carnage.

Apples covered every surface. They teetered in stacks on the table. They rolled across the floor. They bobbed in a bath in the sink. They drip-dried on the counter and their bathwater dribbled onto the floor. Apple bruises and apple cores cut from fruit now burbling in pots simmering on every burner lay in mounds around the ancient stove. Apple seeds crunched underfoot and she worried lest someone's foot would slide out from under them as her children scrambled through it all, trying to keep up with a production line that seemed to have degenerated into a free-for-all. Then she took in David's set features. *He doesn't look like a happy camper,* she concluded.

"So, David, how's the, uh, applesauce coming along?"

"Don't ask," he mumbled darkly.

"That bad?"

"David, how does this look?"

She watched him glance distractedly into Casey's bubbling brew. "Looks good to me, kiddo, but then what do I know?"

"I got all these old margarine tubs out, David, and I found the lids, too. Is this enough?"

David's eyes seemed to measure as they swung from the simmering pots to the apples still gathered on the counters and then to the containers waiting on the cabinet top.

"It's kind of hard to tell, isn't it, Mark? This cookbook I found says the apples will boil down, but it doesn't say by how much. We'll have to play it by ear."

David worked with numbers for a living. Numbers were exact. You always knew exactly where you stood with numbers. Annie had fled from that kind of precision. She seemed to enjoy buzzing through life by the seat of her pants. A certain grimness settled in as he realized he had set himself on a path to personal insanity unless he could disentangle himself from the endearing, ensnaring personalities surrounding him—and quickly.

"Do you want me to take over here, David?"

David contemplated the offer skeptically, sure it was a trick of some kind. "What's the alternative?"

"Go put your feet up in the living room," she insisted. "I think I even have a beer in the back of the fridge left over from friends who dropped by during the summer. I'll finish up in here and join you when I get everybody bathed and pj'd."

David sighed audibly. What was done was done. If he sank today or sank tomorrow, what was the difference? He heard the resignation in his voice as he said, "No, you've got to be as tired as I am. You get the baths going. I always finish what I start."

Annie wondered if that applied to relationships, as well. If it did, what did he see as their future?

She pulled Stevie out of the pots and pans cabinet and sent an apologetic smile across the room to David when he jumped at the ensuing clatter of lids against kettles. "Come on, honey," she cooed. "Time to get cleaned up for bedtime."

"Want a story."

"One."

"No, no. Want *lots* of stories."

"Two," she bargained, flushing her three youngest out of the kitchen and up the stairs. The nightly bartering with her eighteen-month-old seemed suddenly silly with David looking on.

"Is that lots?"

"Yes," she assured him.

She left David resolutely straining apple mush through a colander and wondered if he'd make it through the full two weeks of vacation for which he'd scheduled himself. After tonight, he'd probably take off for some campsite in the Canadian wilderness, preferring bears and wolves to temporarily fathering her brood.

Chapter Five

David hummed tunelessly as he attempted to dry his hands on a soggy dish towel some two hours later. He was alone in a quiet kitchen. Annie had briefly reappeared once the children had all been tucked in, but he'd sent her off to bed an hour earlier when her fatigue had her saving the seeds and skin and tossing the strained sauce. He had intervened in the nick of time.

After flipping off the kitchen lights, he felt his way back into the living room where the unappealing, lumpy sofa awaited his pleasure. It was heaped with the pillows and blankets Annie had scrounged up the night before. He looked at it with a fatalistic sense of déjà vu before he slipped out of his soft wool shirt and jeans and flipped open a sheet and two blankets. Crawling in between the layers he'd created, he tried to get comfortable. It wasn't easy.

The sofa was too uncomfortable to allow anything other than a light dozing. Hours later, he was immediately aware of the soft scuffling of slippered feet coming down the staircase. Annie didn't look his way as she entered the room. He watched through slitted lids as she slipped ethereally across the room to the front picture window. Annie lifted a corner of the curtains back and David wondered what she so intently searched for in the triangle of inky blackness. He heard her small sound of unhappiness and saw her curl into the overstuffed wingback next to the drapes. Still holding back a section of drapery, she sat in the chair and stared out. Every now and then she shivered, but she continued to sit and study the monochromatic study in black framed in the window.

"Annie," he finally questioned softly. "What are you doing?"

Her head spun in his direction. "I'm sorry, David. I didn't mean to wake you, but this is the only east-facing window I've got."

David just knew that was supposed to clarify things. Somehow, though, he couldn't quite get a grip on how. "Annie, what does the direction of the view have to do with anything? There's no moon tonight and you haven't got any streetlights. It's pitch-dark. Why are you trying to look out the window at all? There's absolutely nothing to be seen."

She looked rather forlorn as she returned her gaze to the nonexistent view. "There's not a sign of the sun yet, is there?"

David checked the luminescent numbers on his watch. "It's only four o'clock. The sun won't rise for another two hours, at least."

"If it comes up at all."

He sat up on the sofa. "What?"

Annie continued staring at the blanketed eastern horizon as she talked. "I mean, maybe this is the morning where it just doesn't come back."

The house seemed suddenly cool. David pulled the blankets up a bit. He struggled to follow her reasoning, but felt more as if he'd been plunked down in the Twilight Zone. Any minute now, Rod Serling would announce in that wonderful, sonorous voice of his, "Consider this. You are visiting a friend out in the country. The sun cannot rise without her presence and encouragement. One morning, even her strength is not enough. The sun simply does not return. You have now entered the Twilight Zone."

"Annie, of course the sun will rise. It'll be there. It's just too early right now."

He saw her shiver and pull her robe more tightly around her shoulders. "You have to wonder if it doesn't ever get tired. So tired it won't bother rising again."

Ah, the light in his head, if not the sky, dawned. Annie was transferring her own emotional fatigue onto the inanimate things around her. He had no idea what to say that would be comforting. Much to his chagrin, he found himself slipping into a scientific explanation of the sun's and earth's relative positions in the solar system. "Think, Annie. The sun doesn't go anywhere. It's the earth turning and revolving around the sun that just gives the impression of sunrise and sunset." It was all wrong. He felt like a jerk. Annie's soul needed soothing and all he could come up with was a lesson right out of a grammar-school earth science class.

Annie sank back into the chair. Her arm dangled over the wingback's side, its pale thinness oddly emphasized against the chair's dark bulk. "It's so weird. And hard to explain. On one level, I know the sun doesn't actually rise or set."

David saw her lean forward for another searching glance into the night.

"But on some other level—and it's only been the past few months that I've been concerned about it—I just can't seem to get past what my eyes seem to see. And I worry about it.

I end up coming down here every morning and just sitting here, waiting to make sure the sun makes it back one more time. It's awful.''

As well it would be. David tried to imagine the depth of Annie's pain. Her world must be dark indeed that she needed to personally ensure the sun's—and light's—return each morning. If he wasn't in his underwear and unwilling to shock her in her present state, he'd get up and sit in the wingback, with Annie in his arms, and they'd wait for the sun together.

As it was, he didn't know what to do. There was Annie, no more than a few feet away, vulnerable and needing someone.

He wanted to comfort her. He'd made the decision to be as much help as possible during his stay. He just didn't know if he could pull it off right then without making his own needs obvious. His body was already reacting to the picture she made there in front of the window. Good grief, he was a sick person himself. It was hard to imagine anyone becoming . . . uncomfortable in a situation like this.

Well, he decided philosophically, he'd just have to be strong. Snagging his pants from the sofa end table, he wriggled into them under the covers. He did not want to have to explain to any childish apparitions what he was doing in his briefs with their mother cuddled on his lap so early in the morning. There'd been enough trouble explaining things to Casey the night he'd arrived, and he'd been totally dressed then. Once he finally fumbled the top snap into its mate and pulled the zipper up, he felt free to peel the blanket off and, at long last, pry himself out of the prison-like sofa.

Annie protested when he turned on the end table lamp. ''David, the light's glaring on the window. Now I can't see out at all.''

He turned on the floor lamp next to her wingback. "You don't need to see out. I will personally guarantee that the sun will come back, but not for a while." He took her hands, preparing to hoist her out of her seat. "You and I are going out to the kitchen. I'll heat up some mugs of cider and we'll talk." The best thing to do, he reasoned, was distract her. Keep her occupied until he could point out dawn's returning light. "It's been, what, ten years since you left the company? You can fill me in on all that missing time. And I'll fill you in on what I've been up to, too."

He managed to get her up and moving, and he flipped on every light switch they passed on their way to the kitchen in an effort to dispel some of the gloom in both the house and her mind. "Did you know," he began as he set a steaming mug of cider in front of her, "that I've worked my way up to branch manager since you left?"

"I know," she responded. "You mentioned it earlier. You must be so proud. That's quite an accomplishment."

"Oh, I intend to go a lot farther. That's why I'm taking this vacation. I needed to get away." Charitably he left "from your father" unsaid. "I should get another promotion sometime this year. Then who knows how long it might be before I can get away again?"

She'd known since David first appeared that he ran on the fast track. Why did hearing it put into words depress her so? "There's always something going on in the business world that makes it tough to get away, isn't there, David? That's one of the reasons I hated it. Actually, I'm surprised you didn't go a lot farther once you scraped together a two-week time block. Hawaii, Las Vegas or someplace."

David's surprise showed. "Do I look like the Las Vegas type?"

She studied him. "Kind of. Maybe not. I don't know."

Kind of, maybe not, she didn't know? Disconcerted, he assured her, "Annie, I've never gambled in my life unless you count putting a dollar into an office betting pool on—" Oops, he'd better shut up. That betting pool had been on how many addendums her father would try to add to his latest contract with the company. "At any rate, a dollar here or there is not considered major gambling. Not Las Vegas style."

"Oh." Annie shook her head, showing her understanding.

Oh? That was it? He'd *oh'd* her. Peering intently at her over his own mug of cider, he continued. "Job security. A steady income you can depend on, that's where it's at. Nothing is worth jeopardizing that. My parents never had that. The pressure got to my dad. He took off when I was three. My mom tried, but she had no education or training. She ended up working three jobs. My aunt says she died from sheer overwork."

Annie was shocked. She'd had no idea. They'd known *of* each other when she'd worked there, but hadn't really *known* each other. Obviously she'd missed out on a lot. "David, I'm so sorry—"

He waved away her interruption. "Hell, I didn't mean to make you feel bad. You feel bad enough as it is. I guess the point I'm trying to make in my own convoluted way is that a dependable, steady income can go a long way toward easing anxiety. Especially when a pack of kids are depending on you for every crumb that gets put in their mouths. Maybe you ought to consider coming back. You're a different person now, older. A decent paycheck you can count on showing up the fifteenth and thirtieth of every month might make you feel a hell of a lot better. Think about it. I'd hire you."

She blinked back tears as she rose and went to the sink. She washed out her mug and set it there. Clearly neither one of them was much good at pegging people. She'd misinterpreted key clues to David, but if he thought she could go back to the city without curling up and dying, he was just as obviously misreading her, as well. She picked up the mug she had just rinsed, rinsed it again and put it back in the sink a second time. Next she looked at the stack of clean kettles piled next to the sink and did a double take. "Were all those dirty?"

"Every one of them. Look at that mountain, Annie. With the kind of salary you could earn, you could hire a housekeeper and buy your own damn applesauce in a professionally processed, germ-free glass jar from a grocery store like normal people do."

"I'd be in high heels every day, wearing a shirt with a floppy bow tie that strangled me again. My kids would be raised by a baby-sitter. Furthermore, I like putting up applesauce."

"I could tell."

"This year's been different. I've been under somewhat of a strain." Out of the corner of her eye she spotted a blob of sauce David had missed when he'd sponged off the counter. She cleaned it up herself. "My children will have wonderful childhood memories from all this."

He hoped not. He'd just as soon be left out of memories of tonight's fiasco. "They'd have wonderful memories of Northstream, as well. They'll just be different." David only had twelve days left. How much could he accomplish in that time frame? Once back in Northstream, he wouldn't be of much help to Annie. And in his estimation, she *did* need help with the kids—Vic could provide that, and if she came back, she could also enjoy a bit of culture while escaping from all this . . . nature.

Annie was still busy being overwhelmed and defensive. "No, it wouldn't work. The kids would have to be reoutfitted from head to toe in order to fit into Northstream."

David was no longer used to having his suggestions questioned. At least, not to his face. "I make far more now than

I ever thought possible. Way more than one man needs to live comfortably. I'll help." He'd make sure Vic did, too.

He followed her as she began trailing out of the kitchen and wandering toward the living room. "No, this is my responsibility, not yours. The kids are all settled into school here, they have their own little friends. The upheaval might be too much."

Although frustrated and secretly suspecting the upheaval might be harder on the schools than the children, he decided not to push any further right then. Catching up to Annie, he took her hand in his. "Okay," he said, although he had no intention of accepting this as the final word. Wisconsin was simply too far away. "Let's go back into the living room. We'll sit on the sofa and wait for the sun together."

After David opened the drapery a bit, he joined her on the lumpy couch. He hooked the coffee table closer with one foot and wrapped the blanket around them both, then put his arm around her. They leaned back and put their feet up on the table, snuggling silently. The uncomfortable position seemed to be outweighed by the security of being held in his arms.

Annie dozed off and David watched the sun come up by himself.

The morning light, though, did little to improve Annie's stubbornness, David found the next day. She absolutely refused to listen to reason. Annie helped him pull the storm windows out of storage and line them up against a wall of the garage. They argued the subject up one side and back down the other while they worked.

"Wow, these windows are really dirty," she said, eyeing the cobwebs and dirt clinging to the row of dingy glass.

"I'd noticed the same thing," David agreed as he wiped some of the grime off his hands and onto his jeans.

Then Annie made some observation about how there was a big difference between accepting a little help around the place as a payback for meals and taking advantage of some poor sap for everything she and children who weren't even his needed.

That made him grit his teeth. He was not "some poor sap." True, the thought of dealing with all those children frightened him, but no way would he let any of them suffer. What's more, he could well afford to help her out until she was back on her feet. He informed her of that salient fact. He was *not* a sap.

That wasn't what she meant, she told him as she pulled the hose into position, and he very well knew it.

Women. They were unbelievably exasperating. How was he supposed to have known that? Maybe sensitive-and-in-touch-with-his-emotions Craig might have known it, but David was just a nonunderstanding, typical nose-to-the-grindstone working slob. He took the hose from her and gave the control a vicious twist that sent water spurting over the windowpanes. It ran from the glass down onto the ground where it puddled in the dirt. He felt like turning the hose on Annie. It would serve a dual purpose, both cooling off her temper and appeasing the devil in the back of his mind that wondered what Annie would look like in a wet T-shirt. Although how he could even think in terms of sex when he was as mad as a hornet, he had no idea. Right then he was even angry with his poor sainted mother for working so hard that he felt obligated to help another hard-working mother out. Now that *was* totally unfair.

He indicated the growing puddle with his free hand. "This is all going to turn into mud, you know, Annie. If the kids get into it, it will get tracked all through the house."

"I'll give them all rakes. They'll be so occupied piling up leaves to jump in, they won't even be aware that a great mud-pie opportunity has passed them by."

"Look at them," Annie directed twenty minutes later. She pointed to her frolicking children, all squealing in delight while rolling in a heap of crisp yellow and orange leaves.

David straightened slowly and obliged her by turning his gaze onto the group. He recognized the shape of the leaves. Maples. Amazing that she didn't try and tap the trees and boil down her own damn syrup. "They certainly seem to be having a good time," he observed noncommittally, unwilling to put any ideas into her head.

"How many kids in Northstream do you know unsophisticated enough to have the time of their lives jumping in a leaf pile?"

"I don't know any kids in Northstream, period. I leave at seven in the morning and don't get back until seven or eight at night. The house is basically an investment for me. It's a four-bedroom central-entrance brick colonial, almost four thousand square feet. It needs people who actually live in it and use it as more than a place to crash at night before it could honestly be called a home." David pulled a damp rag across his forehead, taking off the top layer of sweat and grime with it. "There's an idea. You could stay there until you found a place of your own." Damn, he was tired. Keeping up with Annie was tough stuff.

He wiped his throat next. "Anyway," he expounded, "leaf jumping is fairly universal, I would think. It's not like Northstream's another planet."

Annie shook her head vigorously. "You're wrong, David. For these kids, it would be. Don't forget, I grew up in Deermeadow, which is right next door. Those kids have ballet lessons on Mondays, piano on Wednesday, scouting on Friday and gymnastics on Tuesdays and Thursdays. They grab a fast supper and rush out again to the local children's theater play rehearsals. If there's a night off from that, they carpool to swim team, or basketball, or soccer, or hockey, or little league, or tennis practice at the club."

David felt a bit stunned. "It can't be that bad."

"Believe me, I lived that way for years. It is *exactly* that bad. It's not what I want for these guys. Even if it was, do you have any idea how expensive that is? Not just the lessons, but the equipment they'd need?"

"I said I'd get them anything they needed."

"Two hundred dollars for hockey skates, a helmet and safety pads? And that's secondhand. I priced them for a peewee league that was forming here last year."

Two hundred dollars? Good grief. He turned off the hose spigot and squished his way through the soggy ground over to her side. "Listen, I'm too tired and hungry to argue anymore. You win." And she had. She was actually more stubborn than he. "I was only trying to figure out a way to help you once my vacation is up." And he still would, damn it.

Hell. He'd gotten too close to her. There was some kind of magnetic field humming now between their two bodies. Annie must have felt it, too, for that hardheaded woman reached up and pulled his face to hers.

It was a natural, uncalculating gesture when she kissed him. "Thank you, David," she said.

As a gesture meant to soothe his temper, it left a lot to be desired. The kiss zinged its way down his legs, knocking out all his muscles' normal chemical impulses as it went. His legs and arms were left obnoxiously weak.

His annoyance grew with his body's response. Now he was angry with himself as well as with her stubbornness. He did not want to feel these things. Physically helping her get the family back on its feet, yes. Tying his emotions into a knot worthy of the *Queen Mary*'s anchor line, no.

Possibly his body's reactions were due to fatigue. He hadn't slept worth a damn the night before. Parts of him were hot and he leaked what felt like steam—from a long morning of physical work, he hoped. Other parts were iced down and chilled—from the running hose? He'd probably be sick by nightfall.

"Let's go eat," he said. "I think I've got low blood sugar or something. I need to get some food into my body." But he didn't step away, instead he let his arm drape across her shoulders and he kept her there by his side. With his arms and legs acting so strangely, he told himself, it was just common sense to keep a crutch close at hand.

Shortly after lunch, David discovered he had a fear of heights. Annie of the electrical body and knock-'em-dead kiss had located an ancient wooden extension ladder in the hinter regions of the garage. The initial frisson of fear had feathered down his spine with his first good look at it. "This is it?"

Annie gave him an odd look. "You wanted a ladder that would reach the upper-floor windows, right?"

"Yes, I guess that's what I asked for," he responded glumly. He should have been more specific and requested one that had come off the assembly line sometime during this century. The concept of slowly wobbling his way up to the second story while maintaining a grip on both the ladder and the bucket had a trickle of sweat dribbling down his back that contradicted the cool fall afternoon.

"Well..." Annie prompted, motioning toward the old relic hanging on hooks along the back garage wall.

Man, David thought in disgust as he struggled to lift the heavy wooden monstrosity and release it from the hooks holding it captive.

He hoped Mary Ellen McGee was enjoying the beautiful fall weather they'd been having. It would be her last, if David had his way. And Annie, she would owe him a major debt when he was done with this task.

Every time he battled his way up the ladder and hung a window while carefully looking only straight ahead and never down, every time he fought the ladder to a new position under a different opening, he thought of a new way to collect on Annie's mounting debt. Gradually he came to realize the only fantasies that seemed to satisfy the size of her obligation centered around a revitalized Annie handing over her virtue on a solid sterling platter.

"Next job on the list is installing a lock on her bedroom door," he decided as he once again fought with the ladder, this time back to the garage, thank God. "That way, when the debt paying gets serious, the kids won't be able to disturb us." The sun had given up an hour ago. David was frozen through, dead tired and had dishpan hands. The skin on his knuckles cracked and hurt where they curled around the ladder's rungs. "I'll toss all her clothing out the window and keep her in there with me for a week," he muttered with a certain amount of relish as he heaved one end of the ladder back up onto its hook. "She'll be wanting me, begging me, before I'll take her. Then I'll let her take me and we'll alternate giving up our respective virtues every hour on the hour for the rest of the week or until there's no virtue left and we're both thoroughly bad. Whichever comes last."

The thought of such an idyllic happening gave him the strength to hoist the other end of the ladder onto its hook. He dragged himself into the house, convinced that all that was keeping him alive was the fact that he was too tired to summon up enough energy to die.

Dinner, when it was finally served around seven-thirty, was hot dogs. David gratefully settled for three of those and a handful of chips. Then Annie spooned baked beans on his plate. He ate them only to set a good example, but he found even they tasted good. For a special treat, Annie had made root-beer floats to go with the boiled dogs. David wondered what he'd ever seen in real beer. The black cow slid down his throat. The melted ice cream beautifully coated the parched, dry spot way in the back. The entire sublime con-glomeration—hot dogs, chips, beans and root beer—sat in a pool of contentment in his stomach, sending "you're mellow" signals up to his brain. He left the kitchen to sink into the living room sofa. Putting his stocking feet up on the small brass-and-glass coffee table, he let his head fall back. A sigh escaped his lips as his eyelids drifted shut.

Sleep began fogging his brain almost immediately. It was an out-of-body type experience, sort of. He could feel it stealing over him, could feel his arms and legs disconnect themselves from his conscious control and become heavy, lifeless weights. Gradually he became aware of a weight on the weight. It was several seconds more before he got one of his eyelids to respond to his command to open.

Through bleary eyes, he studied what appeared to be a hand resting on his one thigh. Odd. It was awful small. He ordered his head to turn to the right and eventually suc-ceeded in doing so. He checked to his left, as well. Nope, it wasn't one of his. Too close to sleep to overly worry, his eyes glassed over again.

The hand shook his leg. A voice spoke, sort of angelic-like. "David?"

Boy, this was getting otherworldly. Probably an angel of the Lord, come to express God's gratitude for what a great guy he'd been lately. "Mmmph?"

"Mom says to come bothuh you for a while. She's twying to do the dishes and Stevie is in the way."

David forced his eyes open once again and he did his best to focus on the source of this announcement. Finally, by following the hand to its arm, the arm to its shoulder and proceeding on up from there, he found Amy's decidedly unangelic head. It was a moment before he spoke. Even then his words sounded slurred. "Only Stevie was in the way? Not little Miss Amy?"

"Nope. Not me. I didn't do nothing. It was all Stevie. He kept stealing huh bubbles and smushing them on the flooh." A pint-size piece of trouble was unceremoniously pushed forward, his face displaying the most mutinous bottom lip David had ever seen.

He tried to rally his tongue for a second attempt at speech. He managed, "Hi, Stevie." A moment later, he got out, "What's up?"

David watched with a certain detached graveness as Stevie burst into tears. "Mommy and Casey *bad,*" he hiccuped. "They *dumb!*"

Evidently the sins committed against the little tyke were manifold and compounded greatly by the sheer stupidity of the sinners. One could only commiserate with Stevie's frustrations. "Come sit by me," he offered. His arms had still not reconnected to his somatic nervous system—they refused to listen to his commands to move. Under those conditions, he wasn't sure what kind of haven he could provide, but it had to be better than the trials the soap bubble thief had suffered in the kitchen with his bad, dumb relatives. But how to convince Stevie?

"Didn't I wash all those windows for your mother?" he asked as the toddler hesitated.

Stevie wiped his eyes with the back of a balled fist before nodding reluctantly.

Finally David got his arms to move. He held them out in a come-to-me gesture. "That proves I'm good." At least, he hoped it did. He worried that it could just as easily be a sign of stupidity that would relegate him instead to the same category of low-IQ individuals from which Stevie had just escaped.

Being less than two, however, Stevie's reasoning power had yet to fully develop and he finally climbed up onto the sofa next to David and snuggled into his side.

David wrapped his left arm around the little one and settled back into the sofa, determined to recapture the sleep point—that moment in time differentiating slumber from wakefulness—that had just escaped through no fault of his own.

Stevie popped his thumb into his mouth, put his head down on David's chest and appeared content to settle in for some serious cuddling.

David's eyes drifted shut and he felt a distant foggy mist call his name. It was bliss. "Oh, no," he exclaimed as his eyes popped open. There was a decided dampness seeping through his pants and shirt along the left side.

He gazed down at the most likely source of moisture. Amy had not exaggerated her claim that Stevie had been in the dishwater. He hoped it was dishwater. It could just as likely be an inside job, he supposed.

Two huge innocent blue eyes stared back up at him.

"Stevie, you're all wet."

There was evidently no ready response for such a charge. Stevie continued to suck his thumb and look limpidly back up at him.

David glanced at the watch on his wrist. Eight fifty-four. He must be getting old to be totally wiped out so early. He sighed. "You need a complete overhaul, kiddo. And it's past your bedtime. Your mom needs to give you a bath, clean diapers and pajamas." He thought about that. Annie was out in the kitchen putting away dishes and scrubbing kettles. She ran this race around the obstacle course of the campground and motherhood every day. It was probably how she'd maintained that figure that still knocked him cold even though she'd been through five pregnancies. It probably also made her tired every night. Just as tired as anything he could claim. Thinking about Annie exhausted, trying to bathe five overtired children, twisted something painful inside his chest.

To complicate matters, there was no doubt all the children needed baths. And there was only one other adult in the house who could take over the chore. He eyed Stevie once more. Would the kid catch pneumonia in his wet clothes if he waited another twenty minutes for his mother to finish up out in the kitchen?

Consciences were hellish things. His was quite busily working on him. It did not let up until he sighed and hauled himself out of the depths of the sofa. He was here to help, wasn't he?

"Come on, Stevie," he said as he lugged the little one toward the stairs. "You too, Amy. Let's round up the rest of the gang and get the bath brigade started."

"Don't wanna."

"You don't want to play in some nice warm bubble water for a while, put on a clean diaper and neato jammies with feet on the bottom?"

"No."

"Too bad. It was only a rhetorical question. We're doing it, anyway." The only remaining question in David's mind was how the hell he was supposed to go about deducting this—and he considered it his biggest corporal work of mercy to date—from his income tax as a charitable deduction.

Chapter Six

Annie couldn't remember ever being so tired. Even the awful fatigue that had accompanied her depression hadn't seeped into her very bones like this. The staircase loomed as high as Mt. Everest and she thought she would scale it with no less difficulty than climbers encountered on that peak in Nepal.

"Listen up, feet," she ordered. "Do your thing. Get me up there." A puff of air gusted out audibly as she thought of how nice it would have been to have asked David to handle the children's baths. Unfortunately she was so far in his debt after everything he'd done for her the past two days, she doubted she could dig her way out with a pickax and shovel.

There hadn't been a sound from the front of the house for twenty or thirty minutes. He was no doubt asleep on the living room sofa by now. He'd stared off into space through most of his hot dog, seemingly eating more by force of habit than any kind of concentrated effort. He hadn't even commented when she'd caught herself sticking the salt into the refrigerator and leaving the ketchup in the middle of the kitchen table with the napkin holder.

"Anyway, they're not his children, they're mine," she reminded herself as she paused halfway up the stairs to regroup for the final assault. She was surprised at the regret she heard in her voice. David was all wrong for her, she acknowledged for the million and tenth time. He was quite caught up in running the corporate rat race. His life was organized around color-coded neckties and backboned with a rigid business structure. The creative free-spiritedness she considered her essence would curl back in on itself and die should she hook up with such a man.

Of course, teaming up with another free spirit hadn't worked out all that well, either, she admitted as she consciously picked up one foot and set it on the next step. There'd been no substance there, nothing solid a person could lean on. Her mind whirled while she recognized she didn't know *what* she wanted or needed in a man. All that mental gymnastic work was no doubt contributing to her fatigue, as well. She tried to shake off her strange mood and move her other foot. It was much harder to manage than the first. She forced it.

There was a real ruckus being raised on the second story, she noticed as she hauled herself up the final few stairs. It seemed to be coming from the bathroom. God, she'd kill them all if they'd decided to give themselves baths and had water all over the floor again. There was little doubt in her mind that it was extremely dangerous when the water came down through the living room light fixture.

It was the bane of every mother's existence that there was nothing surer than the knowledge that if she got busy, the children got busier. Bracing herself for soggy bedlam and another major cleanup, she made the turn into the bathroom. She felt a lecture attack coming on.

Her tongue was primed. "Listen, you guys, you *know* you're not supposed to…" Her words sputtered to a halt as she took in David's form draped over the tub as he built the little ones' mounds of shampoo bubbles into towering elegant coiffures straight out of the 1800s. Everyone was dissolved in giggles, with old lady Casey far and away the furthest gone and sporting the most outlandish do.

Annie stared in amazement, her lecture lost. There was only a minimal amount of water on the floor—she doubted she'd have done so well—and no dirty clothes at all. They'd all been deposited in the hamper. It was a miracle, and her heart swelled with reluctant feeling for the man who'd brought it about.

"Look, Mom. David says I look just like Marie Antoinette."

David glanced up and gave Annie an engaging grin that tore at her sensibilities.

"I may change professions," he said as he eyed Casey's hair critically. "I think I've found a new field." He leaned back over the tub to make a slight adjustment to a sagging curl.

Annie snorted at him before responding to Casey. "You look tremendously elegant, honey. But I think you'd better get your head rinsed now. Marie Antoinette lost hers on the guillotine, you know."

Casey pushed her nose high up in the air and looked out at her mother from slanted lids. "You're all my slaves," she announced. "And if you're not terribly careful, I'll have your *heads.*" Then she ruined the snotty effect by laughing sillily and sticking out her tongue.

"No," said Annie as she knelt by the tub, transfixed by the change in her daughter. "You're supposed to say, 'Let them eat cake,' if you're going to be Marie Antoinette."

The worried expression was gone from Casey's face and eyes. She looked just like an eight-year-old should. Carefree, goofy, and with not much else on her mind other than the bubble fest going on around her. The weight her daughter had carried since Craig's death and Annie's ensuing chronic depressed state had disappeared. Somehow David had done that. She glanced sideways at David while she picked up the small plastic pail kept by the tub and dunked it in the water before unceremoniously dumping it over Casey's head.

"Hey, you ruined my hairdo," the child sputtered while water ran in rivulets down her face.

"Garbage happens, Ms. Antoinette. It's part of life," Annie informed her offspring unfeelingly while mercilessly dumping a second bucket over her head. "Stand up and I'll wrap you up in your royal robe."

"I'll have your job for this, lady," Casey snootily informed her when she was standing.

Her mother draped a bath towel over her thin shoulders. "No, Casey," Annie told herself. "You *had* my job, you poor little tyke. You were trying to be mother, father, daughter and everything else for a while there. Now I've got my job back, thanks to David." She leaned over and kissed him right there in front of the children.

He gave her a confused but pleased look. "What was that all about?"

She shook her head, not really able to explain.

"Kissing! Mom, that is *so* gross!"

Billy was standing in the tub, dripping water on his siblings' heads. "Wanna robe, too!"

"Okay, champ, you've got it," David responded. But he stole another quick kiss before shaking out another towel and holding it for the next family member to emerge from the tub.

"Ooo, icky. Did you see that guys? Mowh kissing. Kiss me, too, David."

David helped Amy out and mummified her in a towel. "I thought it was icky."

"It's okay foh kids," Amy allowed, "but not gwown-ups."

"Ah, I didn't understand," David said, placing a smacker dead center on the child's forehead before blowing raspberries on the side of her neck.

Amy dissolved in giggles and threw her arms impetuously around his neck. "Do it again," she asked and broke up once more when David complied.

He was so good with them, Annie thought sadly. So good *for* them. But he'd be gone in a week and a half. She was so much better just since his arrival, there'd be no real excuse to stay in touch. Craig's absence had left her with a lot of work around the campground. When David left, she'd be left with an aching hole. She'd use the work to fill it. There was no other option.

David, despite Annie's urgings, worked right by her side until all five children had been pajama-ed, de-snarled, storied and bedded.

"Take your shower first, David," she insisted. "You're the guest."

"I was going back to my campsite tonight to sleep there," he told her, startled by her assumption he'd be staying the night again.

"Oh, no, don't do that," she protested. "It's too late to be hassling with all of that. I don't even know if your sleeping bag is dry. I forgot to check on it, we got so busy. Your blankets downstairs are still folded on the floor next to the sofa. Just sleep there. After all the work you did today, you deserve a real bathroom and a heated, comfortable sleeping space. Come on," she urged. "Otherwise I'll feel bad."

Hell, he thought. She certainly knew which buttons to push. "Okay," he agreed. "Just for tonight." Maybe she didn't want to be alone. He'd see her through the night and then he was getting the hell out of there. At least if he could separate from them at night he figured it might help keep emotional entanglements to a minimum, although he worried it might already be too late for that.

"Take your shower, David. The hot-water tank's had enough time to recover. Then go downstairs and sleep. In fact, sleep late in the morning. I'll keep the kids quiet."

She made it sound as though sleep would be easy to achieve on a too-short couch with only a plaster ceiling separating him from the reality of some of the more prurient daydreams the past forty-eight hours had inflicted on him. He settled for nodding in resigned acquiescence and going downstairs to retrieve clean sweats from his duffel bag.

David found little advantage in her courtesy of allowing him to go first. Conscious of Annie waiting exhausted in her room and unsure of the hot-water heater's capacity, he decided against lingering under the heated spray and attempting to steam the aches out of his muscles and joints.

So this is what sharing your life would get you, he told himself as he quickly ran the soap bar down an arm and over his chest. He worked the thin film up into a decent lather over his thatch of chest hair and laughed as he stepped back under the spray to rinse it all away and smiled as he thought of the beehive he'd created with Amy's hair.

But it wouldn't be all good times and playing in the tub, he warned himself. He'd seen the three little ones throw some pretty decent temper tantrums, Mark putting an ice cube down Casey's back for no good reason other than sheer devilment, and there had been teeth marks right through the plastic packaging of the hot dogs when he'd taken them out of the refrigerator to boil up for dinner.

"Chicken pox," he said out loud as he leaned over to soap the hair on his legs. "Flu, strep throat and algebra," a subject he considered listed in its proper place with other diseases. "Boy-girl garbage, girl-girl garbage and boy garbage of all types." He balanced on one foot like a flamingo while he washed the other and he thought of some of the stunts he himself had pulled off. "It's a damn wonder I'm still around at all," he told the cracked ceramic tile in front of him.

Switching to the other foot, he commiserated with Annie's horror as she'd described Mark coming home from school earlier in the week with a note from the teacher that he'd indignantly handed her.

"It wasn't my fault, Mom. I fell out of my seat and she got all mad at me for disrupting the class!"

"You didn't get hurt, did you?"

"Nah, of course not."

Annie had related to David that she'd been relieved at first, but the more she'd thought about the circumstances, the odder she found them.

She said she'd asked him, "How did you fall out of your seat in the first place, Mark?"

"It wasn't my fault, it was all Timmy Burkmeyer's fault. She didn't do anything to Timmy Burkmeyer. It's so unfair!"

"Timmy pushed you out of your seat?" Annie had told David she'd thought that did seem rather unfair for Mark to be in trouble if Timmy Burkmeyer had shoved him out of his desk.

"He didn't push me out, Mom. He told me a joke that was so funny I fell out 'cause I was laughing so hard."

Annie had explained that the only reason for her next question was she'd needed a good laugh herself right then, that ordinarily she'd have known better than to pursue this kind of conversation. "What was the joke that was so funny?"

"We were in math, Mom, and the teacher asked how much seven plus eight was and Timmy said, well, Timmy said, 'Naked,' just like that, right out loud. I couldn't stop laughing and I kind of rolled out of the desk and onto the floor. Miss Ostheim said I was creating a disturbance and she made *me* go out into the hall."

"But it wasn't your fault," Annie had said she'd reiterated, for some reason needing to clarify things.

"It was Timmy's fault," Mark had informed her while looking at her as though she were dense for not grasping that right off the bat. "He's the one who told the joke."

"The one about seven plus eight equaling naked."

"Right."

Even thinking about it, David couldn't keep a smirk from forming as he turned off the water. He could never explain it to Annie, but Timmy Burkmeyer and Mark were men after his own heart just then. His latest worry was that such terms as "naked" and "nude" would insert themselves as answers while he was adding columns of numbers back at work. He could see them popping to mind in the middle of a branch meeting, while calling on a customer, or standing in front of the king-size bed in his master bedroom back in Northstream. He was very much afraid that Annie had ruined him. It didn't seem to matter where he was, there was a lot of lascivious nudity being played out in the recesses of his mind.

He stepped out onto the mat and slipped on clean underwear and soft sweat bottoms, then opened the door. Annie stood just outside, her nightgown and robe neatly folded and cradled in her arms. His understanding of the male body's capabilities needed drastic revamping, he realized as he found himself reacting to the sight of her, bedraggled as she was. He tried to recall the headaches of rearing children he'd had no problem coming up with earlier in the bath-room. The computer disk running his brain had evidently crashed. His memory banks were scrambled and thought was lost.

Except for one.

He knew he wanted to kiss her.

A tiny round scar rode right over her mouth on other-wise flawless skin.

Chicken pox, that was one.

The heck with chicken pox, he still wanted to kiss her. Actually, he wanted to do a whole hell of a lot more than just kiss her. He eyed Annie hungrily and realized dinner had only assuaged one type of appetite.

"You're done," Annie commented inanely, and David realized he had failed to conceal his thoughts. Annie was fidgeting uneasily.

"I'm done," he agreed. *Done for, more likely.*

"You didn't need to rush."

"I knew you'd be waiting. I didn't mind." He still stood in the doorway, staring.

Annie looked down at the gown in her hands, looking suddenly shy and awkward. David realized he was blocking the door. He needed to move. He was so overtired, he mightn't be responsible for his actions if she was forced to brush by him on her way to the shower. She was staring at his chest. He looked down and noticed the poor job he'd done drying off. Annie seemed mesmerized by the glisten-ing pearls of water beaded on his chest hair. Her eyes fol-lowed the path of a droplet heavy enough to roll down his neck and David took a deep breath and stepped aside while he could.

"You're very, um, clean," Annie commented.

David closed his eyes and prayed for strength.

"Yes, indeed. Very. I'll just go in and…wash up, as well. Then we'll both be clean." She smiled brightly and closed the bathroom door on him.

David took a deep breath and had to hang on to the banister to make it down the stairs. Once in the living room, he hunkered down into the sofa and covered himself with three blankets, determined to actually saw logs in blissful, oblivious sleep instead of dreaming of Annie. The sofa felt great, for a bed of nails, and he was out as cold as a computer room suffering a power blackout.

He sank into a sleep so deep, his brain developed the bends. That was the only explanation for the tricks his mind played on him while he was defenseless from his subconscious. He dreamed of Annie. An Annie unfettered by children and responsibility. Unfettered by clothing, as well. Wow.

They were together…making fresh-flower headbands out in some meadow. She wore nothing but two strategically placed iridescent streamers that floated in the breeze. David grabbed, attempting to snag an end and free her body to the warm meadow's sunlight and his own touch. There, he had it. His breathing became shallow in anticipation.

"David? David, what are you doing? David, stop that!"

"Hmm? What?"

"David, let go of me."

He shook his head groggily. "Annie, is that you?"

"For heaven's sake, who'd you think you were grabbing? Of course it's me. Let go!"

David managed to get his sleep-dilated pupils down to size and brought them to bear on the subject under his hands, a major accomplishment under the circumstances. Sure enough, right in front of him, brought into focus through a squint, was Annie, tormentor of dreams, preventer of slumber. He looked at her a little dopily. Damn, she had that stupid flannel nightie and robe on again. He would speak to her about it at once.

He wound up his tongue and managed to sound amazingly petulant and accusatory when he said, "You took off the streamer things. Put them back on."

"What?"

David started fumbling with the hem of her gown. "They must be under here. Don't worry, I'll find them, just hold still. Damn, where'd you get this thing, the Manhater's Resale Shop?"

Annie slapped at his hands and straightened her spine indignantly. "This is a perfectly good nightgown. I bought it *full price* at a maternity store with a section for nursing mothers when I was expecting Stevie. It's cold when you get up in the middle of the night to nurse a baby and this gown is very warm."

"I'll just bet it's warm. Nothing can touch you while you're wearing that thing, not even a breath of air. How the hell is the baby supposed to get anything?" he asked snidely. He sat against the sofa back and rubbed his eyes. He was finally starting to wake up, but his tongue was still operating on its own, letting Annie know his disappointment with the disappearance of his dream.

"My guess is you're still asleep. I've never seen you act like this before." Annie had her hands on her hips now and was definitely glaring at him.

"And for your information," she continued, "there are slits on both sides for the baby to nurse through. What did you think, I'd sit there and tease him by only letting him get so close and no closer?"

It didn't sound so farfetched to David. It certainly captured the essence of his mood at the moment. He leaned forward and gave his eyes one final scrub with his hands before refocusing on her. He was sure it was bad for his health to be drawn from a deep sleep twice in one night. If the fatigue didn't get you, the loose tongue it generated probably would. "Hell, Annie, I'm sorry. You're right, I think I was mostly still asleep." And those slits *did* sound interesting. Rather strategically placed, were they? He examined her gown with new interest. Where? He was awake enough now to have the sense not to ask directly. "What are you doing down here, anyway?" He glanced at his watch. The numbers glowed eerily up at him, although they seemed harder to read than normal. Finally he was able to announce, "It's only 3:30."

Annie sank into the armchair by the picture window and said, "I know."

She knew? He sat forward in alarm. "You're not—"

"Going to sit and make sure the sun has the strength to come back one more time to shed a bit more light even though it's a couple billion years old and probably tired as all get out? No, I'm not. For the first time in months, I'm fairly confident it will make it."

"Then what?"

"It's been almost a year since I've been able to sit and enjoy the dawn without that awful sense of panic."

David's chest tightened around her words. She was so dear to him already. His life loomed emptily before him after this vacation, which just went to show he was probably on the verge of a major depression himself.

Now that he was more fully awake, the nightgown was just right for the kind of person she was. He held out his arms and she came to him on the couch.

He hugged her briefly and settled her back into the sofa, leaving her there briefly while he went and tugged on the drapery draw cord, opening the curtains. That done, he returned to her, squeezing back in between Annie and the sofa arm. He worked at positioning their bodies. His efforts led to his using the sofa arm as a headrest, his body semireclining. Annie lay half on her side and half on top of him, wedged next to him, the whole length of her body, right there, against his whole length. Her head lay on his chest. He pulled a blanket up.

He was inordinately pleased that she trusted him enough to lay in such a position with him. "Comfortable?"

"Yes, thanks. You?"

"Mmm."

The room was quiet for a few moments.

"David?"

David had such a sense of peace and contentment, he found it hard to respond, barely managing another, "Mmm?"

"What are we doing like this?"

"Waiting for the sun together."

"Oh. It's nice."

"Yeah."

They lay there a while longer, enjoying the silence. It was a rare commodity in Annie's home, David had found, and he treasured it for that reason.

He readjusted her position slightly and found his feeling of mellowness suffering in the process. Damn, she felt good. Tension—lower body tension—began taking precedence over other sensations. He began thinking about those nursing slits in her flannel nightie. Mightn't what was good for the gosling be advantageous for the gander, as well? He let his hands start to roam. They investigated the side seams, pleats and fabric folds all across her upper body.

"What are you doing now?"

"Nothing."

"It doesn't feel like nothing."

"Yeah? What's it feel like?"

"Something. Definitely something."

David laughed. It sounded low and husky even to his own ears. But he didn't stop his searching. The openings had to be there somewhere. She'd said so herself. And the anticipation was killing him.

Annie shifted. David could feel a certain tautness creeping into the body blanketing his own. It was good to know she wasn't totally immune to what he himself was experiencing.

"If you're looking for the sun," Annie said a bit breathily, "it's out the window, not there."

"You sure?" David questioned. "There's a lot of heat to be found right here, I'm discovering." He brazenly put his hands right over the flannel area that should have been covering her breasts and cupped her warmly.

Annie jumped a bit, as though she'd been jolted.

That pleased him.

"Oh, God. Here, David, put your hands here in these folds." She took his hands and guided them right to the slits.

David took it from there. He let his hands go where his eyes couldn't see, enjoying the strictly tactile sensation of their contact with warm satin. It was so delicious, he shivered right along with Annie at the intimate touch. Annie's breasts were solid and real under his hands. It was no dream. It was . . . a piece of the sun.

Annie snuggled back a little farther into him and almost melted there against his chest. His arms were around her, true, but the casual observer would see nothing untoward. Any child wandering in would never notice that his hands disappeared at the sides of her gown. "I never realized the potential of this nightgown before. You can get quite fresh and no one would be the wiser. Do you have any idea," she asked him, "how difficult it is to be naughty or bad with children underfoot? I've got to tell you, it's been years since I've managed it. And, David, it feels so good. I could stay like this all night."

His chuckle rumbled against her back. Damn, so could he. "Why don't we?"

She sighed. "Wouldn't it be lovely?"

He laughed again. "Yes, Eliza, it would."

Her answering laugh was so low and sultry, David could only groan in response. He had to conserve the rest of his energy in order to maintain his control. It was important for Annie to relax and feel comfortable with him. It had been a long time for her. He groaned again and shifted his position slightly, seeking something more comfortable. Hell, it had been a while for him, as well, and this was too important to spoil by rushing.

They lay for a while in what David hoped Annie would interpret as companionable silence. Personally he was feeling a bit muzzy brained from the concentrated effort he was exerting to relax. Relaxing would probably be easier if he could force himself to remove his hands from the dark warmth where they lay buried, but he decided the extra effort would be well worth it.

"David?"

"Hmm?"

"You know anything about chemistry?"

"Very little. Just the basic core stuff required for someone majoring in a nonscience."

"Oh. Too bad."

"Why?"

"No reason."

"Come on, why?"

"No, just forget it. It's too silly."

"You've got to tell me now, or I'll go nuts all night wondering."

"Well, I was just wondering about the human flash point. I mean, we're not doing anything but holding each other and I think I'm about to self-combust. I read an article about somebody doing that once, but I thought they'd just made it up. I must say, I've never felt like this before."

She hadn't, huh? Good. Maybe he could give her something Craig hadn't been able to. God knew it wouldn't be poetry. He'd spent the afternoon yesterday in a bookstore in town thumbing through instruction manuals and rhyming dictionaries. The experience left him doubtful that there was a poem in him waiting to be pulled out, so he'd take any edge he could get. He had to make a conscious effort to relax the possessive grip his hands had taken on her.

"It's quite an amazing feeling, really. Just extraordinary."

She snuggled her bottom more tightly into him and David took in a deep breath, holding it for a long time. He smiled, though, when he finally released it. For a long time, he just held her, enjoying her closeness and warmth. The serenity of that predawn time seeped so thoroughly through them that they drifted off, once again missing sharing the return of light.

Chapter Seven

Annie became gradually aware of her name being called off in the distance. No, not her name, her role.

"Mom? Mom? Mom!"

"I found her, Casey. She's in the living room sleeping on the sofa with David."

She was? Groggily Annie opened her eyes. She was!

"Oh, yeah, you're right. Here she is."

"Shh. Can't you see they're sleeping?"

"Why's she sleeping with David?"

"I don't know. You'll have to ask her when she wakes up."

"You ask her. Her eyes are open now. Go ahead."

Yes, they were. Wide open. She wished they'd stayed shut until she'd had time to think up a good reason as to why she was on the couch sleeping virtually on top of poor David.

Thinking of David, she gave him a good look. He couldn't be suffering too badly, she supposed, as he was sleeping right through the grand inquisition here. And inquisition it was, complete with three interrogators lined up in front of the couch staring at her.

"Hi, guys." She sat up and pushed the hair out of her face.

"I looked for you in your own bed, but you weren't there, Mom. How come you slept down here with David?"

Inquiring minds wanted to know.

Annie shrugged lamely. "We were talking." She thought it best to leave the nonverbal communication out of her explanation. "And I guess we sort of fell asleep in the middle of the conversation."

"That's really dumb," Mark declared. "I wouldn't fall asleep if I were talking to David. He knows a lot of cool things." Mark's eyes suddenly widened. "I know, I bet you were sexing him. That's so boring, people fall asleep all the time. That's why you have to do it lying down. It's so gross, though, Mom, how could you do something like that without barfing? Are you going to have a baby now?"

"Don't be stupid," Casey directed as though one had a choice. "Sexing doesn't work unless you're married. Isn't that right, Mom?" She turned to her mother for confirmation of the facts of life.

Amy jumped in to defend Mark before Annie could come up with a good response. "Maybe they got maywied last night aftuh we went to bed. Did you, Mom? Then it could wohk."

Annie could feel David's chest start to shake under her supporting hand. The rat was awake and enjoying her predicament. Obviously he didn't understand the seriousness of the matter. Kids talked. The fact that she'd slept with him would be all over their respective schools. Parents hearing the tale brought home by their children were bound to put their own interpretation on the story. She'd have a reputation in nothing flat unless they were very, very lucky.

She held up one hand in a traditional traffic director's gesture. "Stop. Wait just a minute here." When she had their attention, she proceeded. "All that happened is just what I said. David and I were talking, and we were so tired from all the cleaning we did yesterday we fell asleep practically right in the middle of a word."

"Which wohd was it?"

Annie stared at Amy, slightly nonplussed. Their questions never ceased to surprise her. "I don't remember," she finally admitted. "But I do know it takes a whole lot more than sleeping next to each other on the sofa to make a baby." She looked at her two oldest offspring. "You guys know that."

"Yeah." Mark nodded in agreement. "I remember you said the guy has to— Oh, it's too gross. I'll never do that."

"You can't get a baby unless you sex somebody," Casey informed him, sounding none too happy herself.

"Well, I'd never do *that*," Mark informed her, growing red in the face at this injustice. "And nobody can make me. It's too sick for words."

"I think this is enough discussion on the subject. I don't want you telling anybody else, not even your best friends at school, that I fell asleep on the sofa with David, understand? That's personal and private and just between us, okay?" She looked around hopefully at the surrounding ring of faces and she swung her legs up and off the sofa. "Now who wants some breakfast?"

"Me!"

"Me!"

"Mom, remember that funny tape we saw when we rented a Buster the Big Hearted Bear cartoon from the video place and you said they must have mixed up their tapes?"

Annie was halfway through the dining room, moving toward the kitchen like a mother hen with all her chicks trailing behind, peeping away as they came. She was determined to ignore Mark and was most unhappy to realize he hadn't put the ten minutes he'd seen of that particular movie out of his mind. "I've got some pancake mix in the pantry," she said loudly. "We could whip up a pile of those."

"I get fuhst batch!"

"Second!"

"There were more than two people naked together in that room and—"

"Mark! Not another word, do you understand? We'll talk about this later, okay?" *Much later.* First she had to get herself back under control. David had looked mighty good lying there on the sofa when she'd checked back over her shoulder to make sure the gaggle of little ones was following as she left the room. Now was not the time or the place, more was the pity. Breakfast. She needed to concentrate on breakfast.

"I'll tell you what, Mark. You can get the syrup out of the refrigerator and make sure the little ones don't drown their pancakes. How's that?"

"Hey, that's my job!" Casey protested.

"This morning, it's Mark's job. You can make the orange juice."

Moderately mollified and distracted, everyone set about their tasks while Annie breathed a tentative sigh of relief. She knew better than to think the serenity would last long. Sooner or later, this latest family interest in her love life would be dragged back out and shaken like a dusty rug. Children had an unerring instinct for those topics that would raise the biggest flak. Hopefully she'd have worked out a few answers herself by then.

Unfortunately David strode into the kitchen before she'd come up with any. He was wearing jeans that fit him in such a manner as to set back Annie's control over her inappropriate mental meanderings by days. Maybe weeks. She could feel her pulse start to race and hoped he would attribute her flush to the heat from the range top. The pale yellow sweat-shirt loosely covering his chest should have been an instant turn off with its bright blue company logo boldly embroidered center front. What should have been an unhappy reminder of a joyless time in her life was interfering with her breathing instead. She suspected it was the way he had the sleeves pushed up to reveal a pair of beautifully sculpted, hair-dusted forearms.

The man was inherently indecent, Annie decided as she determinedly flipped a pancake. Even fully clothed, David had her libido going into overdrive. Old ladies in tennis shoes would shortly be marching with painted poster-board signs on her front lawn, chaining themselves to the pickets of her front porch railing, while demanding David be locked away in an effort to protect their daughters and female grandchildren. Her name would be in the newspapers. Her campground and photos of her home would appear on the ten o'clock news. She'd be ruined.

To top it all off, David seemed totally unconcerned with her upcoming downfall. He was whistling. "You certainly sound cheery this morning," she said with a touch of asperity. He'd been the cause of a lot of discomfort for her this morning, both mental and physical. He could at least be sporting a bag or two under his eyes. In fact, now that she examined him more closely, David's marvelous blue eyes were darn close to twinkling and his early-morning cough sounded suspiciously like a chuckle cover-up to her. Her eyes narrowed.

"What's the matter with you, Mary Sunshine?" David inquired. "Get up on the wrong side of the sofa?"

"There is no right side of a bi-occupied sofa when there are five children in the house," Annie muttered as she walked from the stove to the pantry door, opened it and stared inside. "Damn, I mean, darn, what did I want in here?"

David came to peer over her shoulder. His breath feathered down her neck. She shivered even though the house was warm. "What's the problem?" he asked.

Annie exploded. "Three times I've come over here to get something, although God only knows what, I certainly don't. I open the darn pantry door, forget what I need, walk back to the range top, remember, go back to the pantry for whatever it is and promptly forget again." She ran her hands through her hair in an extremely distracted manner. "It's not so bad down here. The pantry's only a few steps away. But this happens all the time. I'll go upstairs to get something, forget, go back downstairs, remember, go back up and forget again. I've got to tell you, those stairs are killers when you do three to four trips up and down in a row. I swear, sometimes I think I've lost my mind and will never find it again." And she refused to turn around while David was so close. One look at him, and she'd drop the *sometimes* and replace the *think* with *know*.

David dropped his hands onto her shoulders. Annie stopped breathing.

"Let's look at this logically. Instead of retracing your steps over and over, we'll think it through."

There spoke a businessman, trying to apply logic and managerial techniques to pancakes. No wonder she was upset with herself for her inexplicable attraction to him. "David, I—"

"Whatever it is, you think of it when you're over at the stove. Can't be salt or pepper, not for pancakes. Butter and syrup would be in the fridge, not the pantry. Um, platter? Napkins? Powdered sugar?"

"Napkins, that's it. Thank you, David." She expressed her gratitude even though she wasn't feeling particularly appreciative.

"It's okay." He reached around her, took down the package of napkins and handed it to her.

Billy padded into the kitchen on footed pajama soles. He looked owlishly about and spoke around the thumb in his mouth. "Hi, Mom. Hi, David. Whath's for breakfatht?"

Annie looked at her son, still sleepy and warm looking. It pleased her to inform him that his favorite was being served. "Pancakes. Here. You can put the napkins around as your job." She handed the package to the tyke. Billy accepted them semigraciously and wandered by the stove to sniff appreciatively on his way to the table. "Mom, the bubbles on the top all popded. Didn't you say that meant they should get tuwnded?"

"Oh, my gosh," Annie wailed and raced back to the stove. "Thank God, they're not burned." She flipped the pan full of cakes and turned back to David who had followed her to the stove. "You know how I said sometimes I think I'm losing my mind? Well, forget it. It's over and done with, I'm convinced I've lost it."

"I wouldn't worry too much, if I were you," David told her kindly. "You're not retreating into yourself the way you said you did after Craig's death. You're coping. And who wouldn't be distracted with all this commotion going on one hundred percent of the time?" He cocked his head in the direction of the brood of children swirling around the kitchen table.

"Mom, Casey's being a miss bossy pants again. Tell her I don't have to do what she says."

"You two will have to work things out," Annie informed her oldest son, refusing to become involved in their arguments. "Just make sure the table is set by the time these pancakes are done." She turned back to the stove and said more quietly, for David's ears, "Yeah, they're something all right. I'm just not always quite sure what."

David stuck around long enough after breakfast to help Annie gather up the laundry. He lugged it down to the corner of the basement where her ten-year-old washer and dryer lay sulking. Annie saw the laundry through new eyes when it rode in someone else's arms.

"You've got a lot of dirty clothes to wade through here, lady," David commented as he dumped it on the cement floor in front of the washing machine.

Annie eyed the mound dubiously. "I do it every other day," she returned a bit defensively.

"I'm not criticizing, merely passing comment. You've also got a lot of people industriously creating this pile for you. Your kids are good at dirt."

"Yes," Annie agreed, still not sure if she should take offense or not. The fact was, her kids *did* excel at dirt. Did that turn David off? Why was she worried if it did? "I've never really measured it before, I've always just kind of grabbed some and thrown it into the machine. There's probably no more than the typical four to five loads here."

"You realize that's almost a load per person?"

"I never really thought about it," Annie mumbled as she hefted an armload up and into the washer. "I'll tell you what I *do* think, though," she confided. "I do the laundry every other day. There should only be two pairs of underwear each, right?"

David nodded his agreement as he tossed darks to the left and whites to the right, separating the clothes into smaller piles that were less intimidating than the original Everest-like mountain.

"There's always more. And socks. There should only be twelve pairs, but there's not. I think this laundry is not only physically grimy, it's soul is in the gutter, as well. I think it mates at night."

"The socks are sexing each other?" David questioned doubtfully.

"You *were* awake! You *did* hear!"

He defended himself. "I just didn't want to interrupt such an important parent-child discussion. I'm sure the kids found it extremely informative. I know I did."

"You rat. I'll get you for that."

"I can hardly wait." He held up a black-and-white striped sport shirt. "You want this in the lights or darks?"

"I've never been able to figure that out. Make a pile for mediums and put it there."

David tossed it onto a blank spot on the floor. "Never would have figured you for a middle of the roader."

What did he mean by that? She was too chicken to ask. Instead she held up three sport socks, each with a different stripe from its neighbor. "Look at this," she directed, continuing when David obediently raised his head. "If they're going to mate, couldn't they at least have the courtesy to pick a similarly striped partner?"

"I beg your pardon?"

"I'm serious. A large blue stripe gets fresh with a big red stripe and they produce a socklet with smaller size red and blue stripes. Then I've got three socks, none of which match at all. I've got a whole basket full of singlets over there."

She dangled the offending socks in front of him and found herself wondering about the differences in their coloring. If she had a child with David, would it be blonde or be blessed with David's brown hair? Blue eyes or brown? Then she knew she was nuts to be even fantasizing about adding to the mayhem surrounding her.

David appeared to give the tubes hanging from her fist his serious consideration. "I can see that you have a serious problem here. These socks definitely have filthy minds. Personally, I'd get rid of them, quick. They could be the reason for the kids being so preoccupied with our activities on the sofa. They might be just taking a cue from the socks. Come on, I'll help you gather them up before the children are ruined."

"Oh, shut up." Annie tossed the offending mismatches into the tub. She poured in the soap, shut the lid and spun some dials. "I'll deal with the rest of this after church." Maybe she'd get her own mind out of the gutter in the prayerful atmosphere of the nearby town's small house of the Lord. She obviously had sex on the brain if she had sunk to accusing her laundry of lewd and lascivious behavior.

She was jealous, that was all. Jealous? Good God, of a sock? She was sicker than she'd thought.

Suddenly tired, she reached up and pulled the chain of the overhead light. Their corner of the basement was reduced to shadows. "I've got to get back upstairs and make sure everybody's getting dressed," she told David. "Are you coming to church with us?"

David looked down at her for a moment before speaking quietly. "No. I'm going back to my campsite. I brought a little work with me, I'll go through some papers while you're gone."

"Oh." She stood there uncertainly. "You're on vacation. You shouldn't be doing paperwork." Biting her lip, she added, "You shouldn't be doing all this stuff around here, either. Just stay at your site and relax for the rest of your time here and don't worry any more about us. We're fine." She let her hand worry the zipper pull on her robe.

David put his hand over hers, stopping her. "Hey, it's okay. Nobody hog-tied me to that wreck of a ladder yesterday. I did it because I wanted to be with you and help you out a bit while I could."

Annie looked at him doubtfully, wishing desperately it was true, yet not understanding why.

"No, seriously. All that physical labor was a great release."

"Of what?" She inched closer, unwilling to give him up just yet.

"Tension. Stress. Mental fatigue." And it hadn't done a thing for any of those three items. Since coming here, he was not only tense, stressed and tired, he was frustrated, as well. He looped his arms around her back and tugged her closer. "Now quit worrying about it and kiss me. I won't see you for a whole hour or two."

She began fiddling with the neckline of his sweatshirt, adjusting it, smoothing out any wrinkles. "Oh, David, I don't know. This is all so confusing for me."

"Here, then. Let me do the work." He lowered his lips, gently settling them over hers.

She sighed and cuddled closer.

"See how easy it is?" He kissed her again. Softly.

The kiss did little to ease her inner state of confusion and it exacerbated a lot of physical symptoms she'd been having trouble with since David's arrival Friday afternoon. But she enjoyed it, anyway.

"Mom? Mom! Where is she? Mom!"

Mark's voice drifted through the floorboards overhead. "Has anybody seen Mom?"

David sighed and leaned his forehead against hers. "We're about to be discovered."

More distant yelling. "I think she's in the basement doing the laundry."

"Yes," Annie agreed. "I think we are." But she didn't move. Not yet.

The basement door swung open and crashed against the stairwell wall. "Mom, you down there? Stevie put his shirt on upside down and he won't let me fix it. He looks really dumb. And Billy put the seat from the old potty chair on his head to be funny, only now it's stuck there. Can he go to church like that?"

David started chuckling helplessly. "With the potty seat on his head?" he questioned. He threw an arm companionably around her and guided her toward the staircase.

"Come on, Mom. Sounds like you've got your work cut out for you."

"It's Sunday," she grumbled. "I thought it was a day of rest."

"Not for parents," David informed her. "They don't get any days of rest until the nest is emptied. Then that's all they get, I guess. My mom told me it was a case of feast or famine." Only his mother had never had the opportunity to find out for herself and David didn't know if he could wait that long for a stretch of uninterrupted time with Annie, either.

They started up the stairs.

"I have a neighbor," Annie told David, "who insists I'm going to be bored and lonely when they're grown and gone, that this is the best time of my life. I have to tell you, there are days when I find that an extremely depressing concept."

"Mom, did you hear me? Are you coming?"

David stayed long enough to make sure greasing Billy's head with petroleum jelly was enough to release the potty seat. He put them into Annie's car and waved them down the driveway after instructing them to say a prayer for him. He figured he would need more than one to make it through the next week and a half.

Then he wandered down to enjoy the peace and quiet of his tepee tent for the hour and a half until they returned. Instead of retrieving his briefcase from the car's trunk, however, he pulled out his bag from the bookstore. He retrieved his black thin framed glasses from the dash and sat at the rickety picnic table thumbing through the items he'd picked up. A rhyming dictionary. He'd never heard of such a thing, but it appeared interesting. He picked up the second book. *Poetic Magic, a Guide to the Mystery of Poetry Writing*. The clerk had recommended that one.

Once he'd flipped through both manuals, he simply stared at them for a while. He took off his glasses and chewed the earpiece. This was really a stupid idea. Probably one of the dumbest he'd ever had. He couldn't write poetry.

Snapping the book shut, he tapped its cover impatiently. Casey insisted her dad's poems used to make Annie smile. David wanted to see Annie smile. Flowcharting his thoughts like only a true born-and-bred programmer would, David knew, if *p* implied *q* and *q* implied *r,* then *p* implied *r.* In other words, David would write a poem for Annie. He sighed.

Sometimes a logical mind was its own burden. Iambus? Trochee? Spondee? Anapest? What the hell were those? He was far more comfortable with COBOL, FORTRAN and C language. As far as he knew, what logically flowed from amphibrach and amphimacer bore a close resemblance to gibberish. Oh, hell. He'd write her a damn poem. He'd write all of them poems. They'd be inundated with poetry. He'd think of it as practice. This way, if he ever ran into a woman as kind, as caring, as good looking, as down to earth as Annie was, but with a love of the city and the time to devote to a relationship with a man, he'd be ready. Annie was good practice, that was all, practice.

He stuck his glasses back on his nose and opened the book yet again.

Iambic pentameter seemed big. Shakespeare himself had used it, and if it was good enough for him it would suffice for David's purposes. Okay, five feet per line, each foot consisting of a short-long voice stress combination. No problem.

Uh...

"David, what are you doing?"

He jumped as the curious young voice broke his concentration. Swinging his head around, he found Casey staring at him. "Casey! Are you guys back from church already?"

"Yeah, Billy found somebody's old yucky gum stuck under the pew in front of us. Mom tried to get it away from him only Billy got mad and wouldn't let her have it. He waved his arm all around trying to keep it away so he could have it for hisself, only it flew out of his hand and landed on the lady in front of us.''

"My God," David said, both horrified and fascinated.

"Yeah, He was right there, Mom said, watching the spectacle we were making.''

"Was the lady mad?" David asked cautiously.

"Nah. It was stuck good and tight in her hair, though, but she said she'd cut it out when she got home, that she'd had six kids of her own and not to worry, she'd seen it all.''

"That was lucky," he commented, not believing it for a second. The poor woman had lived through the graying antics of a half-dozen children and now someone else's were dumping on her. She'd probably go directly home after church, lock herself in a nice, quiet closet and weep all afternoon as she realized there was no escape from this particular form of madness. But it seemed Casey was not finished yet.

"While Mom was apologizing, Stevie got away from her and went down the center aisle, right up onto the altar and started shaking the cross. Mom made Mark go get him. The usher said we were creating a disturbance and Mom said we had to leave before she committed murder in God's own house. She said there was nothing like going to church with all of us to put her into a totally non-Christian frame of mind.''

"She was just kidding, honey," David assured Casey weakly.

"I don't know. A man honked at us 'cause she waited so long at the stop sign at Main and Third on the way home. There were no cars coming or nothing.''

"Why'd she do that?"

"I don't know. I asked her, but all she said was that it was all our fault. She said she wouldn't sit around waiting for

stop signs to turn green if we didn't get her so discombooberated.''

David nodded. "Uh-huh. I see." Only he didn't.

Casey crawled onto the bench next to him. "Well, I don't.
A stop sign can't turn green. Only a stop-and-go light can.
And I didn't do anything to discombooberate her. That's
why I came over to see you. I could tell she was mad and was
gonna make us clean our rooms." She glanced at the blank
paper in front of him. "You never said what you were doing, David."

Trying to be romantic. No, no, that wasn't it. He was
merely trying to make Annie smile, give her an emotional
boost to make her feel better along with the physical one
he'd been giving. Yeah, that was more like it. And it certainly sounded as though Annie could use a smile right
about now. "I'm writing a poem for your mother."

Casey leaned against his arm as she studied his empty le-
gal pad. "But there's nothing on the paper."

"I'm using blank verse."

"What?"

He rolled his eyes. "Nothing. I'm still thinking about
what I want to say."

David fiddled with his pencil and squinted at his paper
pad for several silent moments. "Okay," he finally muttered. "What we need here is something that fits into ta*da*
ta*da* ta*da* ta*da* ta*da*."

Casey glanced up, eyes askance. "I've never heard a poem
like that before. Daddy never said ta*da*."

That showed how much old Craig had known about
writing poetry. "That's called the meter, sweetie. Now we
have to substitute words for that beat."

Casey appeared confused. "Oh. Do the words hafta
rhyme with ta*da*?"

"No, no. You're missing the point."

"David, are you getting discombooberated?"

"It's a distinct possibility," he muttered. "Okay, here goes," he said a little louder. "Most of these examples here seem to go in for cataloging features." Annie's mouth immediately came to mind. "Uh, Her lips are like a glist'ning rose."

Casey looked up expectantly while he repeated the line carefully, testing it. "Her *lips* are *like* a *glist*'ning *rose*. It's a foot short."

"How do you know how tall it is?" Casey asked, clearly impressed with David's abilities. "I didn't see you measure anything."

"I'm one ta*da* away from being another Shakespeare. Hell. Pretend you didn't hear that, kiddo." He shrugged. "So I'm not Shakespeare. We'll forget pentameter and go for..." He flipped several pages. "Here it is, tetrameter. Now there's another spanner to throw in the works, it says here. Pattern. We have to have lines rhyming in the pattern: *ababbcbcc*."

"What happened to ta*da?*"

"We'll get back to that in a second. This next line is a freebie, but after that we get into trouble." He chewed the end of his pencil thoughtfully. "Let's see. What else has she got besides a mouth?" He did tend to fixate there, he realized.

"Eyes."

"Hmm?"

"She's got eyes."

"Yeah, gorgeous blue ones." He straightened and harrumphed. "I mean, yes, you're right. She definitely has eyes." He slipped an arm around Casey and gave her a squeeze. "Thanks. You're being a big help."

Casey sat up straight and preened. "I am? She's got ears and yellow hair, too."

He made a production of noting that in the margin. "Right. We won't forget those." He thought about marking down the discovered territory he'd found behind the slits in her flannel nightie the night before so as not to forget those, either, but decided he was unlikely to disremember that particular treasure. He wondered how good a reader Casey was. Maybe he could slip a line in about white, white breasts without her being any the wiser. He eyed the child speculatively.

"How about this, David? Her eyes look like two smushed blueberries."

"Ah, not bad. It needs a little refining, but it's not bad."

"Write it down," Casey requested eagerly.

What could he do? He looked into Casey's pleased, earnest expression, picked up his pencil and wrote it down.

Things degenerated from there. Annie's hair became strands of spaghetti, her nose a lump of salt and flour dough. David and Casey were laughing hysterically over feet made of twelve-inch rulers when Annie and the rest of her brood came upon them.

"Ruler doesn't rhyme with rose, you goof," David was saying.

"Yeah, well, blueberries doesn't rhyme with dough, either," Casey responded.

They both jumped when Annie cut into their wrangling.

"So this is where you disappeared to, Casey. What are you two up to?"

PLAY "LUCKY H
AND GET . . .

- ★ **Exciting Silhouette Special Editio**
- ★ **"Key to Your Heart" pendant nec**
- ★ **Surprise mystery gift that will de**

THEN CONTINUE
LUCKY STREAK
SWEETHEART OF

When you return the postcard on t
send you the books and gifts you q
free! Then, you'll get 6 new Silhou
novels every month, delivered righ
before they're available in stores. I
them, you'll pay only $2.96* per b
43¢ off the cover price—plus only (
entire shipment!

Free Newsletter!

You'll get our subscribers-only ne
look at our most popular authors a
novels.

Special Extras—Free!

When you join the Silhouette Read
also get additional free gifts from t
of our appreciation for being a ho

DETACH AND MAIL CARD TODAY

SILHOUETTE'S

With a coin —
scratch off
the silver card and
check below to see
how many gifts you get.

YES! I have scratched off the silver card. Please send
me all the books and gifts for which I qualify. I
understand that I am under no obligation to purchase any
books, as explained on the opposite page.

335 CIS AH65
(C-SIL-SE-02/93)

NAME

ADDRESS   APT.

CITY   PROVINCE   POSTAL CODE

**Twenty-one gets
you 4 free books,
a free necklace and
mystery gift**

**Twenty gets you
4 free books
and a free necklace**

**Nineteen gets you
4 free books**

**Eighteen gets you
2 free books**

SILHOUETTE "NO RISK" GUARANTEE

★ You're not required to buy a single book—ever!
★ As a subscriber, you must be completely satisfied or you may cancel at any time by marking "cancel" on your statement or returning a shipment of books to us at our cost.
★ The free books and gifts you receive from this LUCKY HEARTS offer remain yours to keep—in any case.

If offer card is missing, write to:
Silhouette Reader Service, P.O. Box 609, Fort Erie, Ontario L2A 5X3

DETACH AND MAIL CARD TODAY

Chapter Eight

Annie tried to pry Casey away from David's campsite in an effort to give the poor man a bit of peace and quiet on his vacation. "Come on, Casey. I need help back at the house."

"David needs my help, Mom, and my room's clean."

"Clean by whose definition?" Annie retorted. "Yours or mine?"

David turned his notepad upside down over the two poetry manuals and began rising. "You need help, Annie? I can—"

"Sit down," she insisted, pushing on his shoulder. "I was just trying to give you some space."

David glanced around. He could use some. Claustrophobia lurked just around the corner. Children seemed to mill everywhere. The air he breathed threatened to clog his lungs instead of inflate them. On top of that, the tepee tent wasn't all that stable. If it tumbled over, someone could get hurt. However, he refused to simply send them off. From Casey's description of Annie's morning, Annie needed a break as badly as he did.

He took a deep breath. If Annie needed a bit of relief, he would provide it, period. After all, he could go home to his nice, quiet, calm and, best of all, *empty* house. Annie was stuck in this bedlam for another fifteen to twenty years.

He watched as children charged aimlessly but energetically about. They did seem a bit antsy today. Probably the nicest thing he could do for Annie right about now would be to give them a workout and wear them out for an early bedtime. "I tell you what. Let's all—" he thought fast "—take a walk."

"Take a—"

"Yes." David nodded decisively. "Didn't you tell me there were some nature trails around? We'll go for a walk. Then later we'll come back and build a fire. A cookout, hot dogs over a camp fire, that's what I'm in the mood for. With s'mores. How about that?" When the breakfast toast had gotten burnt, David's mother had told him charcoal aided digestion. He sure hoped that was correct, as he suspected he'd take in an ample supply tonight. What a man did for his woman. It was embarrassing.

His thoughts stopped short and backed up for an instant replay. His woman? Who, Annie? No, no. Annie was practice.

"Walk! Walk! Wanna go for a walk! David, you carry me?"

"It won't be a walk if I carry you, sweetie. It would be a carry." And it wouldn't tire out little legs, either.

"I get to be leader, I call."

"I was just about to call. You got to be leader last time."

"Too bad, I already called it."

Annie sighed tiredly. "Listen, David, why don't I just get them all out of your hair?" It was a poor choice of words.

It brought back bad memories of church. She shuddered slightly. "I can take them for a walk myself."

David did not miss the quiver, nor the newly compressed thinness of her lips. The way he saw things, he had two options. He could either warn the children to use pebbles and not bread crumbs to mark the trail back, or he could go along and make sure they all made it out of the woods in one piece, thus sparing Annie a long prison sentence for murder or worse. Although spending more time with Annie didn't seem like a particularly good idea from his standpoint, surely he could be strong. After all, the alternative appeared to be consigning the poor woman to jail, which would leave five young children effectively orphaned. The knowledge she'd probably leave them with him for the duration of her term firmed his decision.

"Okay, guys. As soon as you all stop arguing, your mother and I will take you for a walk."

Instant silence.

"Good. Now all of you can run ahead. Down to that tree by the curve in the road. Then come back." He wanted them all tired. Very tired. "First one who finds something starting with the letter *a* gets an extra marshmallow tonight."

They were off.

David and Annie followed more casually. David fought with himself and managed not to take her hand in his. He wondered how long he could keep it up.

"You're very good with them, David."

"I'm just new on the scene. They haven't learned to tune me out yet." He had to believe that. He absolutely did *not* have a way with children.

"I don't know about that," Annie began doubtfully.

David cut her off ruthlessly. "I'm sure that's all it is." He took her hand, angry with himself for doing so.

"Look, David! I found an acown."

"That's great, Amy. Okay, everybody," he called. "Letter *b* now."

They strolled silently for a few moments. Children scrambled through the leaves and grass at the sides of the path, scrutinizing everything their shoes scuffed up as they searched.

Annie breathed deeply, taking in the distinctive smell of autumn. Only moments ago, she'd been prepared to commit mayhem on her brood. Now she couldn't think of anything nicer than a walk with David on a gorgeous fall afternoon, her children gamboling on all sides. David was the key, of course, she recognized immediately. His insistence on helping her out lightened her load by way more than half. It was amazing. A sense of contentment, of rightness, filled her, pushing out every negative thought she'd ever entertained. She wondered if David shared it. "So how are you enjoying your break from the city, David? Do you like the country?"

"Sure." David shrugged. "Fresh air's okay in small doses, I guess."

"Oh." She was nonplussed. That hadn't exactly been the ringing endorsement she'd hoped for. She walked on. What had she expected? That he would abandon everything he'd worked for in Northstream and run off to live with her and her menagerie, all on the basis of their two-day reacquaintanceship?

Ruefully she had to admit that was exactly the idea that some self-inflated corner of her mind had entertained. Totally unrealistic, of course. Totally disappointing that things couldn't happen exactly that way. She straightened her shoulders. Well, life did not consist of a long string of walks on perfect October afternoons, that was for sure. She'd cope.

"Ouch! Damn it to hell!" David swatted his neck and brushed something out from under his collar.

"What? What's the matter?" Annie's voice squeaked in alarm.

"Nothing," David muttered as he lifted his foot to step on something. "A bee got caught under the collar of my shirt and the little sucker stung me, that's all."

"Oh, that's too bad," she said. "You're not allergic or anything, are you?" It was typical, of course. Her days were filled with the little drones of life whose whole purpose seemed to be to constantly remind her that even perfect fall days could only camouflage, and sometimes not too successfully, life's blemishes and stingers.

"How the hell would I know if I'm allergic or not?" he grumbled disgustedly while tentatively touching a fingertip to the side of his neck. "I've never been stung before."

"Here, let me take a look." She reached up to fold his collar down.

"Ouch! Damn it, Annie, don't touch it. That hurts."

"Don't be such a baby, I'm nowhere near it. Oh, dear, it looks like the stinger is still in."

"What does that mean?" he asked in alarm. "I suppose the thing is still pumping venom in even as we speak."

"All it means is we need to pull it out," she soothed. "Don't panic. There's very little swelling, really."

"Easy for you to say," he grumped. "It's not your neck that will shortly be swollen to twice its normal size. Geez, we're out in the middle of nowhere, on top of everything else. Do you even have paramedics around here? Maybe I should drive into town, stand around in the hospital lobby. That way there'd be medical people around when I keel over."

Annie had to smile. Men were such babies when they got hurt. "Oh, David—"

"David, there's nothing in this whole place that starts with *b*. We've searched everywhere."

"Oh, yeah? I found *b* for you, see?" He pointed to the smushed yellow jacket with the tip of his shoe. "You can start looking for *c*."

"Cool." Casey started back to announce David's find to the others and then turned back. "Why are you holding your neck?"

"That's how I found the bee. The little so-and-so bit me," he informed the child darkly. "Your mother thinks it's funny."

"I don't," Annie protested immediately. "I just don't think it's...as serious as you do." She lifted his hand and checked the swelling again. It was still localized.

"Lean down, David. I'll kiss it for you."

Annie watched as David carefully picked up her eight-year-old daughter and solemnly presented the side of his neck to her. He cringed slightly when her lips touched the site, but said nothing until Casey was safely back on the ground.

"Thank you, Casey," he told her. "That was very kind of you. It feels better already. You have magic lips." Probably got them from her mother.

"You want me to stay by you and smack any other bees that come around? I could get a big stick."

"No thank you, darling. Why don't you run and join the others," he suggested gently, determined to return childhood to the little girl. "Your mother and I will watch out for each other."

"But—"

He leaned over and pointed to his neck. "Look, Casey, your kiss cured it. It hardly hurts at all. Now I know this is hard for you, but it's the grown-up's job to worry. The kid's job is eat vegetables and run around a lot so when they're older they're big and strong enough to go to school and study hard. Everything else is up to the grown-up, okay?"

The smile that broke over Casey's face after a doubtful, mulling moment cracked a wall in Annie's heart. She watched while David, who'd been moaning away a few moments before, stoically accepted Casey's hug, including the small arms flung around his sore neck, without complaint.

"There's something special between the two of you, isn't there, David?" she asked perceptively once her daughter had run off.

"She's a nice kid." David defended his behavior. "All your kids are easy to like." One at a time.

Annie thought about that. She had been blessed with good children. Juvenility was considered acceptable in people whose age was counted in single digits. She had a few years left to file off the rough edges. Yes, her children were good . . . for children, but that wasn't it. "No, I think I'm right. You've got some kind of special affinity with Casey."

"Maybe," he muttered, shrugging. The action made his neck throb all over again. Damn it, anyway. He felt trapped. The fact that it was a web of his own making did nothing to alleviate the panic he felt. "I just remember that helpless feeling of being a kid trying to take care of the adult in my life." He thought of something and glared at her. "I want you to eat your vegetables tonight."

Her eyebrows rose. "We're cooking vegetables over a camp fire?"

"Damn straight we are. And you're to drink some milk. In front of the kids."

"Yes, sir."

"I'm not kidding."

"I can see that."

"Casey thinks you're going to die because you don't eat right."

"What?"

"Mom, I found a rock with a crack in it."

Annie deferred to David for a ruling on that, her mind whirling. Casey had never mentioned anything that serious to her, and she was her mother.

David was in no mood to split hairs, or crack rocks, as the case might be. "Okay, we'll accept that. Go see if you can find a dragonfly or something," he called.

"Watch out for poison ivy," Annie added automatically as the children tore off into the trees on either side of the pathway.

David rolled his eyes in resignation. Sure. Poison ivy. What else? Why anyone in their right mind would wax lyrical on nature was beyond him. Before they'd even started their walk, Annie had made everyone, David included, tuck their pant legs into the tops of their socks. "To keep the deer ticks from crawling up your leg," she'd said. "You don't want to get Lyme's disease."

Bees, poison ivy, deer ticks, good God, what else? Quickly he glanced around to make sure everyone had followed Annie's instructions. His eyes widened. Holy smoke, the tops of Casey's feminine version of sport socks showed three narrow bands of pastel color. Three! The socks in Annie's basement had gotten into group sexing!

His breathing shallow, his eyes reeled down to Annie's legs. He swallowed a moan. Cotton-candy pink, baby yellow and pale blue diamonds in an argyle pattern held her pant cuffs captive. There was only one possible explanation for tri-toned argyles. The socks in the laundry basket had degenerated into something more perverted than group sexing.

David put a hand to the back of his neck. It was still warm around the bee sting, but less swollen. Could the venom be affecting his brain? Maybe he was allergic. He'd never been turned on by thoughts of wearing apparel before. Never indulged in anthropomorphism. A sock was a sock. Always was, always would be. Hell. He picked up his pace. The kids weren't the only ones needing tiring out if there was to be any sleeping done tonight.

Annie looked at him curiously as she quickened her step to keep up. "David? Is anything wrong?"

Wrong? What could possibly be wrong? He dragged a hand through his hair. None of this was Annie's fault. "No, honey, nothing's wrong. I promised the kids marshmallows for s'mores and I was just wondering where to go to get some. You got any ideas?"

Annie eyed him cautiously. That was an awfully dark scowl for a marshmallow. "Sure," she allowed. "I should have some left in the camp store. We can use those."

"Great."

She'd taken care of his concern, but somehow he still did not have the appearance of a happy man, Annie thought. "Uh, no problem."

They walked on in silence. David gradually relaxed and began seeking the beauty around him. Dappled sunlight danced through the surrounding woods and over Annie. It frolicked in her hair. Suddenly, David had the second line to his poem. Her hair a playground for the sun. "Her *hair* a *play*ground *for* the *sun,*" he mouthed to himself, counting the meter.

"I'm sorry, I couldn't hear you. What did you say, David?"

"Hmm? Oh, nothing. Nothing at all." Four feet exactly. He congratulated himself on his cleverness. Nothing to this poetry stuff.

"I need to get back," Annie informed him regretfully. "One of the neighbors put in a late crop of snap beans and brought a bushel full over for me to put up. It'll take most of the afternoon to get them ready for freezing."

David stopped in his tracks and stared at her. Why he would have assumed that Annie would buy her beans in a bag from the frozen-foods section was beyond him. She'd yet to do anything predictable since he'd arrived. "That applesauce fiasco wasn't enough for you?" he asked in as neutral a tone as possible. "You're going to spend the afternoon putting up beans?"

Now what had she done? Cautiously she nodded. "Well, yes. That's what I'd planned. Is that a problem?"

"Is that a problem?" he mimicked under his breath as he stalked ahead, leaving her to follow in his wake. "What is she, nuts? Is she crazy?" He called the children out of the woods. "Come on, kids. It's time for more family fun. We're going to spend the rest of this gorgeous afternoon inside the kitchen snapping green beans. Doesn't that sound like a good time?" He continued the mutter to himself all the way back to the house. "The woman's lost her mind. She needs to get in line for a brain transplant and I'll be right behind her. I can't believe I'm actually going to do this." The fact was, however irritating it might be, if Annie wanted a bushel of beans snapped and parboiled, he'd lend a hand. It was no wonder he seldom took vacations. This had to be the most exhausting experience of his life.

He turned around and backpedaled his way down the trail. "Annie, if I promise to go into town tomorrow and buy you a case of canned green beans, can we trash the ones your neighbor brought you?"

"David, you do not need to do this. I can handle it."

He snorted his opinion of that. "Right. I'm supposed to lay around and bask in the warm sunshine, all the while knowing you're in a hot steamy kitchen dealing with the beans from hell?"

Why not? It's exactly what Craig would have done. He'd have sat down at the picnic table by the back door and written her some stupid sonnet, oblivious to the fact that it would have been far more helpful if he would have at least kept an eye on his own children while she worked around the place. "Seriously, I can—"

"Not while I'm here, you won't." He cut her off abruptly. "The two of us together will get it done in half the time."

David cringed when he saw the beans by the back door. Did the neighbor hate Annie? Was he one of those types that actually believed misery loved company? "I thought you said this neighbor of yours brought one bushel of beans over. There are two baskets sitting there."

Annie explained the two baskets. "Each one of those holds a half bushel. So, yes, there are two, but there's only one bushel full here."

David picked up one basket and started down the back stairs.

"Hey, where are you going with those?" Annie called, half-afraid he was headed for the camp dumpster.

"We'll do it out here on the picnic table," he answered. "That way we can keep an eye on the kids at the same time."

"Oh," she responded blankly. "Good idea." And it was. David supervised animal relay races for the children while he and Annie snapped beans side by side. Sunlight cast a warm glow over her boisterous brood as they became elephants trumpeting toward the finish line and then crabs scuttling on their backs. Orangy-red maple leaves drifted down over the scene along with leaves from a yellowed ash. David's warmth next to her as he tried to develop some kind of an efficient bean-snapping rhythm blocked the slight chill developing in the air as the afternoon progressed. It was one of those days she'd treasure some lonesome and cold winter night.

The size of the bean pile still waiting to be done surprised David. No more than a couple of handfuls remained. It hadn't been all that bad. The children's laughter and Annie's company had made time pass quickly. "Why do you do this?" he asked, finally calm enough to be genuinely curious. "You can't save that much, can you?"

"At store prices, this is, I don't know, maybe thirty-five dollars worth of beans."

"But your time is worth something," David quickly interjected. "Between the two of us we've already put in about four hours, I'd guess, and we're not done yet, are we?"

"No. We still have to wash them, parboil them, dunk them in ice water to stop the cooking and divvy them up into plastic bags before we can actually put them in the freezer."

"Then it's obviously not time efficient, so why?"

Annie lifted her face to the late-afternoon sun and thought. "It's just a part of life here," she finally decided. "One of the benefits of living in the country is the freshness of the produce. When you get it right off the vine, the bush or whatever, it's like a different species from the one you get in the store. It makes you want to save some of the summer's and fall's goodness to enjoy during the barren winter. These beans will have special meaning on Thanksgiving." She spoke slowly, having never put any of it into words before. "There's a connection, too, between you and generations of farmers and pioneers who performed these very tasks way back into time. Of course, for them it was a matter of survival." She looked at him, to see if anything she said was making sense.

He returned her look. "It would be like living in the city and not participating in the museum programs or going to the theater."

"Yeah, I guess."

David studied the bean in his hand. He'd lived in Northstream all his adult life. He'd yet to make the trip into Chicago to see any of the museums. He'd heard the sky show at the Adler Planetarium was excellent. The aquarium with its controversial whale tank and the Field Museum were practically next door to the planetarium. The Museum of Science and Industry lay only fifteen minutes down the Lake Shore Drive from that point.

He wouldn't care if he never snapped another bean in his life. Suddenly that bothered him. Annie was living her life. He was . . . just kind of floating on down the stream.

The kids were finally slowing down, David noticed. Maybe they'd get tired yet. They'd also notice empty stomachs before too much longer. He rose and picked up a basket of snapped beans. "I'll go put these in the sink and rinse them for you. Then I'm going to try and start a camp fire. Do you put up your own hot dogs or shall I rifle the camp store for some of those?" he teased gently.

Annie stood and fished a set of keys from her back pocket. "Get some marshmallows and chocolate bars from the store, but mark it down on the inventory pad by the cash register so I remember. Get one of the grates out of the supply closet in the back right-hand corner of the store." She dangled a different key. "This one will open that. We had hot dogs last night. We'll do a one-pot meal instead. That way we can dump the vegetables right into the main course and keep everybody happy."

David followed Annie's plan of attack like any good corporate soldier. Twenty minutes later, he was back behind the house laying wood out in a relatively grassless spot.

"Hi, David."

David glanced up from his task. "Hi, Case, hi, Mark."

Casey hung her thumbs through the belt loops of her jeans and balanced on widely spread feet. "Whatcha doing?"

"I promised you guys we'd cook out tonight, remember? I'm getting the fire ready."

Casey looked around. "Where's the bucket?"

"What bucket?"

"The fire bucket."

David put a hand to his forehead and tried to think. At times it was hard to believe Northstream, with its streetlights and sidewalks, existed a mere hour and twenty minutes down the highway. Certain things were so alien, it might as well be another planet.

Why would Annie build her fires in a bucket? The woman's mind did not work along the same lines as anyone else he knew. He considered the fact she was even then in the kitchen trying to bag up thirty pounds of beans the perfect illustration of his point. Who else would even want to attempt something like that? Well, he was going to build a normal fire and to hell with buckets. "To tell you the truth, Case, I think I'll just build the fire right here on the ground and not use the bucket. Just for a change, you know?"

"You can't," Mark broke in.

"Sure I can. Watch." He piled another log onto the haphazard stack. "What we need is kindling, not a bucket."

Casey's voice rose in pitch. She sounded agitated. "David, it's not safe. Don't do it."

He tried to reassure her. "Honey, I'll be very careful." Maybe the cookout hadn't been such a good idea if Casey was going to get all worked up about it.

"Come on, Casey, we'll go tell Mom on him. She'll make him get the fire bucket and the blanket, too."

Mystified, David watched the two scurry off intent on their tattling. The fact that Mark was firmly on Casey's side instead of sniping at her said something, but he wasn't sure what.

He stood and tested the early-evening breeze. He may not build his fire in a pail, but he knew enough to lay the logs out so that the first two formed a V and the cross log that went on the end was into the wind. He was laying kindling up against the cross log when Casey and Mark slapped the back screen door open and came struggling out with a heavy bucket between them.

"Don't worry, David," Casey called. "We've got the fire bucket."

"Yeah, and I've got the blanket under my other arm," Mark added.

Weird kids, David thought. Really weird. "That's great," he responded. Something slopped over the side of the pail as the panting duo worked their way down the stairs to the yard. It was wet, not glowing. "What's in there?" he asked as he went to relieve them of the heavy bucket.

"Water!" Casey seemed amazed he hadn't known. "Mom says accidents can happen and you should always be prepared, especially around fire. If somebody gets too close and their clothes catch on fire or something, you should have water and a blanket nearby. She makes me put my hair into a ponytail, too, but she just sticks hers down inside the back of her shirt. I don't think that's very fair, do you?"

David immediately mentally apologized for every uncharitable thought he'd had. Annie was making sure her children grew up safe and in the environment she thought best for them. She'd made a lot of sacrifices to do so and deserved his respect.

The children circled the area until they'd found enough rocks for a credible fire ring. David lit the tinder and, once the fire was going, set up the grate.

It was dark by then and Annie came out the back door, her arms laden with food items and children.

David moved to help her, concerned lest she fall on the steps.

"Oh, thanks, David."

It annoyed him that she seemed surprised by his offer of help. No wonder she couldn't sleep nights. She probably spent them brooding over the impossibility of being everything to everybody. How would she manage when he left? "You're welcome," he said through gritted teeth, feeling trapdoors doing their best to snap shut. "What is all this, anyway?" He indicated the big pot stuffed with cans, jars and a package of ground beef.

"The makings of goulash," she informed him, looking around the area with pleasure. The air was crisp, but not cold. True, it was dark, but the fire and David beckoned. The kids would all be in a good mood, feeling they'd really gotten away with something, having a cookout on a school night. This would be fun, the kind of night that made memories. Her step lightened as much as it could with one child in her arms and another hanging on her sweatshirt sleeve.

"What's the dish detergent for?" he asked.

"To soap the pot," Annie explained as she emptied the pan's contents onto the picnic table and picked up the squeeze bottle of detergent.

"You're not going to do it now, are you?" David asked in alarm. Good God, everything would taste like soap.

"You do the outside, not the inside," she assured him as she overturned the pot and squirted the puddle onto the cast-iron bottom. "The soot from the flames washes right off that way."

"Oh." Of course. Silly him.

He helped her set the heavy pot on the grate and watched, fascinated, as she browned ground beef, stirring to prevent burning. She added diced green pepper. He opened cans of tomato sauce and corn. A couple of handfuls of the fresh green beans got tossed in, as well. Annie let a few pinches of various spices drift down into the brew. David recognized basil. It actually smelled good, he realized as he sniffed the air appreciatively.

And it tasted even better, David acknowledged when they all sat down to eat. "This was great," he finally admitted out loud as he sopped up the last bit of juice with a slice of buttered French bread.

"I'm glad you liked it," Annie said. She rose and, armed with thick pot holders, attempted to lift the pot off the grate. "Are you ready for s'mores yet?"

"Yeah!"

"All right!"

"Wicked!"

"I don't know, I'm pretty full."

Annie looked at David, amused, as he wrestled the heavy pan away from her. He set the grate aside, as well.

"I'm afraid you're outvoted, champ. Everyone else appears to have saved room."

"A bunch of bottomless pits." He grunted as he carried the grate to a safe distance to cool. But he helped Amy and Billy toast their marshmallows without turning them black.

"Thankth, David."

"You're welcome, tough stuff," he responded gravely as he made a sandwich from graham crackers, chocolate bar and hot, gooey marshmallow. "Here you are." He watched as Billy greedily attacked his treat and shook his head. "It looks disgusting," he confided to Annie.

"Yeah, they're pretty bad," she agreed, nibbling on her own. "Have a bite and judge for yourself." She held hers out to him.

David studied it. Marshmallow oozed out the sides. Chocolate, melted by the hot marshmallows, was beginning to follow. Carefully he bit from the exact spot Annie had. "It's awful," he pronounced.

Annie licked a swirl of escaping chocolate. "Yes, but there's something about them. You know they're not good for you, not what you need. You know they don't even taste that great, but you keep coming back for more. Once you've had one, you can't put it down or stay away next time. It draws you."

David held her wrist while he leaned for another bite. Annie had a definite philosophical bent at times, he thought, and yeah. He knew exactly what she was talking about.

Chapter Nine

When the proceedings reached the point where Casey and Mark were deliberately setting their marshmallows on fire, saying they liked them black, Annie reluctantly rose. "It's late," she murmured, the quiet night seemingly requiring subdued tones. "You've all got school in the morning."

David smiled as children groaned. Some things were universal in town or country and on down through the time. "Last one in the tub's a rotten egg," he called and the evening's silence was shattered with scrambling, teasing, raucous children.

"Not it!"

"Not it!"

"It won't be me, eithuh."

The screen door slammed three times, then a fourth.

"Look what you've done," Annie rebuked with a smile. "You've started a riot."

David shrugged his shoulders.

She watched the movement like a hypnotized mouse watches a hawk.

"At least I got them as far as the second floor for you."

Regretfully she scooped up Stevie. "Yes, and I need to go oversee. Just leave everything as it is. I'll take care of the cleanup when I'm done up there."

David watched her retreating back and felt ... what, a bit of anger? He would certainly not be leaving her with the cleanup when creating the mess had been mostly his idea in the first place. Shouldn't she know him better than that by now?

"Her *eyes* are *blue* but *can*not *see.*" He grunted as he hefted the pot to carry it into the kitchen, determined to find out if the crazy idea of soaping a pot before using it worked or not. "Right number of ta*das,* but it doesn't rhyme with *rose* and it's not exactly romantic." He lugged the leftovers inside, not exactly feeling romantic, either.

By the time Annie got back downstairs, he had the leftover goulash put away, the bowls rinsed and stacked in the dishwasher and the pot washed. The soap idea had worked pretty well, he'd grudgingly admitted.

"Everything's done," she said in a wondering tone that grated.

"Not everything. I haven't had the time to get the fire bucket or blanket in yet."

Annie went to stand at the back door and looked out. "The fire's died down to coals," she observed. "Perfect for toasting those last few marshmallows." She turned her head to contemplate the six white blobs sulking in the bottom of their plastic bag. "What do you think?"

What did he think? He thought those marshmallows there in that bag on that table were the embodiment of Annie's philosophical appraisal of the lure of s'mores. Her thesis could be widened to encompass his life of late in general, his fascination with Annie and her brood in particular. He was full, and they weren't what he needed right now. "Let's do it."

David grabbed the bag before he had time to think twice and lit out the back door with Annie in tow. He caught the screen door before it could bang and eased it carefully shut. The kids were asleep and he wanted them to stay that way. Then he and Annie were down the back stairs, giggling like...kids. "I feel like an escapee from a Saturday morning cartoon," he said, laughing.

"I know what you mean," Annie agreed as they arrived breathless at the fire ring. "I've often felt I lived in one. It's gotten cooler," she said with a shiver.

"Hang on a second." David retrieved the blanket from next to the bucket of water. Flipping it open, he motioned for her to sit on one edge. When she complied, he pulled the other edge up over their shoulders, effectively encasing them in a warm woolen cocoon. "There. What did my mother used to say? Snug as two bugs in a rug."

Annie struggled to keep the blanket over her shoulder while threading marshmallows onto a skewer. "I never heard that one before," she admitted.

"Stick with me, kid, I'll take you places." He reached for his own skewer. "What kind of blanket is this, anyway? It's really warm."

"Old army surplus, one hundred percent wool."

"Ah."

They sat side by side, warmed by the coals, wool and body heat, silently toasting marshmallows the slow way. They gradually brought them from white all the way down to a deep golden brown without once setting them on fire. Annie turned to feed him the one she'd toasted. It was melted through to the center and dissolved in his mouth. He wondered if you could make love like that, a long, slow, drawn-out roasting of the senses that didn't burn, just left you feeling melted down to the core.

He pulled his off the stick and held it to her lips, wondering if he'd succeeded as well as she, and if he'd be able to hold off in love making long enough to ensure she melted like that.

"You want another?" he quietly asked in the dark.

"Yeah, sure. I guess." Annie could feel the intimacy building. With the children in bed, her natural built-in buffer was gone. It was David and her—they were undistracted and alone under that blanket. She didn't know if she wanted things to continue spiraling or, more importantly, if she could emotionally handle things should they do so.

She threaded another marshmallow onto her stick and leaned forward, letting her hair screen her face from David. It was up to her to decide what she wanted here.

So what was it?

David turned to her with another marshmallow. She took it. As she bit into its melted depths, David's eyes caught and held hers. Glowing coals simmered there in a warming reflection of the embers in front of them. Suddenly the blanket seemed stifling.

"Annie?"

She understood the unspoken question, but remained unsure of the answer.

David's head began to slowly lower.

She swallowed quickly. There was no time to use her tongue to sweep her lips clear of sticky residue, his own mouth and teasing tongue were already there. His lips touched, then his tongue traced the contours of her mouth.

There was a gratified, "Mmm," only she didn't know which of them had uttered it.

The immediate sensorial assault scared her with its intensity. She recognized instinctively that tonight was different. Different than it had ever been before. The moon shone benevolently down and the stars winked in approval. Reduced to coals now, the fire threw nothing more than a soft glow, as though it, too, wanted perfection for the coming interlude. Crickets serenaded from nearby. It seemed all of nature conspired to keep David and her together tonight.

She was in deep trouble, floundering in the night, the stars and David. What did she want? She'd better make up her mind quickly. One thing for sure, David didn't seem to be sharing her doubts. He continued to lean farther into the kiss, teasing her mouth, with the effect of pushing her gradually down onto her back.

David groaned. "You taste good."

Annie was caught by surprise with the breathlessness of her voice as she responded, "So do you." She touched his mouth wonderingly with a fingertip.

David took that tip into his mouth and sucked gently.

Annie's heart had steadily climbed out of her chest from the moment she'd first realized David was going to kiss her. It was now firmly lodged in her throat, making breathing difficult. "We ought to...to put out the fire," she murmured.

"Yeah," he agreed. "Let's put out these flames."

"No, no. Those flames. Over there. And we need to bring in the blanket and things."

"Right. The blanket. Good blanket. Warm."

Annie totally lost her train of thought just as David's night-cooled lips settled back over her own.

What had she ever found frightening about the dark?

It enveloped her now, cradled both her and David in its private cocoon. David covered her with his body and pulled the blanket snugly around them both. The night held them while the moon hid behind a cloud as though too shy to witness their intimacy.

Annie's hand lay limply next to her head. David worked his way down her throat, but was continually drawn back to her mouth.

"Damn, but you taste sweet," he swore. He let his hands slide down her body, down to the cuffs of her rolled-up jeans, down to her slim ankles. "You're lethal, you know that? Absolutely, totally lethal." His mouth ground against hers while his hands rose to her waist and played with the hem of her sweater before sliding underneath.

Annie's decision made, she held his head with hands that roamed restlessly through the short hair at the base of his skull. She arched slightly, allowing him to pull up her sweater. "Wait," she panted as her world spun. "Hang on just a second, there's a rock in my back."

Impatiently David rolled, putting himself on the bottom. He doubted he'd feel anything under the size of a boulder right then. Her words served to reinforce his view of her as a delicate princess. One who needed him to be on the bottom, buffering the pebbles now and then. "Is that better?" he asked.

"Yes." She looked down into his face and could once again see the reflection of the burning embers in his eyes. Or was it a reflection?

She ran her hands over his shoulders.

He ran his up her ribs.

They moaned simultaneously when he reached her breasts and he circled her nipples with his fingertips.

"Oh, my God."

"Yes, I was thinking along similar lines," David all but panted as he reached behind her for the clasp of her bra.

He seemed to have trouble with it. Annie felt a trifle frantic as she arched her back and reached her arms behind to do the job herself. David took the action as an invitation and lowered his mouth to one breast, sucking it right through the flimsy material.

You could die from this kind of pleasure, she thought. Only why bother when she'd found heaven right here?

"Mom? Mom, are you out there? Billy says he feels sick. He snitched that last chocolate bar without asking, you know. Maybe God's gettin' him. Mom? You hear me?"

"No," David groaned as she pulled free and hastily readjusted her sweater. "No, no, no, no."

"I'm sorry," she said, caressing his face with butterfly fingers. "I'm so sorry."

"Mom! Billy's sick!"

"I hear you, honey. I'm coming. Go on up and stay with him until I get there."

"I've got to go," she said to David, shivering as she gave up the blanket and David's caresses.

David recognized she had somehow instantly metamorphosized from siren princess back into her mother role. There was no point in trying to recapture the mood. "I'll put the fire out and take care of things out here." He sighed.

She leaned and gave him a distracted kiss. "Thanks. I appreciate it."

He ran his finger down the side of her face. It was some small comfort when she shivered in response, but not much.

He lay there and watched as she scurried into the house. Then he placed his arm over his eyes and called upon his mental reserves. Eventually he was able to rise and take the water bucket over to the coals. Steam rose as he began dribbling water over the glowing wood. It singed his eyebrows, curled his hair.

"Just like Annie's kisses," he muttered morosely as he stirred the coals and dribbled more water. He made sure the embers were completely extinguished before he folded the blanket and set it and the bucket up on Annie's back porch. He turned his back on the warmly lit windows of Annie's house and slowly made his way back to his own abandoned-looking campsite.

Melancholia settled over him, holding him as securely and snugly as the sleeping bag he pulled up to his nose. "It was a damn close call," he finally told himself, wanting to feel relief. "You didn't have anything to use," he reminded himself. "Imagine a shotgun wedding to a mother of five. I'd have been the father of six!" He shuddered and finally drifted into sleep, sure he faced eight hours of nightmares.

He hadn't known they were expecting twins. That's why his brow rose in surprise when the nurse pointed out two bassinets in the nursery.

He pressed closer to the viewing window. A pink-wrapped bundle topped with blond hair lay in the bed adjacent to a blue-blanketed bald bundle voraciously sucking a bottle nipple stuffed with cotton. "Poor little guy," he murmured, watching as his son pumped away on the empty nipple. He glanced around the nursery, prepared to knock on the window to gain the nurse's attention if necessary. "They should bring little David in to his mother. What a dirty trick to play. He needs the real thing."

And Annie was the genuine article. She had what his babies needed, she had what he needed. Why she—

"David?"

"Hmm?" Blearily he opened his eyes. Children surrounded him. "Oh, good. You're all here. Come see the twins. They're really something."

"What twins? David, what are you talking about?" Casey and Mark edged closer. "The bus is coming soon. We ran down to see you to find out if we could do another cookout tonight. Please?"

David propped himself up on an elbow and wiped his eyes with his free hand. He tried to clear his mind. Still muzzy, he squinted at the children's forms, dark against the morning light let in by the open tent flap. Gradually his surroundings sank in. "The tent. I'm here in the tent. No babies, I'm in the tent."

Casey leaned down and put a hand to his forehead in a gesture stolen from her mother. David doubted she knew it was a fever check.

"Are you feeling okay, David?"

"Yeah, I'm fine, honey." He took her hand away from his forehead and planted a kiss on her palm. "I must have been dreaming, that's all." He sat all the way up. "You two better run before you miss your bus."

"But what about the cookout?"

"We'll have to see how the day goes, okay?"

Dissatisfied with the answer, reluctant to start another school day, the two dawdled inside the tent.

"Go on now," David directed. "Shoo. I'll see you both later."

He sat there, blinking in the morning light streaming through the tent flap, and thought about his dream. He was in deep trouble. He ran an unsteady hand through his hair as he acknowledged that the most frightening part of the whole thing revolved around the fact that the dream hadn't, didn't, seem at all nightmarish.

Evidently he didn't even have enough sense to be scared.

It was depressing, that's what it was. Depressing.

He worked around his campsite most of the morning, but found he could only reorganize a meager amount of supplies so many ways, so he took a walk through the grounds.

There were fifty-eight campsites, he discovered and wondered if that was enough to support her.

Of course, he didn't know much about campgrounds, but as he looked around appraisingly, the place seemed to be edging toward—well, shabbiness. The picnic tables were old. On a few of the sites, they listed to one side or the other. Fire grates were bent out of shape or just plain missing.

He looked closer. Shabby wasn't right. No, the entire grounds seemed to be more slipping into a genteel poverty than anything else. The acreage was immaculate; no garbage littered the grass or wooded areas. The grassy sites were cut short and the sandbox sites were level and weed free. He turned in a full circle. "How the hell does she do it all?" he wondered out loud. "It must be killing her to see everything going downhill while she breaks her back over it."

He wandered back to his tepee tent morose and discontent. He liked to take charge of a situation. Draw up a battle plan, issue orders and turn the thing around. "This place requires a massive infusion of cash, though," he said helplessly to the listing picnic table in front of his tent. "I can't afford it. Not as much as would be needed."

He sat at the table, restlessly drumming his fingers over its surface. Actually he had the money, but it would mean cashing in most of the portfolio he and his investment counselor had been carefully building up. His savings had been invested conservatively in low-risk, blue-chip stocks and bonds. Campgrounds had never once appeared on his analyst's list of recommended investments.

The angry tattoo his fingers beat out matched his mood. That portfolio was damned important to him. It represented his protection from ever again having to eat Thanksgiving or Christmas dinner from a diner doggie bag at the end of his mother's long shift. It meant security to him just as surely as his large four-bedroom brick colonial in Northstream assured him he'd never again live in a roach motel masquerading as a studio apartment.

He couldn't sell it.

He couldn't bear to do nothing, though, to watch Annie worry or suffer, either.

Restlessly, he drove into the small town to poke around some more, but he'd seen most of it the day before. He checked in with the office, using the town's only public phone.

He sought Annie out later that afternoon. She was in back of the house hanging out sheets.

"What's the matter," he asked, immediately concerned. "Did the dryer break down?"

"Hmm? Oh, no. I just like the way the sun makes them smell. When you go to sleep on them, you're surrounded by sunshine and the outdoors."

"Uh-huh, well, I've been to town again. There are a few more things for you in the trunk of my car. I'll just put everything in the kitchen."

He turned in retreat, but came back again. "Annie, I checked in with the office while I was there. I need to go back and work out a couple of sticky things that have come up, so I'm going to have to cut things short here." He shrugged helplessly, and that was exactly how he felt. Helpless. Helplessly torn between the growing emotional attachment and what he considered a nonbiased assessment of his and Annie's needs. He couldn't father a brood of five.

To top things off, he began to suspect he couldn't write poetry to save his soul, and Annie needed that kind of thing. Deserved it. And what did David need? Damned if he knew. He thought he needed his career, the safety of a regular paycheck, the city. Darn it, he still did. He would shortly be out of here. Once safely back in Northstream, he'd be able to maintain a better perspective. Think about things. He'd send her some money, treats for the kids once in a while and call occasionally to make sure the packages had arrived. That would work out much better.

He lugged in two heavy boxes filled with peace offerings to his conscience and left to dismantle his campsite.

Annie stood at the clothesline, sheets snapping around her, and wondered what had just happened.

Nobody went to all the trouble to plan a two-week vacation and then called it off after what amounted to a long weekend. Surely somebody in the office could handle whatever crisis had come up. Good Lord, her one remaining friend from the office, Mary Ellen McGee, had been there for years. Surely she—

He just didn't want to be there anymore.

She was surprised by how much that hurt. The children would miss him. *She'd* miss him. She tried to be fair. It wasn't easy. She lectured herself. Children, even good children like hers, could be hard to handle en masse for some people.

She hadn't thought David was one of them, though.

She seldom received social invitations. People assumed five children would dismantle their homes in less time than they'd taken to build. She understood. So why did she feel tears welling up like a faucet needing a new washer?

"Maybe it's not the kids. Maybe it's me." She entertained the idea forlornly. Suddenly the air didn't smell as sweet, the sun lost its warmth. She flushed red, embarrassed by the idiotic, intimate thoughts she'd entertained about David lately. Then she pulled the sheets down off the lines, deciding to simply throw them in the dryer instead.

"Where's David?" Casey questioned eagerly as she hopped off the school bus that afternoon.

"He said he'd think about another cookout," Mark announced buoyantly as he bobbed out the door.

Annie was taken aback. "Oh, well, he had something important come up at work." *Hah.* "He had to go back." *Double hah.* "I really think one cookout on a school night is enough, don't you? It would lose its specialness if you do it every night." Unlike making love with David. She was quite sure that would never lose its specialness no matter how often they indulged their appetites.

She spent the afternoon pacifying the children. They made caramel apples. From scratch. It took forever for the candy thermometer to reach the proper temperature. Usually they all enjoyed the task. This particular afternoon, the sluggish mercury was the cause of impatience and short tempers.

"Okay, that does it. Everybody up to their rooms for a cooling-off period."

"I didn't do anything to him, Mom. I shouldn't have to go to my room. He poked me for no reason."

"I did not! She's been bugging me the whole time. I've hardly had any turns stirring at all."

"Like I said, I think we all need a cooling-off period." She held up her hand to prevent the denial forming on their lips. "And if you don't, I do. I am very close to blowing my stack. It won't be a pretty sight if I do, so if you're half as smart as I think you are, you will all head out of here as fast as your little legs will carry you and without further argument."

"Mom? Billy stepped on my foot and I know it was on puhpose."

"Out. All of you. Now."

This kind of petty squabbling never used to bother her. It did today. David had run interference and laughed with her at the kids' inherent childishness over the weekend. Suddenly, without him, their silliness didn't seem so funny. It was pathetic how much she'd come to rely on David in a few short days.

Finally. Two hundred and forty-five degrees. She ladled hot caramel over the washed apples in the quiet kitchen. Inevitably some dribbled from the spoon onto the stove top and waxed paper under the apples. She knew not to touch it. From personal experience, two hundred and forty-five degrees hurt like hell. Annie stared at one of the small blobs. Shouldn't she have displayed the same common sense while David was around? He'd done her a favor by taking off, and she'd continue to tell herself that until she believed it.

Unfortunately for her analogy, when that caramel cooled a bit, there was little in heaven or on earth that tasted as good. No comparison to the store-bought stuff. It was the real thing.

Chapter Ten

David glanced up at the knock on his office door. "Yes?" he called as he slipped a paper into his rhyming dictionary and hastily tossed both into a desk drawer. He took off his glasses.

The door opened about a foot. His second in command, Mary Ellen McGee, cautiously stuck her head around the wooden barrier as though prepared to quickly pull it shut again and run should the necessity arise. David smiled grimly. He had not been a happy camper around the office during the four weeks that had been marked off since his return from vacation. He really needed to get a grip on his behavior.

"Come on in, Mary Ellen. I won't bite. Promise."

The gray-haired, perfectly groomed woman sidled halfway in, still partially shielding herself with the door. "What about throwing things? Do I need my body armor?"

He grimaced. "It was only one time and I never actually let go of it."

"Speaking of your paperweights, where are they?" Her eyes nervously roamed the room.

"In my desk drawer. See? There's nothing to worry about. Now come in and tell me whatever you've come to say. I'm feeling decidedly frayed around the edges this morning and you seem intent on pulling the remaining threads."

"Who me?" Mary Ellen protested as she came farther into the room. "I'm just trying to protect my own hide. Lock the drawer that has the paperweights and put the key out of reach."

David's eyes narrowed. "Why? What's going on? Did Carver make another stupid math error on a contract? Why can't he ever make a mistake in our favor? How much damage—"

"Calm down, calm down, it's nothing like that," Mary Ellen soothed as she slid into a chair across from David's desk.

"Then what is it?" he questioned, pinning her with his eyes. "Why am I going to want to fling paperweights around?"

"In all honesty, I don't know." Mary Ellen sighed. "But for one solid month, any time Victor Glenn's name comes up, you go into a frenzy. What is going on between the two of you? To be blunt, you've become almost irrational on the subject."

"The man's a jerk," David proclaimed defensively, fidgeting with his glasses frames.

"He's always been a jerk. You've never had any problem keeping him in perspective before. What gives?"

David set his glasses back down and picked up a pencil from the desktop holder. He tried to balance it across his index finger, glowered when it tumbled off, then sighed. He supposed Mary Ellen deserved an explanation of his less than exemplary behavior of late.

"Remember when you set me up to meet Annie Cronin a few weeks back?"

She nodded. "For all the good it did me. You barely had time to figure out who she was and then you were back. I can't figure out what went wrong." She shook her head in puzzlement. "I know she's Vic's daughter, but you still seemed so right for each other, or so I thought. Both lonely, needing somebody." She pursed her lips thoughtfully. "I really expected things to click."

David snorted. "Take it from me, Mary Ellen. The woman is not lonely. Not with that brood of hers always around. And by the way, if you ever try anything like that again, I'll break a minimum of two legs and an arm."

Mary Ellen nodded. "Not as bad as I thought. I was figuring at least two of each, so you have to know how sure I was things would work out. And furthermore, you can be lonely in a crowd, David. You know that. And what Annie needs, she's not going to get from a three-year-old."

David couldn't seem to make the pencil balance on its eraser end in his palm, either. He scowled. "If you're talking about sex, forget it."

Mary Ellen leaned forward. "Sex, shmex. Annie needs somebody without a lisp to talk to. Someone to hold her when the night gets dark, and help her when the health department quarantines her house because all five of the little ones come down with chicken pox. Somebody who doesn't mind singeing his fingers a bit helping those rascals make s'mores."

He refused to become involved in a discussion of s'mores. It was bad enough that he dreamed of them at night. He shook his head. "And you thought this paragon was me? Well, think again. When and if I ever succumb, I'd like a little adult companionship out of the deal myself," he explained stonily. "You can forget my doing it as a corporal work of mercy. It would be an insult to Annie, for one thing. She can do a lot better than pity."

Mary Ellen sat back, obviously puzzled. "You sure covered a lot of territory in two days, if you know so much about her."

David flipped the pencil over one finger and under the next as he worked it down one hand. "The campground was fairly deserted this time of year," he explained carefully. "I spent some time with the kids and Annie."

Mary Ellen eyed him speculatively. "All right, I get the message. You don't want to talk, but what does any of this have to do with Vic?"

"He's a horse's rear," David announced, determined to start watching his language lest something untoward slip out should he, by any chance, see the children again.

"Did he show up or something?"

"No, he did not show up," David ground out.

"You didn't like Annie? She's a horse's rear, too, and you figure it's his fault for passing down equine rear-end genes? That's not very fair-minded of you, David."

"Oh, be quiet, will you? Annie's a delight. Kind and considerate the whole time I was there."

"Still as cute as she used to be, too," Mary Ellen stated with some satisfaction.

David nodded in discouragement. "Yes, she is. She's an absolute knockout."

"You liked her."

"I liked her."

"A lot."

"A lot. Maybe." The pencil snapped in his fingers. He looked at it in surprise before dropping it in the trash. "Hell, I don't know. There are a few extenuating circumstances, let's just say. She's got five children, to start with. Five, count them, five."

"I know. Raising them by herself, too."

He nodded glumly again. "A hunting accident. Can you believe it? A stinking hunting accident. And now Annie's up there struggling to raise five children and running a campground on a shoestring budget all by herself."

"I still don't get it. How come all the animosity toward Victor Glenn? How does he figure in this?"

"I helped as much as I could while I was up there and I've sent a few care packages since I've been back. But damn it, I shouldn't have to be doing this. Her family should be there for her," David protested feeling sorely abused and frustrated.

"In other words, you're attracted to Annie and feel obligated to help. You resent both of those items."

"Listen." He bristled. "She's turned into some kind of nature child up there. She's obviously in her element and it's certainly not mine. On top of that, Annie's in some kind of funk and who can blame her with what she's been through? The last thing she needs is some guy coming on to her."

"How do you know what she needs?"

"I just do, that's all." Although Annie hadn't exactly run in the opposite direction the few times he'd been unable to sit on his more carnal impulses. He shook his head impatiently. No, that just made it more imperative to keep his distance. At this point in his career it was essential to stay away from a woman with an antipathy the size of Annie's toward the business world.

"Of course, it would sure put a crimp in your career plans if you settled down in rural Wisconsin and lost your mobility."

Her eyes watched his face. She'd picked up on the central issue right away. She was sharp, he'd give her that. He knew she was waiting for some betrayal of emotion. He tried not to satisfy her curiosity by squirming. It was hard, though. "The first transfer I turn down will put my career on permanent hold, and we both know it. If I don't put my career first, the company sure as hell won't."

"You *are* in a bind," Mary Ellen commented sympathetically. "You're the kind of person that would need to try and help, just as I thought."

"Hell," he growled. "My mother died struggling to take care of me under a similar set of circumstances, which, I might add, is exactly the possibility that is giving Annie's oldest girl nightmares." He snapped another pencil. "Mary Ellen, I should fire you for doing this to me."

"I'm sorry, David. I really thought you'd go for her."

He scrubbed his face with his hand. "I can't concentrate on business, and you want to know why? I'll tell you. It's because her little girl, Casey, has got me writing poetry because Annie likes poetry and maybe she'll eat her vegetables if she's happy and get her four food groups in every day and not die, after all."

"We are getting very heavy-duty here."

"Tell me about it." He stood and went to the window, with its landscape in motion picture of the adjacent Edens Highway. He shoved his suitcoat back and watched the traffic heading on up to Wisconsin with his hands on his hips.

"Just because I'm terminally curious and can't stand not knowing, uh, how's the poem coming?"

"Lousy."

"What have you got so far? Maybe it's not as bad as you think, although I have trouble picturing you as a poet, to be truthful."

"You and me both," he growled as he stalked back to his desk. He reached into the drawer and virtually threw the book with his poem in it at her.

Mary Ellen let the book skid across the desktop until it threatened to land in her lap. She stopped it and pulled out the paper extending around the perimeter. She began to read it out loud:

"Her lips are like a glist'ning rose,
Her hair a playground for the sun.
Her eyes set me to compose
A poem for her, my special one."

"What's wrong with it?" Mary Ellen asked when she finally looked up.

David threw up his hands in frustration. "That's over a month's worth of work. I need six more lines. I wanted to send it to her for Christmas." Then he felt obliged to point out, "And the meter's all wrong in the third line. 'Her *eyes* set *me to* com*pose*.' Hear it? I've written a poem with a stutter. Ta*da* ta*dada* ta*da*. Now that I think about it, it's a whole beat short on top of everything else." He raked his hand through his hair in frustration. "I can't do this, I can't be what she wants. And honest to God, except for the fact they're both crazy, I can't believe she's related to that cutthroat, Vic."

"Oh my gosh, I forgot!"

David glanced up sharply from his perusal of his work. "What?"

"Vic. The reason I wanted the paperweights locked up. He's on his way over."

David threw up his arms. "That's just what I need right now. Oh, hell, maybe it's not such a bad idea. I can throw the paperweights directly at him, cut out the middleman, so to speak."

"Now, David—"

"What the devil is he coming here for?"

"He says there's a problem in the latest batch of figures and he wants it cleared up before he leaves on vacation."

David sank back into his chair. "Sure, that jerk feels obligated to ruin our day before he goes on some luxury trip, while his own daughter's shoestring operation is about to snap it's so badly frayed."

David glared as Mary Ellen remained silent. "Get Carver in here," he directed. "Tell him to bring a copy of our latest proposal to Glenn's company."

Mary Ellen rose and went to the door, looking pleased that the paperweights were still in the drawer. "Have fun with dear, sweet Vic," she told him as she left.

David sighed as the door whispered quietly over the carpet and closed with one well-bred, low-toned click. Certainly a far cry from the constant slamming of Annie's back door or the slapping of the screen as it swung shut.

He sat behind his desk and pulled toward him the paperwork Carver had snuck in and left.

He read the first column, then stopped to rub his eyes and reached for his glasses. Ever since his ill-fated vacation, pages full of numbers reminded him of Mark's joke about seven plus eight equaling naked. He tried to clear his mind and found it almost impossible. It did not help that this particular page of numbers belonged to Victor Glenn, which brought to mind his daughter Annie, which brought him right back to thoughts of naked and nude, with Annie in the starring role. "Hell."

Sheri, his secretary, announced Mr. Glenn, and David directed Sheri to show him in. He got up from his desk to greet Annie's father.

After the better part of two hours, Carver's job was safe. Vic Glenn was simply in an argumentative frame of mind, wanting to quibble over every bit of data entered on the thirteen-page contract.

Didn't the man have anything better to do with his time, David wondered tiredly after doggedly pointing out that WCN had cut Vic's company a more than fair deal with the original contract. David was determined to stand his ground. If that old geezer Glenn wouldn't help out his own daughter, the least he could do would be to leave enough of a profit in the deal for David's commission check so that David could.

"Why can't you knock another couple thousand off the price of those three machines?" Vic asked, pointedly adding, "I throw a lot of business your way. You make up in volume what you lose on the individual sale."

"We've already taken that into consideration, Vic. The prices quoted here are more than reasonable, lower than anything you'd get anywhere else."

"I still say—"

David was almost grateful when the intercom buzzed, although Sheri knew not to disturb him when he was in a meeting. "Yes?" he answered the summons gruffly.

"You've got a phone call on line one, David."

David sat back and stared at the instrument in surprise. That was Mary Ellen's voice floating into the office. "Where's Sheri? Is this more bad news?" he asked, unable to imagine what Victor Glenn must be thinking of an office where the assistant manager answered the telephone and interrupted client meetings after clear instructions not to.

"It's a very tearful little girl who would not accept Sheri's explanation that you were in a meeting and couldn't be disturbed. Sheri passed her to me and I'm taking full responsibility for interrupting. It's Casey, David, and she's really upset."

David sat bolt upright in his chair and punched the button for line one, cutting off Mary Ellen's explanations. Across from him, Victor Glenn harrumphed his annoyance. David ignored him. "Casey, honey? What's the matter, sweetheart?"

His heart thumped in his chest when his initial response was a hiccup and a slight sobbing sound. "Casey?" He all but strangled the telephone as he waited.

"David? David, they wouldn't let me talk to you. You said I could call if I needed you when you sent me your card with the number on it."

"I know, it's my fault. I forgot to explain things to my secretary. Now tell me why you called." Damn, he thought. He needed to be there and comfort her through whatever was bothering her. What could he do from here?

"Kennedy, this is unprofessional. We're supposed to be having a business meeting here. Man's got to learn to keep his personal life separate if he's going to get ahead."

David gave Vic Glenn an irritated glance and pointed his finger at him. "You be quiet. I can't hear what she's saying." He removed his glasses, leaned back and closed his eyes as he attempted to focus only on Casey's call, not really caring how Vic felt at being told to shut up by a business associate who should be currying his favor.

"And she hasn't eaten her vegetables since you left and now she says she has the flu, but she hasn't gotten out of bed in three days, not even to make sure we're safely on the bus. She always makes sure we're safely on the bus, and she makes throwing-up sounds all the time only she says there's nothing left in her stomach. David, that doesn't make any sense, does it? How can you—"

David was already up and moving. He let his head clamp the phone between ear and shoulder while he opened his briefcase on the top of his desk and began throwing papers into it. Vic's figures, he threw into the top drawer, refusing to even consider altering them. "Don't you worry, sweetie, I'm on my way." He remembered Casey's fears and reassured her. "Nothing is going to happen to your mother. She's going to be just fine. I personally guarantee it." He hung up the phone and hoped he could live up to his word.

"Say, now, just a minute," Vic Glenn blustered. "We're negotiating a contract here. You can't go running off because some kid calls and says her mother's sick."

"Watch me," David answered as he pushed the briefcase shut.

"Son, business has to come first. You're not even married. You got some kind of common-law arrangement going nobody knows about? Who is this?"

David had his briefcase in hand and was ready to walk out the door. "You want to know who it is? I'll tell you. The caller was an eight-year-old girl named Casey. Ring any bells? No? She's one of your five grandchildren. I met her on a brief vacation I took several weeks ago."

David nodded in satisfaction at Vic's startled look.

"That's right, *your* granddaughter. The mother she's worried about is your daughter, Annie, who is evidently so ill she hasn't gotten out of bed in three days."

Vic rose ponderously from his chair. "My Annie's sick?"

"She hasn't been *your* Annie since you wrote her off for daring to pick a different life-style." David walked to the door. "I'm leaving now. Your daughter needs *somebody*. Looks like she'll have to settle for a virtual stranger." He opened the door. "By the way, the figures on that contract are firm. Take them or leave them."

David strode out the door, swearing as he marched through the outer office.

Behind him, a door opened and a voice imperiously called, "Wait. I'm coming with you."

Just what he needed. Vic Glenn's company for the trip up to Wisconsin.

Mary Ellen McGee met him by the parking-lot egress. She was breathless and harried. "Here," she said, shoving some money into his hand. "Casey told me what was going on. I took up a quick collection from the people who remember Annie."

David sighed. "Mary Ellen, you know that's against company policy. You're not allowed to take collections in the office. You'll have to give it back. I'm not jeopardizing my job over this. I can cover any medicine or food Annie needs."

"Neither one of you will pay for a damn thing for my daughter. I'm her father. I will take care of her myself."

David and Mary Ellen both turned to Vic with a look that spoke volumes. "Give me the money," David said to Mary Ellen. "I'm sure Annie will appreciate the gesture more than some father who hasn't seen fit to contact her in years."

"She's the one who left and refused to come back when I needed her," Vic protested.

"And that makes it okay." David shook his head in disparagement as he slid into the car. "Get in if you're coming and let's get out of here."

"I never understood where I went wrong with Annie," Vic fretted as though she was already dead.

David swung onto the connector ramp between the Edens Highway and the interstate tollway. If the backups at the tollbooths between that point and the border weren't too bad, he'd be there in an hour. He edged his foot down a bit on the accelerator. Maybe less. "Nothing went wrong with Annie," he came back. "She's a wonderful mother. You should see her with that pack of pistols she's raising. She's also a good cook, kind to living things and doesn't spit, smoke or swear. What more could you want?"

"I worked my tail off building a legacy for my daughter and grandchildren. She spit in my eye and walked away from it all."

David had a little trouble understanding anyone walking away from that kind of gift himself, but he wasn't going to admit it. Not now. "Did she really spit in your eye?"

"Figuratively, yes, she did. I gave her time to move out and be independent. But then when her mother died, she wouldn't come home. She refused."

He could see it still galled the other man. "She didn't want your life-style or your business. You tried to cram them down her throat. Living in the country instead of operating in the business world doesn't make a difference as to what kind of person you are. You succeeded in what was important. She's loaded with guts and gumption and she's a good person."

"I should never have let her go."

"You couldn't have stopped her. But you should have stayed in contact."

"She wouldn't come when I needed her. She went back to that camp place right after the funeral."

David rolled him a look of disbelief. "Oh, come on, you were angry and you pushed her away."

Vic sighed and sounded old. "Maybe. How much longer?"

David glanced around. They'd already shot past Lamb's Farm and the Great America amusement park outside of Gurnee, Illinois. "We're almost to the border," he said. "Slightly over half an hour to the campground."

Vic shifted in his seat. "A campground. Who'd have thought any daughter of mine would turn into a nature child? Probably lives in a tent by now. Given up bathing."

David shifted lanes, steering around a triple trailer truck and the You Are Leaving Illinois, the Land of Lincoln signpost. "Come on, Vic. She's your daughter. She owns the place, has a nice Wisconsin stone-and-clapboard farmhouse. It's small, dated, but she keeps it maintained. The whole campground is well groomed and picked up, but I've got to warn you. Money's obviously been tight for a while. The grounds and the house have a tired look to them."

Vic remained quiet for a while. David was off the main highway and driving along the gentle swells of the county road leading to Annie's when he next spoke.

"How bad are things?"

"Hard to say. Annie hasn't actually confided in me, but my guess is they're bad."

"She should have called."

"In her shoes, would you have?"

Gruffly Vic inquired, "Is there enough to eat for her and the kids?"

David considered the question. "Yes, I think so. Nothing gourmet, but she does a lot of home freezing and canning and there's meat. No steak, but plenty of ground beef and hot dogs, that kind of thing."

Vic thought about that as David swung into Annie's driveway and immediately hit a pothole.

Vic hung on to the dashboard as he yelped, "What the hell was that?"

"Annie's driveway needs a little work," David explained as he braked abruptly. "I forgot and came in too fast."

He bounced much more slowly through the apple orchard and on up to the house. He watched for the children as he went. "You've got to be careful coming in here," he lectured Vic. "One of the kids could be out playing and run in front of the car."

Vic gave him an odd look, as though to point out it hadn't been him taking the turn too quickly, but said nothing.

David braked by the front door and turned off the ignition. "Come on," he said. "Let's go in and see how bad things are. I wonder if Casey knows the name of their family doctor?"

"Do they even have doctors out here?" Vic questioned as he pulled his large frame out of the car and looked around in disbelief. "I feel like I'm in a different world entirely."

"From Northstream, you are," David assured him.

David glanced up as the front door slapped open and Casey came hurtling across the threshold and down the steps.

"David! I knew you'd come. I just knew it. What took you so long, though? I've been waiting by the window forever and ever!"

David thought about the time he'd made. He was lucky to be here at all instead of the state lockup, but he was sure the time-lapse had seemed like an eternity to the waiting child. "I'm here now, kiddo, so let's go see what's up with your mom. How does that sound?"

Casey noticed the stranger with him and took a reticent step back, using David as a shield of sorts. "Who's that?" she asked uncertainly. "Did you bring the doctor? I wanted to call one, but Mom said no."

"And she may be right, we'll have to see." He swung the child up into his arms to soften the impact of an introduction to an unknown grandparent. "Sweetie, this is a friend of mine from work. He also just happens to be your mom's very own daddy. You know what that makes him?"

Casey shook her head.

He turned to Vic. "What does that make you? The grandfather, Grandpa Vic, Gramps? What?"

Vic watched the child with eyes David knew could pierce. They were soft and liquid now.

"Pop-pop," he pronounced slowly. "I'm your pop-pop." And he reached out to gently touch Casey's wild fire-engine-red curls.

David managed not to laugh, but he did startle. "You want to be called 'pop-pop'?"

Suddenly the eyes were piercing again. "That's what Anne called my father and what I called his. You have a problem with that?"

"Uh, no, not at all." He cleared his throat. He just had trouble thinking of Vic Glenn, business mogul, as a pop-

pop. "Well," he stated briskly. "Let's go check up on Annie." He gently tickled Casey and succeeded in coaxing out a giggle.

Other children attached to his legs like leeches as he progressed through the house. David tried not to let his impatience show. He wanted to get to Annie, but the children needed reassurance. As usual with this group, he was torn.

The little ones clung to him and peeked around his legs at Vic. David climbed the stairs with a child on each leg and one in his arms. His own natural perversity was becoming a constant state of amazement to him. Here he was, angry at the attachment forming against his will with Annie and her brood, and at the same time fiercely glad it was he the children were clinging to and not old Vic.

"Shh," he cautioned outside Annie's bedroom. "She might be sleeping."

"She's been sleeping all the time since she got sick," Casey agreed. "How much sleep do you need, anyway?"

"Sleep's the best thing when you're ill," Pop-pop informed her, a bit pompously in David's opinion. "Gives your body time to fix itself up."

"Oh." Casey nodded wisely, but she looked to David for confirmation.

He nodded to her while he pushed the door open as quietly as possible.

Chapter Eleven

Annie woke slowly. Cautiously she checked her symptoms. Lousy. She felt lousy, but definitely better than she'd been feeling. Relieved, she turned onto her side and opened her eyes.

She blinked and opened them wider. Maybe she wasn't recovering, after all. In fact, she must have taken a decided turn for the worse. She was hallucinating.

Her eyes were convinced David was standing on the edge of her bed. She recoiled as this surreal David reached out and brushed hair back off her forehead. A tactile hallucination. Panic set in as she tried to think how to deal with this latest plague.

"How are you feeling, honey?" her dream asked.

"I thought I was getting better until you appeared," she complained. "If I'm going to start having visions, why couldn't it be the Blessed Virgin instead of you?" she questioned querulously. "At least then I could claim a miracle instead of one more graphic illustration of a failing mind."

"Your mind's just fine," David soothed with a grin. "But it's late afternoon now and the light's failing, plus you're still half-asleep. Let me assure you, I'm real and I'm here."

While it was nice of her apparition to try and reassure her, she was unsure how much verisimilitude to assign to the word of ghost. Instead she reached for the nightstand light switch and sat up. She put a hand to her forehead.

"Cool," David informed her, reaching to adjust a pillow behind her back. "I've been checking the past few hours."

"You've been here for a while?" she questioned stupidly, leaving her hand where it was. Impossible. Some sixth sense would have told her. She'd have woken up.

"Yes. Casey called this morning, worried about you. You've been ignoring the vegetables and fruits part of the four food groups again."

Annie groaned. "That's what you think. My stomach hasn't ignored a darn thing I've tried to feed it in three days."

"So I hear, so I hear. Well, take heart, sweetie, Uncle David is here to see you through."

"Great," she groused. "Just what every woman wants. The man she's interested in assuming a paternal role and seeing her at her absolute worst." She knew how she felt. It didn't take much to extrapolate from there how she looked.

"So you admit you're interested, huh?"

"Oh, God." She closed her eyes in embarrassment and wondered again why it couldn't have been Mary or some saint come to visit.

She felt the bed shift and opened her eyes. David was gone. But he was back shortly with a basin and washcloth that he set on the nightstand. "Here," he told her as he dipped the cloth into the water, then handed it to her. "You can wash up a bit. There's no easy way to tell you this, so I'll give it to you cold. Your father's here. He was in my office when Casey called.''

Annie's hand stilled in the midst of rinsing her face. Blankly she repeated, ''My father? Here?''

''He insisted on coming. He's downstairs, but will probably be barging in any moment.''

''You're kidding, aren't you?'' she pleaded hopefully.

David sighed. ''Sorry, but no. Tell me where your brush is and I'll get it.''

''I must look pretty bad,'' Annie worried, ''if you're going to all this trouble so seeing me won't upset my father.''

''You look like somebody who's been sick for a while,'' he informed her gruffly, retrieving the brush from the dresser where he'd spotted it himself. He did not want to tell her how worried he'd been during the hours since his arrival. He'd watched her like a love-starved prince who'd come across Sleeping Beauty. Unfortunately David's kiss lacked the restorative powers of the prince's in the fairy tale, so he'd sat by her side holding her hand, helpless to alleviate her symptoms.

He'd tried a few kisses while she slept, anyway, just in case, and he tried another now, leaning to gently plant it on her forehead. ''You're already looking better. I'll go get your dad. He's entertaining the kids downstairs.''

Annie glanced at him weakly. ''My dad? My dad is entertaining my children?''

''Your dad,'' David confirmed. ''They think it's funny the way he's pacing up and down and growling at the furniture in his way.''

The world had gone crazy, Annie thought dizzily when David was gone. Then she cringed. She'd been determined that she and Craig would make it on their own, steadfastly resisting even her father's emotional blackmail when her mother had died. Time had stretched since then into eight years, and their relationship was still stalled at a perfunctory exchange of cards on appropriate holidays. She knew her father was still waiting for her to come to her senses, which would translate as moving back to Northstream, preferably into his house with him, and could just imagine what he thought of her small, worn home with three days of dirty dishes located—hopefully, at least—in the kitchen, although probably not the sink, and as many days of laundry laying anywhere someone had stepped out of them. Toys and school papers were no doubt strewn everywhere. She sank back down into the covers.

Her father rapped once on the bedroom door before coming in and standing uncomfortably by the side of the bed. "Anne," he said, nodding gravely once.

"Dad," she acknowledged.

He stood there, looking down at her. She doubted he missed the rumpled sheets on her bed, the sag in her mattress or the hairline cracks in the wall behind the headboard. Her father didn't miss much.

"Damn it," he burst out. "You should have called. I didn't know things were this bad."

"Dad, you were as mad as a hornet the last time I saw you." She pleated the sheet between her fingers. "How could I make my first call back a plea for help? I wanted to make it on my own, without your money, before I contacted you again." She shrugged helplessly. "I wanted to be able to say, 'I did it.' I didn't want you to say, 'I told you so.'"

Her father sighed and grinned sheepishly. "The temptation is strong, Anne. Believe me, I'd say it if it wasn't so damn sad to look where our stubbornness got us. The only thing I ever really cared about, gone for eight years, grandchildren I've never met, a business that means less and less to me each day."

Annie looked at her father uncertainly. She'd left a vigorous, sure-of-himself CEO. He'd been a man confident in his decisions both for himself and those around him, especially her. She'd held that picture in her head for eight years. This melancholy, doubtful old man with the paunch bore little resemblance to her memories. All she could think to say was "I never should have let my children go all these years without knowing their grandfather. I'm sorry, Dad."

She about slid off the bed and onto the floor, convinced she'd relapsed and was hallucinating for the second time, when Vic admitted, "I never understood you, child. Still can't figure out what was so awful about having a multi-million-dollar corporation handed to you. But I shouldn't have pushed the way I did. I should have respected your wishes. I'm sorry, too, Anne."

Wordlessly Annie reached and took his hand in hers. If this was a dream, it was a pretty darn good one. She struggled with tears.

"Now," her father said in a much more brisk tone, the one she remembered. "What's going on between you and young Kennedy? If things are getting serious there, maybe something could be worked out in that direction. Good head on his shoulders, tough negotiator. Not ready to take over a company, by any means, but I've got a few good years left in me I could spend grooming him—should he be going to end up in the family."

Annie began laughing helplessly.

Vic looked at her with concern. "Now don't go getting all hysterical on me."

She laughed all the harder. Her father would never change. Not really.

"Women," he sputtered. "Who knows what to make of them?" He eyed her speculatively. "I feel I've got to warn you, though. Kennedy's anything but stupid. Young, but last time I looked that wasn't against the law."

Annie brought herself back under control, although an occasional chuckle still shook her. "No, Dad, there's no ordinance against being young."

"Thing is, he knew you were my daughter. Gave me what for in his office this morning, I can tell you."

"Of course he knows. So what? Don't forget, he was in the office, although in a lesser capacity than he holds now, when I was there."

"Perfect example. Look how he's worked his way up through the ranks there. Boy's got a lot of ambition, make no mistake. Taking all that into consideration, don't you find his timing in showing up here a tad suspicious?"

Annie sat up, supporting himself on a locked elbow. "Just what are you getting at? Spell it out."

Vic sat on the edge of her bed. "All right, I will. I'm wondering if he's using you to come in the back door at Glenn Associates."

"No," Annie whispered the denial immediately. "No, I'm sure he's not."

"It's not necessarily a bad idea," her father hastily assured her. "I used your mother to get a toehold in the business world. Never gave her cause to regret it. Managed to find myself a hell of a mate, too. Kennedy's good stock. If he's willing to take on that army you've got putting him through maneuvers downstairs right now, you could do a lot worse."

Pride overrode every other emotion. Annie sat up straight in the bed and pushed her hair back behind her ears. "I am *not* a charity case," she announced. "I will never marry out of a sense of gratitude that some man deigned to bother with me and put up with my children so he could get a job. Those children are my pride and joy, and I, myself, am not chopped liver." To tell the truth, though, that was just what she felt like right then. There was no need to tell her father that, of course. "I won't combine access to the company with the children and myself in any kind of package deal."

"All right, all right. Don't go getting yourself sick all over again. Just consider it a word to the wise and don't be surprised if he mentions the possibility of a job jump when he proposes. I'm going back down and relieve Kennedy again. Boy's been working his tail off since the minute we got here. You get some more rest."

Annie lay back, stunned. Either she was incredibly naive or her father terribly cynical. She sighed and sniffed a bit, then rubbed her still-sore stomach. Her dad still didn't get it. David couldn't use her to come in the back door of his company. Annie ran a campground now and she wasn't going back. Rural Wisconsin was a bit too remote for a vice president of a Northstream company.

Annie was still too weak to get up, so she lay on the bed and fiddled with the coverlet. What to do?

Her door edged open and David's head poked inside.

"Hi."

"Hi." He came inside. "You're awake. Good." He motioned behind him and all her children filed in one by one. Casey had a box with two cutouts hacked out of the long sides. Mark carefully juggled a plate upon which a single piece of toast rested. Amy carried a glass with an inch of liquid in it, Billy a napkin. Stevie had his blue blanket in one hand and the thumb of his other hand in his mouth.

Annie struggled back into a sitting-up position with David's help. Annie realized the cutouts in the big box were for her legs as David positioned it over her lap as a sort of bed tray. The plate went on the box, the napkin on her chest. David handed her the glass. "Warm ginger ale," he informed her. "That's what my mother always gave me when I was sick."

"Must be good, then," Annie said, taking a tentative sip. "Mine always made hot lemonade."

"Yuck."

"Yeah, I never much cared for it, either." Her eyes ate up David. If she'd been confused about her feelings before, she was far more so now, after her little talk with her father.

"Are you okay now, Mommy?" Casey inquired gravely.

"Yeah, if you're gonna throw up, call me, okay?" Mark instructed, feeling brave now that adults were back in control. "I've never seen a grown-up barf their guts up before."

Her son seemed to be developing definite tendencies toward voyeurism, Annie worried. "I'm feeling much better, Mark. Sorry to disappoint you."

"You're better? It's okay, I'll go get my Wizard's Secret Spells game instead. I'll let you play with me."

"And I'm gonna get my puzzle. We can wohk it on top of the box."

"No. We're going to play Wizard's Secret Spells on the box."

"Want a book. You read me."

Annie looked helplessly at David who firmly took over, shepherding her flock out the door.

"Thanks for carrying all the stuff up here, guys. I couldn't have done it without you. Go on downstairs to Pop-pop now. I'll bet he's dying to play Wizard's Secret Spells, do a jigsaw puzzle *and* read. Your pop-pop is such a great guy, he can probably do all three at the same time. Scoot now. I'll be down in a few minutes, too."

"You're mean," she informed him the moment the children were out of hearing range.

"What did I do?" David asked, contriving to appear innocent.

"Siccing five children on an old man who hasn't been around a kid in umpteen years. You're mean. And bad."

David shrugged. "He deserves it."

Her answer was serious. "David, it wasn't all his fault. I've got my fair share of stubbornness and pride."

He refused to allow her to shoulder any more guilt. "You? Nah, I know you both, remember? He's an old goat's hind end, and you're so beautiful you probably don't even have a hind side. It had to be all him."

Annie smiled in spite of herself. Unconsciously she primped a bit, straightening her nightie and brushing her hair back with her fingers. "I know what I look like when I've been sick. I'm lucky you haven't left the room screaming in terror."

She expected a lighthearted denial, a continuation of their bantering. Instead, he sat down beside her and gently touched her cheek.

"You were so pale when I got here, Casey had to point you out in the bed. You blended right into the white sheets. I was scared to death. Damn it, Annie, you should have called."

"That certainly seems to be the consensus," Annie agreed, remembering her father's identical words.

"Well, you should have."

"Why? Why should I have? You were a camper here for a few days. Was I supposed to go through my old registration forms until I found somebody who'd come take over while I was sick?"

David recoiled as if she'd slapped him. "That's all I was? Just another camper on a long list of previous campers?"

"What else?" she whispered. "What else are we to each other?"

David shot off the bed and restlessly investigated her dresser, picking things up and setting them back. Hell if he knew what they were to each other. "I bought you a case of bananas when I went to the grocer's this afternoon," he finally told her as though that action somehow defined their relationship.

"What?"

"You were out of a lot of things, so I went to the store. They were culling all the overripe bananas and sold me a huge box. I thought you'd be pleased."

"You bought me an entire case of brown mushy fruit? You thought that would make me feel better?"

He turned on her, frustrated. If she was waiting for a verse in rhyme, she'd better not hold her breath. "Well, the grocery store was fresh out of roses." He returned to her bedside. "And furthermore, I would like to point out that the only time I've seen you excited was over a damn bushel basket of green beans."

"The only time? What about the s'mores and the time we waited for dawn together? And I *enjoyed* putting up the beans. I wasn't *excited* over them. There is a difference." She was angry enough to sit up and swing her legs over the side of the bed. If they were going to argue, they'd do it as equals, not with him towering over her.

"Yes, what about the s'mores and the dawn? I suppose you'd do those with any other camper, as well?"

"You know I wouldn't," she told him. "And we are getting offtrack here."

"Are we?"

"Yes, we are." She needed to be firm, stick to the point at hand. Anything else was too confusing. "The point being it takes three bananas to make a loaf of banana bread."

"Three? That's it?"

"You have any idea how many bananas are in a case?"

"Well, I didn't sit down and actually count them, no."

"A lot. Literally bunches and bunches."

"Oh, ha ha."

"David, I am not well enough to bake thirty or forty loaves of banana bread, wrap and freeze them. They're overripe now. They need to be dealt with today."

"Thirty or forty?" David repeated weakly.

"It's just a guess."

He gathered his injured pride around him like a cloak. "So okay, thirty or forty, it is. I dealt with the beans from hell, I can handle the bananas from Hades."

"Fine, you just do that."

"Fine, I will."

"Pop-pop says you need to lower your voices. You're scaring the little kids."

From the looks of the wide-eyed child in front of them, they were scaring one eight-year-old girl, as well, Annie realized regretfully.

"Tell Pop-pop we're sorry and we'll be good, starting right now," Annie told her daughter with a forced smile.

"Speak for yourself," David growled.

Annie frowned at him, still insulted he'd thought a box of produce would curry her favor. Craig would have picked her wildflowers. He would have written her a sweet poem. He would have... Her thoughts lurched to a halt right there. Craig had known how to make the flourishing gestures, but she'd always found them substanceless when she was caught in the reality of raising a family.

You know, when you thought about it, Annie reflected, mushy bananas were really quite romantic, a lot more so than mushy poetry. At least you could make something useful out of the bananas. The pain she felt at the uselessness of her growing affection for a man intent on big-city rat races run far away from her became a throbbing in her temples. She sat on the edge of the bed and leaned over, rubbing them.

"What's the matter now?" David questioned gruffly, although his concern was evident. "Are you going to faint or something?"

"No, I'm not going to faint or something. My head hurts, that's all."

"Well, lie back down, for heaven's sake," he instructed.

"I need to get up. My back aches from all this resting," she complained. "Besides, I've got to go bake forty loaves of banana bread."

"Oh, for God's sake, I'll throw the damn things out."

"No," she insisted stubbornly.

He threw up his hands. "Okay, fine. Be that way. But Vic and I will bake the bread. I'll carry you down to the living room sofa. You can watch TV with the kids, and if we have any questions we'll come ask you."

"This I've got to see. David?"

"What?" he grunted as he leaned to catch her under the knees.

"I'm sorry I snapped. It really was a very nice gesture."

"Yeah, I can tell by the way you were all overcome with gratitude."

He kissed her softly, giving her plenty of time to pull back. She wound her arms around his neck and sighed. "Much better than an aspirin," she murmured. "My headache's almost gone already."

He delved into her ear with his tongue.

She gasped.

He kissed her chin, then her neck.

She shivered.

"I shouldn't be doing this. You're still weak. Your chills are coming back."

"I don't think so." She gasped softly. "David?"

He lifted his face from the elegant line of her neck. "Hmm?"

"You remember where the slits are?"

"There are certain things a man never forgets," he assured her and proved it by finding them immediately. His hands disappeared into the voluminous folds of flannel. He quickly found the soft mounds of her breasts. Lightly he circled a nipple with his fingertip and frowned when she shivered again. "You *are* cold."

"David, I am feeling many things right now. Cold isn't one of them. Trust me."

He covered her breasts with his hands, gently cupping in an effort to warm. "That better?"

Annie lay back limply. What was it about David that he could lay her low with such a simple touch? "Only if you consider lung failure an improvement over chills. Now I can't breathe." She laughed and tried to press herself more snugly up into those cradling hands. "It feels great. Let's stay this way forever."

David considered that. "Things could get awkward at the dinner table."

"I'll feed you."

They lay there silently, content in their nest of twisted bedding. David occasionally nuzzled her shoulder, and Annie murmured sighs of contentment.

"We've got to go downstairs," David finally said. "Casey will be back up any moment to see what's going on."

Annie cuddled closer. "You're probably right. And there's all that bread to bake."

Several minutes drifted by.

"We really need to get up."

"Yes."

"I mean it."

"You're absolutely right."

"This is ridiculous," David grated another five minutes later. "Where is my willpower? My strength of character?"

"I don't know," Annie said with a smile, "but if you find it, let me know. Maybe mine's hiding out with yours."

"Oh, hell. Half the time when I'm around you I can't figure out if I'm coming or going." He leaned over the bed and scooped her up. "Let's concentrate on getting the banana bread baked."

Chapter Twelve

"I'll sign the stinking contract without another com-plaint if you'll just agree to throw the rest of these horrid bananas out. Hell, I'll *pay* you to throw them out."

David listened to Victor Glenn's complaints, unmoved. The sound of the living room clock chiming eleven drifted into the kitchen and David was tired. He'd been up since six and had been at the office since seven-thirty. With Casey's phone call and everything else between then and now, he wasn't in the mood to be understanding or tactful. "Shut up and mash."

"I've been mashing for four hours!"

"Be grateful we're not dealing with green beans. I've been having nightmares featuring those inventions of the devil for several weeks now."

Vic wielded the masher silently for a few more moments. "Listen, we'll hide the bananas down on the bottom of the garbage bag and go buy bread someplace. She'll never know.''

''No.''

''Damn, you're stubborn. What the hell's wrong with buying banana bread from a bakery?''

Having asked a similar question about green beans a few weeks ago, David was versed in the response. ''You are in the country now, Vic. There are certain requirements to be met here. When you live in the city, you visit museums. It's an unwritten law. When you take up residence in the country, you have to get in touch with your roots. Right now, we are linking up with our pioneering forebears, taking part in bread-baking rituals that stretch back through time to earliest man.'' David went back to creaming the butter, sugar and eggs in his bowl as he spouted Annie's philosophy. ''Can't you almost see that chain of humanity we're hooking up to by baking this bread tonight? It goes back to millions of years B.C. and around the globe, as well, all the way to Mesopotamia.'' He was really getting into this. ''These are your roots, right here in this bowl.'' David looked down at the glop in his bowl and the mush in Vic's. It was a depressing concept now that he thought about it.

''You've gone around the bend,'' Vic pronounced. ''And my arms hurt.''

''Man, you are a wimp. You present this tough facade, but what a piece of candy. Lucky for you I won't be around the branch too much longer.''

Vic glanced up sharply. ''You planning on going someplace soon?''

David looked at him, surprised. ''I've been in my present position almost two years, Vic. You know that. Anytime in the next twelve months I should get the call. Of course, the economy's so slow it'll probably be later rather than sooner, but it'll come.'' David didn't want to think about the sense of relief that washed over him every time he realized the economy had put his career on temporary hold. He should be irritated, impatient. He frowned.

"Annie know you're planning on moving on?" Vic eyed him perceptively.

David beat more vigorously. "Sure. How could she not?"

Vic made a negligent gesture. "She watches you. She cares. I can tell."

David made a scoffing sound. "You haven't seen her in eight years, and you didn't read her all that well even at that time or you wouldn't have fumbled the ball back then."

"I didn't fumble a damn thing," Vic protested. "It was her and her cussed stubbornness."

Snorting, David wondered out loud, "Gee, I wonder where she gets her stubbornness from?"

Vic pointed his masher at him. Banana goo dripped off its tines. "Never mind all that, you're evading the issue. It's possible I went temporarily off the deep end when Frances died. People do, you know. It was lonely as hell in that big house all by myself. Maybe I tried to force her hand. I wanted her to come home! Was that so wrong?" Vic stared off, his banana mush forgotten. "Then by the time I stopped taking her refusal to come home as a personal slap, so much time had gone by. It all seemed hopeless. But I'm still her father. I still want to know your intentions."

"Listen," David protested, not wanting to deal with Vic in the role of protective poppa. "I'm not going to clean up the slop you're dripping all over the countertop, so stick that thing back in your bowl and put a cork in it. I do what I can for her because nobody else does. My mother literally worked herself to death trying to support me, only what good did she do me dead? Once I met this family, I couldn't walk away. Those five little faces would have haunted me." He threw the spoon into the sink with a disgusted motion. "Let's get that last batch out of the oven and rinse the pans. Once we get these four going, there's only one more batch."

Vic spooned his fruit into David's bowl, who stirred it in along with a handful of nuts. "I'm tired. I want to go to bed. Reconciliations are exhausting and it's somebody else's turn to mash."

"Whom would you suggest?" David asked as he ran water over the pans from which he'd just dumped hot bread. "Stevie? We put everybody to bed hours ago and your exhaustion will be miraculously cured after twenty minutes on that lumpy living room sofa. Trust me. You have to be beyond mere tiredness to sleep on that thing."

Vic watched as David stacked the four fresh loaves of hot banana bread with the multitude of others they'd baked that evening. "No sane man would do all this work to use up a bunch of rotten produce," he decided. "You're doing it for her. You love her."

"I am linking through time with my forebears," David explained again through gritted teeth.

"Bull."

"Watch your tongue. You want your grandchildren growing up swearing like sailors?"

"Leave the navy out of this. You love her."

David shoved the refilled loaf pans back into the oven and slammed the door hard enough to rattle the windows. He pivoted and faced Vic. "I don't love her. I won't love her. I will not allow myself to love her."

"I had no idea I'd been dealing with a nut case all these months. There's not a damn thing wrong with my daughter the love of a good man couldn't fix. No reason you couldn't be that man."

David snatched Vic's bowl away from him and put both bowls into the sink. He'd finish linking with the pioneers tomorrow. He'd had it. "You are a male chauvinist. She doesn't need a man. She needs help. I am trying to give her that help. Even if she did need a man, there's no way things could ever work out for the two of us. Open your eyes, Vic.

Your daughter loves her life. I mean, I doubt she loves being broke, but running this campground suits her perfectly. I, on the other hand, dislike almost anything having to do with the country. If God had meant you to sleep out in a leaky tent and struggle to cook food over a bonfire that chars the outside and leaves the inside raw, He'd never have invented houses or modern appliances. Yellow jackets, poison ivy and all the other stinging insects and noxious plants that abound in the great out of doors are God's way of telling a man He's given him a house, so use it and leave the woods to the animals." David drowned the two bowls in tap water. "My career is damned important to me and I can't do a terribly credible job of pushing it along from this distance."

Vic threw the masher into the bowls, spraying water over both of them.

David jumped back. "Would you watch what you're doing?"

"What, you're going to melt? You're so stupid, I'd believe it."

David ground his teeth. Nobody could get to him the way Vic Glenn could. Now that he thought about it, he'd originally taken the vacation that had landed him in this mess to get away from old Vic. Talk about irony. "I am not stupid." At least, he didn't think so.

"Oh, yeah?"

"Yeah. I kept up with your machinations the past two years, didn't I? What does that make you?"

"Never mind me. You're the one who can't see past the bananas on the countertop."

"What's that supposed to mean?" David questioned impatiently as he began shoving cooled breads into plastic bags.

"She'd come back with you if you asked her to, son. Can't you see that? Her eyes follow you wherever you go in the room. It wouldn't take much to get the rest of her body in line, as well."

David slammed the loaf he was working with down on the counter. "Eight years later and you haven't learned a damn thing. You're still trying to manipulate her. I can't ask her to do that!" he exploded. "She hated living in the city. I should purposely set out to make the woman miserable? And you think *I'm* a nut case."

Vic suddenly looked much older. Ponderously he walked toward the door. "I'm going to go steam these bones in the shower. You can wait for that last batch. You've got some serious thinking to do, anyway. You might want to ask yourself whether either one of you will be happy even if you do manage to remain noble and separate."

David remained in the kitchen long after the bread was out and cooled enough to bag. He sat in a chair by the still warm oven and mused over how easy it would be to hate Victor Glenn.

Okay, so he'd been a trifle crabby at the office during the month since his vacation. And twice he'd sat in the living room without putting the lights on late at night, entertaining a touch of melancholy. So big deal.

He rose and checked the back door before he began flipping light switches off. He worked his way through the house in that manner until he stood at the bottom of the stairwell. The temptation to go on up the stairs to Annie's double bed rather than on through to the living room was discouragingly strong.

Vic couldn't be right. He *couldn't* be.

David sighed and turned away from the stairs. He hoped the sofa had grown a few more of its tumor-sized lumps during the month he'd been away—no, no, he was away now, he'd been *home* for the past month. It would be nice if Vic tossed and turned along with David for the remainder of the night. After all, he'd been the one happily dropping bombshells in the kitchen earlier.

Creating a makeshift mattress by folding blankets on the living room rug wasn't hard. Going to sleep on it, well—

In what seemed like a very short time later, David propped up one eyelid and tried to call his senses back to order. Every joint and muscle he checked ached from sleeping on the floor.

"David, Pop-pop says he's gonna take us to his house for Thanksgiving. Isn't that the best?"

He groaned and rolled onto his back, blinking in the pale November morning light. "The best ever, Casey. Good old Pop-pop. What a guy, huh?"

The little girl agreed eagerly. "Yes. He says he's going to take us to a *toy* store."

"Wow." David cranked the upper half of his body up into a seated position and leaned back against the wingback, blinking sleepily. It really upset him the way Vic was shamelessly bribing his way into the children's affections.

He should be feeling grateful that their affections would be so easily transferred to Glenn. It certainly got him off the hook. Gratitude, however, was not what he was dealing with just then. Resentment, yes. Jealously, quite possibly. Gratefulness, no.

"Hi. This a private party or can anybody join in?"

"Hi, Mom. I was just telling David that Pop-pop's gonna take us to his house and then we're going to the toy store."

Mark joined in. "Yeah, David, it's going to be totally wicked."

"Totally," David agreed solemnly, although inside, a small green gremlin couldn't help asking if the kids had forgotten all the things he'd sent in the past month. Rotten little ingrates.

Stevie clambered into his lap. The kid was wet. David refused to think about it.

"All right," Annie directed as she turned to the gaggle of children following predictably enough in her wake. "There's a school day to get through before anybody goes anywhere. Go get dressed, all of you, and let's have breakfast."

David helped Stevie up off his lap and pulled the damp fabric off his skin. "You heard your mother. Everybody scoot."

He blinked up at Annie once the room had emptied. "Your father's trying to buy their affections, you know."

Annie sank down next to him on the floor, letting one hand rest on his thigh. "Yes, I know."

David pointed to the darkened spot on his pants. "Watch out," he warned. Then he asked, "It doesn't bother you?"

Shrugging, Annie responded, "He's got a lot of lost time to make up for, and truthfully, he was always like that. Did it to me, too."

David cocked his head at her. "Did it work?"

"When I was their age? Sure. But it won't for long. He'll have to stand or fall on his own merits before you know it. This'll just give him a head start."

Her philosophical response to Vic's mercenary approach to life probably had some merit, David thought. He decided he needed to adapt a more easygoing mentality, especially as the warmth of her body next to his began seeping through his clothing. *Don't react,* he commanded his body even as the fit of his jeans began to change. *Don't do this to me.*

"How are you feeling?" he asked, desperate for distraction. She was obviously better, or she wouldn't be up.

Annie confirmed his diagnosis.

"Much better. Just knowing you and Dad were here made a difference. I really slept soundly last night."

He yawned unwillingly. "That's good." He ended up grunting, wishing he could say the same.

Annie fingered his pants leg.

"Where'd you get the blue jeans?" she asked. "You were in a suit when you got here, weren't you?"

"Ah, yes," David confirmed as he tried to shift into a more comfortable position. "Yes, I was. Casey got me at the office. But I'd been planning to work out at the end of the day, so I had my sports bag with sweats and clean jeans in the trunk."

"Lucky for you, huh?"

He was torn between knocking her hand off his thigh and running away as far and as fast as he could and handcuffing it there so that she could never remove it. It was a tough decision.

"Yes, lucky."

If she gave any inkling she was aware of what she was doing, David was unable to pick up on it. He found her amazingly naive and innocent for a mother of five. That was all that saved her right then from instant ravagement, children and Vic be hanged.

He jumped to his feet, startling her. Taking her hand, he hauled her up. It half killed him, but he kept his good-morning kiss light. "I'm glad you're feeling better, but you still need to take it easy. You scared Casey and the rest of the kids the past few days."

"And it bothers you that Casey was upset."

"That kid carries a lot of weight on her shoulders. Real or imagined, it's there for her." He didn't want to talk about the bond he felt with Annie's oldest, nor how he would miss Casey—and all the little monsters—once Annie was back on her feet and Vic had entrenched himself more firmly into their lives.

"Yes," Annie admitted quietly. "I know it. I just don't know what to do about it."

"Vic can pick up where I leave off," David assured her, both hoping it would be true and not wanting to actually relinquish the task to him. "Now you come out to the kitchen and talk to me while I get breakfast going."

Annie let him drag her along, not sure why they were in such a hurry, but willing to go along with the gag. "I think Dad's already doing that."

"Good," David said. He needed to get back with other people, even Vic would do right then. His self-control needed the boost an audience would provide, he was embarrassed to admit. "That's good. He'll do fine."

Annie gave him an odd look, which David ignored.

Vic had lunches packed in insulated fabric lunch bags. They were lined up neatly on the countertop along with bowls of cereal.

"Good morning, Dad." Annie smiled. "Looks like you've got everything under control."

Vic stopped slicing a banana and subjected her to a piercing visual inspection. "You look better," he finally pronounced. "Sure know how to add a few gray hairs to an old man's head, though."

Annie leaned forward and kissed his forehead. "Were you worried, Pop?"

"Well," Vic cleared his throat, obviously uneasy dealing with his emotions. "You've invested a lot of time and effort in the campground, plain to see. Hate to see somebody else reap the rewards." He harrumphed again, his eyes suspiciously bright as he continued to visually assure himself of her recovery.

"That's my pop." Annie laughed. "Always interested in the bottom line."

"The bottom line here is that group of hooligans you're raising is going to miss the bus if they don't get a move on. Get them down here, Anne. I don't want them racing down the driveway. Liable to fall and get hurt that way."

"Yes, sir. Right away."

Annie left to call the kids, and David watched one old curmudgeon wipe his eyes and blow his nose.

"Fine woman," he announced, glaring at David as though daring him to disagree.

"Yes."

"Good children."

"The best," David softly agreed.

"Well," Vic said and blew his nose again. "Well, once we get the older two out the door, I'm going to take the three little ones for a walk. Got a chance with them, you know. Casey and Mark might be too old to ever really accept me, but the little ones—there's a chance."

"A good one," David admitted unwillingly. He didn't want the little ones bonding with Vic and he didn't want to be left alone with Annie while Vic took them for a walk.

But Vic organized the morning as efficiently as he ran his business. The little ones were dressed and fed in ample time to walk, not race, with Casey and Mark to the end of the driveway to await the bus. Vic brought up the rear like a good general. David watched them go with a sense of despondency.

He ensconced Annie on the sofa with a stack of magazines.

"David, I'm much better today. I don't want to read. I want to get up and do something. The laundry—"

"No, not today," he told her firmly. "I'll take care of it." He picked up a plastic bag next to the sofa and peeked inside. "Here's some kind of knitting. If you don't want to read, work on this, but you're going to take it easy today."

"It's an afghan I was crocheting as a prize for the PTA raffle." Annie sighed. "It's got to be done in a week and a half." She dumped the bag into her lap. Multicolored squares covered her like rainbow-hued snowflakes. She wrinkled her nose as she retrieved her crochet hook from the mess. "I guess I ought to make a stab at finishing it."

"Fine, you do that," David said, almost growling in frustration at the picture Annie made there on the sofa. "I'm going back out to the kitchen to finish linking with my forebears."

"What?"

"I'm going to mix up the last of the damn banana bread."

Annie swept squares off her lap, letting them tumble in disarray to the rug. "I can do that."

David put a hand on her shoulder and forcibly held her down. "No. You stay here."

"Let me at least help."

Victor Glenn was crazy, going off on a walk and leaving David alone with his daughter. Where were his protective paternal instincts? "No, I need you to stay here while I'm in there."

"What—"

He sighed tiredly. "Annie, just do it. For me."

Annie subsided, puzzled. "All right, if that's what you want."

David nodded his thanks and went out to the kitchen. By the time he was done with the last of the bread, he had consigned each and every one of his ancestors to the fiery pits of the netherworld, with a particularly deep, dark hole reserved for any of them that had participated in any part of the bread-baking cycle whatsoever.

Vic Glenn walked in as David rinsed the last dirty loaf pan. Stevie was half-asleep in his arms. Amy and Billy danced around his legs, having obviously lost the last bit of shyness around their newly found grandfather.

"Lunchtime," Vic announced. "And we've got to be quick about it. I don't think Steve, here, is going to last much longer."

David glanced at the teapot-shaped wall clock. Ten minutes to twelve. "Hot dogs, chips and carrot sticks," he decided. "Maybe some hot chocolate. That quick enough?"

"Sure, sounds fine. You all go wash up," Vic directed the children. "Your hands are dirty from playing in the leaves. I'm going to help David. Don't suppose Anne has a microwave hidden around here anyplace," he questioned hopefully.

"Get serious," David returned.

"Afraid you'd say that. Well, we'll dig out some pans and boil the little devils."

They were both used to being in charge. That was the problem, David decided as he and Vic attempted to work around each other in the kitchen. They were both a lot better at issuing orders than following them. Within ten minutes, he wanted to strangle the other man.

"That's way too many hot dogs, Vic. We're not feeding an army here."

"What are you talking about? I put on two apiece."

"Stevie'll eat one, if you're lucky, same with Amy and Billy. They're little kids. They've got little tummies. Annie's stomach might get queasy, we'll give her something bland, instead. You should only eat one with your high cholesterol levels and mine's edging up there. I'll only have one, too. Put half of those back."

Vic frowned at the skimpy pot of hot dogs heating on the range top, clearly unconvinced. "Man, what an old maid. What's wrong with cooking a few extra just in case?"

"Annie can't afford to throw food away and I don't get enough commission off my sales to you to do it, either."

"Well, I do. I'll take full responsibility for boiling up a couple of extra dogs."

"No," David insisted stubbornly. "It would bother her."

"And that would bother you." Vic sighed as he put the hot dogs back into the refrigerator.

"Oh, and make sure you cut Stevie's hot dog the long way, into sticks. Children choke on the circles."

"Now he's a child-rearing expert," Vic murmured wearily.

David carefully poured an inch of milk into the bottom of three glasses.

Vic objected, "There's not enough calcium for a gold fish in one of those."

"We'll refill them as many times as they want," David explained patiently. "But you have no idea how far even this much milk can go when the cup gets tipped."

"They're not going to spill," Vic blustered, but stopped dead as he watched David open the bag of chips and spill them into a bowl with the care of a brain surgeon. "Now what are you doing?"

"Fixing Annie's plate," David informed him as he carefully investigated each chip in the bowl. "Ah, here's a big unbroken one, and look! A perfect, large curled-over one." David carefully set his treasures on a small plate while Victor Glenn looked on in amazement.

"You're nuts."

"If I am, it's your family that's done it to me." He found two more perfect specimens and placed them on the dish.

"If you won't let me give her a hot dog, I'm not gonna let you give her greasy chips. You said bland. Give her apple sauce and toast or something."

David thought about the applesauce-making fiasco. Now *that* made him nauseated, but Vic was probably right. He searched the freezer until he found a bowl of their frozen brew and set it in the sink with hot tap water drizzling over the top. He thought about the chips, weighing the greasy factor.

While he studied the plate, Vic reached for a chip.

"Touch one of the chips on Annie's dish and I'll break your arm."

Vic snatched his hand back. "You're demented, you know that?"

"No, these will make Annie feel better," David decided as he remembered his first night with Annie sharing cola and chips in the front seat of his car while the rain came down in sheets around them. "She's had to settle for the broken, crumbly ones since she had her first kid. She'll like that we saved her some good ones."

Vic shrugged. "If you say so. Where is she, anyway? I haven't seen her since I got back with the kids."

"She dozed off on the living room sofa with her knitting. I'll wake her up when the teakettle is hot."

"Sleeping in the middle of the morning," Vic said almost mournfully. "Anybody I know who has been sick at work says it's a twenty-four-hour bug. She's not snapping back the way she should." He reiterated his decision. "I'm taking the kids back with me, just the way I said I would. This will work out better. They can miss a day of school. Thanksgiving's the day after tomorrow, anyway. I'll bring them back that afternoon. That'll give her tonight, tomorrow and the next morning to do nothing but recuperate."

"You can't leave her here by herself," David yelped in alarm.

"I'm not. I'm leaving you here with her. I don't have a car, remember? I'm taking yours."

"Oh, now just a minute—"

"What? It's perfect. She's got to stay here to rest. If I take her, too, the kids'll still be all over her. You've got a meeting with me tomorrow. I'm canceling it, which frees you up to stay with her. If she's not a lot better by tomorrow, I expect you to call an MD. They must have one around here someplace. See what you can dig up," he said as though all David had to do was lift a few rocks out in the front yard to find a doctor.

David panicked. "Listen, Vic, I'm not sure this is such a good idea," he protested as he dug a few spoonfuls of applesauce from the partially defrosted bowl. The teakettle began whistling, further distracting him.

"Nonsense, it's terrific, you'll see."

"No, you don't understand." He tossed a cinnamon-spice teabag into a mug and poured boiling water over it as he considered how to get across the dangers of leaving Annie in his custody to her father.

"Ah, here's my crew," Vic greeted his grandchildren heartily. "Been gone so long I figured you got lost between here and the bathroom."

The moment was gone, David realized as Amy giggled and said, "Pop-pop, you awe silly. Us couldn't get losted in ouw own house!"

"You never know," Vic came back, waggling his eyebrows comically.

David had to accept defeat and he helped Vic pass around plates before taking a tray to Annie.

Annie woke to a hand running lightly up and down her arm. David's voice called gently, "Annie? Honey, wake up. I've got some lunch for you."

Her eyes opened and her field of vision was immediately filled with David. He was close. Perched next to her on the edge of the sofa, he was close enough that she slowly slid into the depression his weight created on the sofa. Through the layers of both their clothing, she was still aware of his body heat and felt fevered.

Struggling upright, she scooted away from the depression. Her hip and the side of her leg still tingled with a slight burning sensation.

She pushed her hair back off her forehead and tried to clear her mind of the errant feelings running rampant there. "Hi," she tried.

David brushed her chest and lap clear of the brightly colored yarn snowflakes she'd been creating. "Hi, yourself. Get much done?"

Annie grimaced. "One square, that's it. I fell asleep almost immediately."

"Best thing for you," David declared.

"Says you," Annie said, thoroughly convinced that some uninterrupted time in David's arms might prove highly curative, certainly more so than a boring nap.

"Yeah, says me. Now prop yourself up and see how this tea and applesauce go down." He handed her the plate and set the mug on the coffee table by her.

"Applesauce and chips?" Annie asked as she got her first look at the odd menu choices.

David shifted uncomfortably. "Well—yeah."

"Pretty weird," Annie commented as she picked up her first chip and dipped it into the applesauce. "Who fixed the plate, Amy?" Her hand paused halfway to her mouth and she stared at the chip in her hand. Her eyes shifted from the chip to David and back, then she began to get teary. "Oh, David," she whispered as she looked at the three remaining on the plate.

"Hey, now. There's no need to cry," David said uncomfortably. He took the plate away from her and gathered her in his arms, then had to twist awkwardly to fish his handkerchief out of his back pocket. He offered it to her.

Annie didn't have any handkerchiefs in the house. She didn't even have tissues. One box had been used for diapers and blankets for myriad dollies. Another box had been stuffed with cotton balls and tied up around the house as ghosts. A third box had been stuffed down the toilet. She'd never been able to figure out why, she'd just stopped buying them. Noses were blown with bathroom tissue around there, had been for a couple of years. She took one look at the pristine white hankie and cried harder.

"Here, here," Vic blustered as he walked into the room. "Leave you alone for ten seconds, Kennedy, and you've reduced her to tears."

"I thought she'd like them," David protested, sounding puzzled. He held out the plate to Vic. "Get this out of here, I don't think she's ready for food."

"Chips on a sick stomach, no wonder she's upset. Probably can't stand even looking at them." Vic reached for the dish.

"No," Annie got out between sniffles. "I want that. It's the sweetest thing anybody's ever done for me. I'm going to eat every one of those potato chips. I don't know how you kept them away from the kids, but—"

"Oooh, look, Billy, Mommy's got thwee gweat big puhfect chips on her plate."

"Those are your mother's, Amy," David informed the tot without taking his eyes from Annie.

"Mommy, can I—"

"Sure—"

"No, Amy. Today, we're putting Mommy first. She gets them."

"But—"

"She gets them."

Amy went back to the kitchen and lugged her own plate back into the living room. She'd eaten her hot dog and had nothing but chips and applesauce left. "Okay, Mom. Heah's a good one of mine. You can have it. I twied dipping it in the applesauce like David said. It's good."

Billy silently offered one of the dog-eared ones he typically hoarded.

Stevie finally donated one with a crack.

Annie smiled through her tears and realized she'd never felt so loved. David had managed it with a handful of potato chips, a hankie and a box of old bananas.

Chapter Thirteen

Annie waved from the front stoop as her progeny pulled away in David's shiny green Mercedes. They'd never been separated before. The house and campground seemed to develop echoes and shadows even as she and David stood signaling their goodbyes.

She wore jeans and a bulky sweatshirt and David had wrapped the afghan from the back of the sofa around her like a shawl. His arm rested casually across her shoulders. Still, she felt a nakedness without the children racing around. There was nothing between Annie and the man beside her now. A new vulnerability existed that hadn't before.

"If he so much as puts a scratch in that car, I'll murder him."

Annie leaned into David a bit, relishing his warmth on the late-November afternoon. "He's a good driver, David, don't worry."

He tightened his arm around her shoulder in response to her snuggling. "How do you know?"

She shrugged and turned her face up to the slowly retreating sun. There were no leaves on the maples surrounding the house to block it now. She already felt less lonely, less betrayed by their eagerness to go. "He used to be a good driver," she amended.

David was taking more and more of her weight. He grew alarmed. "Annie, are you getting weak? Maybe we should go in and let you rest some more."

Yes, she was getting weak. A delicious lethargy crept through her veins with David's every rumbled word. "No, I don't want to go in. I haven't seen anything but my bedroom ceiling in days. Let's get our coats and go for a walk."

He immediately protested, "Oh, I don't think that's a very good—"

"Just a short one. To the end of the driveway and back."

"That's probably close to a mile."

"Then let's go in and kiss."

"I'll get the coats."

She'd known he would say that and should have laughed. Instead, it stung. David was being far more mature about the attraction between them than she. He was not immune to it—she knew he wasn't—but he struggled against it, not wanting to give in. Obviously he'd looked down the road and seen a dead end waiting and was attempting to apply the brakes now, before either one of them was hurt.

She'd never been blessed with vision.

She ought to just grow up.

But heck, she was thirty now. If she hadn't grown up yet, was there any hope?

"Here, slip this on and zip it all the way up."

Annie tossed the afghan inside the front door and did as David directed. He'd also brought a hat and scarf. It was one she'd knitted of multihued rainbow yarn for Casey.

He stretched the cap over her head.

"It's not that cold," she told him as her scalp protested. "I don't need all this for a walk to the end of the driveway, for goodness' sake."

"Goodness has little to do with what we're facing here," David informed her, sounding slightly grim as he inspected her. "Now bundle up and let's go."

Their stroll to the road and back took twenty-five minutes, exactly. It was then five-fifteen. They had most of an evening and all of the next day to kill.

She unwound her scarf and stuffed it inside the cap before removing her jacket. "I think I'll make some hot chocolate, then go tackle the laundry."

"You sit down," David directed, hanging up both coats. "I'll get the hot chocolate, and the dirty clothes are taken care of. I made Vic do a few loads before he left."

"You didn't." Annie was both horrified and fascinated. It was hard to picture her father doing laundry.

"Hey, don't go feeling sorry for him. He stole my car." And had stranded him there with his only daughter. The man deserved absolutely no sympathy whatsoever.

David installed her back on the sofa and went to make the chocolate. He brought it back into the living room and set the two steaming mugs on the coffee table before sitting in the wingback adjacent to the sofa.

Annie sipped. "So. How's the business world?"

David warmed his hands on his mug. "Fine. Just fine."

Annie nodded. "Uh-huh. Good, good."

David stretched his long legs out in front of him and studied the tips of his sport shoes. "Yep, fine."

"You said that," Annie said with a touch of asperity as she searched for another, hopefully more stimulating, topic. She finished off her hot chocolate, still uninspired and growing depressed at the insight that she communicated through and about her children. Without them, there was a real dearth of conversational material.

David grabbed her mug the second she set it down and rose to rinse them out in the kitchen. "Why don't you take another nap," he advised. "I'll see what's available for dinner."

"I'm not tired," she said. "And let's have black cows for dinner."

He sat back down. "What?"

"You heard me, I want a black cow for dinner."

"Annie, a root-beer float will probably kill you."

Annie waved his objections away with her hand. "No, it won't. I'm much, much better."

"A root-beer float as the main course wouldn't be good for you even if you were in the pink. I was thinking about a can of chicken noodle soup and some crackers."

"David, I have suddenly realized that I don't have to set a good example tonight. My children are gone and, while I miss them, I can also do whatever I want without worrying they'll follow suit. Now let's take my car into town before the stores close and get some root beer, some vanilla ice cream and a jar of hot fudge sauce. Oh, and whipped cream . . . and chopped walnuts."

David was getting sick just listening to her.

"Then we'll stop and get a movie at the video place. A real movie with real people, not cartoons."

"I really don't think—"

"No, David, it'll be great. You'll see. This'll be more fun than sitting around staring at each other all night and I'm much, much better." She stood and twirled around to prove her point. Instead, she got dizzy and had to steady herself on the sofa arm.

David sat in his chair and groaned. "Your father's going to kill me."

Annie would cross that bridge later. Right now, the house was too empty without the children. It left David the focus of her undivided attention, and she was unclear if it would be to either of their advantage to do any indulging along those lines. Too much remained unresolved. Following that line of logic, a few distractions would be beneficial. Taking his hand, she tugged him out of the chair. "Come on. It may be another twenty years before another opportunity like this one presents itself."

Reluctantly David rose. "Twenty years?"

"When Stevie gets married."

He didn't know if he could wait twenty years to gain Annie's attention—and chances were he wouldn't have it even then. "I've got news for you. Kids today come back home after college or marriage in an effort to save some money when they're first starting out. Starving to death your first few years of married life has evidently lost its romantic appeal. I saw an article on it last week in one of the weekly magazines I get, I forget which one."

Annie thought about that, then smiled. "That would be nice, wouldn't it?"

David rolled his eyes. Good grief, marriage with Annie would be public domain material. They'd be old and doddering and still never had had a chance to make love on the living room floor. He eyed the rug, remembering how uncomfortable he'd been trying to sleep the previous night and decided it might not be much of a loss, after all.

He slipped into his coat. "All right, we'll do it, but if you get sick in my car— Oh, that's right, we're taking yours. I don't have a car. Your father hijacked it." He held her coat for her. "Let me have your keys. I'll drive. You lean back, close your eyes and rest."

Annie buttoned her coat. "David, if this is going to make you all that nervous—"

"No, no, it's fine. You're right, you may never have another opportunity. I can understand you'd want to make the most of it. We'll take a chance." He took her arm and guided her out of the house, determined to be noble and brave.

But she didn't become ill from a main course of black cows and hot-fudge sundaes. Instead, she glowed. Excitement shimmered in her eyes as they positioned themselves on the sofa to watch the movie they'd rented. "I feel like a kid playing hooky tonight," Annie told him.

Not a kid, David thought with a touch of desperation. Not even an adolescent. Determinedly David placed the bowl of popcorn he'd made between them. If his hands began wandering places other than that bowl, he would sit on them, if necessary. He would not turn Annie's grand escape evening into some kind of sorry sexual escapade.

Grimly, he watched the opening credits scroll across the screen. They'd rented the movie at a drugstore. He didn't even know what she'd selected. He'd been too busy lecturing himself on how it would be best not to buy any protection since he'd only be tempted to use it, which would be an insult to Annie to assume she'd be willing to... Ah, forget it.

He shifted positions. Hell, his mind was willing to forget. His lower body seemed less adaptable, however.

He jerked upright, squinting at the screen. What the devil? The final line of type was barely off the screen and a couple was, uh, performing intimate acts already. "Look at that," he finally breathed in an attempt to be analytical. "I always figured the guys in the locker room were all talk when they described that."

"My word," Annie returned faintly. "All they need is a trapeze." She'd asked Ned to recommend something, explained the kids were out of the house and she wanted a grown-up kind of movie. Was this the way movies were now, or had Ned misunderstood? If she'd given the impression she'd wanted a skin flick, she'd never be able to show her face in the drugstore again.

"What'd you say the name of this was?" David questioned tersely.

The title she gave was a new release. "I've heard of it," he admitted. "A couple of guys at the office recommended it, in fact." They were obviously depraved and he'd never realized it before. He'd have to watch them. "I thought it was supposed to be an adventure flick."

"You've got to admit that's fairly adventurous," Annie pointed out.

"Annie, you shouldn't be watching this kind of thing." The words were no sooner out of his mouth when he realized how ridiculous he sounded.

"I'm thirty years old, David."

He rose and flicked off the VCR. "Well, then, I'm too young. I shouldn't be watching it."

She looked at him oddly. "What's with you tonight, anyway? You've been uptight ever since the kids and Dad left."

"What's with me?" he asked turning to face her. "Let me tell you what's with me. You think you're ever so sophisticated, don't you? Well, if you weren't a very naive thirty, you'd know why I was uptight." He pointed at the blank screen. "You know what watching that kind of stuff does to a man? Especially when he's sitting next to a gorgeous woman? I want to do that with you. All of it. But I can't, because I'm trying to give the mother of five the respect she deserves. I can't make a commitment here, Annie. And what's sex without one?" He stood over her, glaring down, daring her to respond to his reasoning.

"Beautiful?" she responded. "At least, I think it would be with you."

David wilted under her words. He moved the popcorn bowl and sank down beside her. "Ah, Annie," he grated, feeling torn in two as he moved his hand down the side of her face. "What am I going to do with you?"

"Love me?" she asked softly, holding his hand to her cheek.

"But I can't commit—"

"Just for tonight."

He was still caught in an internal struggle. And also relieved he'd gone ahead and bought the protection when they'd been in town. David glanced, almost sightlessly in the direction of the TV screen. If they'd left the movie on, the hero would probably be getting pulled into a mystery about now. The big dope would probably leave the woman and go for the case. David looked down at Annie and knew what he would choose. The guy in the movie needed to work on his priorities. He, David, was a hell of a lot smarter. He moved the popcorn bowl onto the coffee table and held out his arms. Annie slid into them without hesitation. Her trust in him made him shudder.

If this was her one shot at making love on the living room rug, by God, he'd make it special for her—if he could hold out long enough.

He cast about for ideas. It had been a while for Annie, he was sure. She'd be shy. Slow and easy, he decided. That was the ticket. He let his lips settle gently on her forehead.

She sighed and tipped her face up, letting her eyes drift shut.

He kissed her lids, then her nose. His mouth drifted over her cheeks. He followed a roundabout route to a small ear hugging the side of her head. Finally he allowed his tongue to slip out and join the proceedings. He traced the contours of her ear, blowing hotly into it as he did so.

She shivered and brought her hands up to his shoulders where they traced random patterns.

His tongue dipped into her ear at the same time his hand slipped under her sweatshirt. Reminding himself to be patient, he contented himself with letting his fingers play along her back with no more than the occasional foray to the side of her breast.

Restlessly she shifted positions.

He smiled at the small sign of growing restiveness and kissed her mouth for the first time.

Her lips parted beneath his and he slid his tongue through the slight opening, running it along her teeth.

When she moaned softly, he clamped down with a rigid control on his own responses. This was for her. He did, however, permit his hand to slide around from her back to her front where it found much more interesting territory.

He caught her small gasp with his mouth when he finally allowed his fingers to trace the slopes of her breast. Damn, she felt good. He wanted her more than he could remember wanting anything else in his life. It was becoming harder and harder to take his time, but he was determined to do so. "Annie?"

"Yes?"

Her response was soft and breathy. He was barely able to make it out. "Let's go upstairs."

He shuddered when she leaned forward to trace a line down his neck with her tongue.

"To bed?"

He returned the favor. "To the shower." A cascade of water and an upright position might help him maintain control while he worked on making sure Annie lost hers. He suspected she was far enough along now to find the notion of showering together exotic rather than embarrassing. He stood, then lifted her into his arms.

Shyly she looped her hands around his neck and smiled up at him.

That smile almost killed him. He groaned. "Come on, let's go." He took the stairs as though she weighed nothing at all.

Once in the shower, he'd concentrate on soaping her. He wouldn't let her touch him while they were in there together.

And he tried, he honestly tried. But Annie insisted on hot water instead of cool. Steam billowed into the room, clouding his judgment as it filled the air.

Hot water jetted over his shoulders and down his back, heating his blood, raising his temperature, as he discovered the frustrating futility of trying to cool his ardor.

His stance rigid, he determinedly positioned Annie in front of him, her back to his front and picked up the soap. Working up a lather, he began at her shoulders. "Your skin's so soft," he told her as he got into a massage-type rhythm. He kneaded the muscles at the base of her neck and slid his hands down her spine. Hard to believe, after all this time, all the fantasies he'd entertained, she was here with him in the shower, naked, silk under his hands.

"Damn," he muttered as his body reacted violently to the heat of the shower, to the heat of her. The steam in the shower became perfumed as it picked up the scent of the soap he smoothed across her shoulders.

"David?" she questioned, turning her head in an attempt to look over her shoulder. "What's wrong?"

"Nothing," he assured her. He was dying, that was all. "Turn back around." He kept his eyes straight forward, afraid to let them drift down her body along with his hands.

He lathered up again, reaching around her now, and soaped her breasts. He heard her sharp intake of breath.

"David!"

Annie reached for the soap, backed snugly up against him and reached behind with soapy hands.

She found herself fitted right up against David's body.

David froze. He rubbed against her, arched up into her.

She shuddered and again reached behind her, catching the backs of his thighs, holding him against her.

David lathered the down at the top of her legs and let his fingers slip lower, between her legs.

They both gasped. David closed his eyes and panted, determined to regain control, shocked at how close he'd come to losing it. He was not going to push her up against the shower wall and take her here. She deserved better this first time with him. He would do his best to give it to her. He would be the very definition of the new, sensitivity-trained male. It would probably kill him.

Annie had turned around and was planting little kisses all across his chest. He'd burst into flames if she didn't stop; he'd die if she did. "Annie," he puffed, and the steam between them swirled. "Reach up and turn off the tap."

She reached up lazily and complied.

Gently he lifted her out of the tub, setting her carefully on the bath mat by its side. He pulled a towel from its bar and dried her slowly and carefully, himself much more quickly. Taking her hand, he took her arm in his and escorted her out into the hall.

Annie came out of her sensual haze long enough to glance around and whisper, "Look, we're out in the hall, naked, and nobody's saying 'whooee' to us."

He looked approvingly down the length of her body. "Whooee," he said as he guided her into her bedroom, leaving the door open. Leaning against the open portal, he watched her walk to the bed.

"Close the door," she reminded him as he started toward her.

He grabbed a jar of body lotion from her dresser. "Who's going to see?" he asked.

She thought about that. "You're absolutely right. We can make love with the door wide open." She found the idea deliciously risqué.

He gestured to the bed, and then turned down the spread. "Lie down on your stomach." He was pumping lotion into his hand as he spoke, warming it with his body heat.

She shrugged and complied, willing to do anything if it meant David eventually coming to her that night.

"Thank you," he murmured. For a long moment, he simply stood there, filling his eyes with the sight of Annie.

"Now what?" Annie whispered, not wanting to break the mood.

"Now you just lay there," he told her. "I'll do all the work this first time."

"No, David, that's not fair. I want to—"

"Shh." David came down beside her. "You've been sick. Relax. Take it easy. There will be other times." He began rubbing the cream he'd heated into her back.

Annie went limp, unable to voice further protest. The things David was doing felt too good. *Will there be other times?* she wondered. *Will there?*

David was sinking under a sensorial assault. As soon as he'd leaned over her back, the smell of sunshine trapped in her sheets came up to meet him. It was joined by the scent of her soap, the fragrance of her shampoo and the perfume of the body lotion he was massaging in. He was a drowning man.

Reluctantly he turned her over, knowing he wouldn't last long now. He gave up rubbing the cream in. Instead, he began nibbling his way to her breast. He circled the quivering mound with his mouth, managing to avoid the peak until she was shivering all over.

"Whatever you do, don't stop," she panted when he seemed to hesitate.

"Oh, you like this, then?" He circled closer to her nipple, laving the outermost edge of her aureole.

"Yes," she managed to barely get the word out. "I like this. Very much, I like it."

At long last he pulled the crest into his mouth.

When he stopped, she protested.

"Don't worry," he soothed. "This is just a brief detour." He kissed her stomach, dipping his tongue into her navel. Then he smoothed his palms down her legs, catching one leg behind the knee. He raised it up to kiss and draw little designs with his tongue on the sensitive skin back there.

When her eyes were shut and she lay tense and breathing hard, he used one hand to lightly tease her most intimate flesh. Gently he widened her legs and used his mouth on the sensitive skin of her inner thighs.

She cried out, "David!" It was a plea for satisfaction.

He sat up, looking down at her. He touched her gently with a finger and found her hot and damp. Making a place for himself between her legs, he came into her, then held perfectly still, afraid to move for fear of losing all control.

Annie wriggled under him.

"Don't move," he pleaded, taking several long, slow breaths.

"Oh, right," she came back and ran a foot up the back of his calf. "Why don't you just knock me unconscious? That might work." She moved against him again, loving the feel of him inside her.

Sweat beaded his forehead as he struggled to keep the rhythm slow until he was sure she was right with him.

She moaned. "This is unbelievable. I've never, oh my, felt like this before."

Carefully he picked up the pace while rubbing his chest against her breasts, hoping the slight abrasion of his chest hair on her sensitive nipples would increase her enjoyment.

It worked.

Her body arched, her head fell back over his arm.

He'd have done it again, only his brain was no longer in total command of the situation. His breathing rasped in his throat, and Annie sounded as though she'd just run a marathon. Together they strained toward something just over the horizon. Then, there it was, the magnificent reds and golds of a spectacular sunset.

Quite a while later, David stirred. He rolled onto his back next to Annie and pulled the sheet and blanket up. Now that his blood had cooled, he was chilled and didn't want Annie's recovery set back.

He lay there with his arm around her, thinking. "You know, Annie, we may be novices when it comes to love-making, and possibly the most exciting thing we'll ever do is make love with the door open or the lights on, but I'll put what we just had up against the sexual gymnastics in that movie we started watching any day of the week." He turned onto his side to better see her face.

Annie smiled sleepily and cuddled into his side. "I'm glad."

He held her until she'd drifted off, feeling fiercely protective and totally satisfied. He felt downright poetic.

Chapter Fourteen

David came awake during the night and wondered what had disturbed him. A glance at Annie's bedside clock radio gave him the answer. It read five minutes before three, and beside him Annie grew restless.

Carefully he pulled the sheet and blankets up to her chin and tucked them around her, aware she'd fallen asleep before putting on her nightgown.

A rueful smile formed on his lips. As he crowded closer under the blankets in an effort to warm and comfort her, his body reacted naturally. "Well, damn," he muttered.

He nestled into her back and brought his arms around her. Annie needed rest. She'd been ill. It would be selfish to wake her up.

She quieted under his touch.

David did not.

Time blinked by on the digital clock by the bed.

Finally, when it was close to seven in the morning, light began to filter around the edges of the window shades in the dark bedroom.

"Thank God," David breathed as he began to ease out of the bed. He was pleased that he'd been able to give Annie an uninterrupted night's rest.

He slipped across the hall into the bathroom.

Annie woke as the bedroom door snickered shut. She heard the pipes in the bathroom shudder and water begin to pound.

She lay there thinking. The evening before had been too perfect to even have been a dream. She'd really enjoyed showering together. The more she thought about it, the bolder she grew. Finally she sat up, threw off the covers and sneaked out of the room, still not adjusted to being able to do things like walk around naked in the hallway.

Opening the bathroom door, she was disappointed to find David already stepping out of the tub. "Too bad," she said, turning pink at her own audacity. "I had just talked myself into coming in with you."

David thought about what little good the cold shower he'd endured was doing him now that a deliciously blushing Annie had joined him. "Next time," he assured her, wondering in the morning's cold light if there would be one. "But for now, I want to get some breakfast in you."

"Oh," said Annie decidedly nonplussed by his morning-after brusqueness. "Well, okay."

David sighed, reading her with the same ease he read a spread sheet. Would they ever get their act together?

Annie reached for a towel and strove for nonchalance as she wrapped it around herself, tucking the end in over her breast. She then reached for a second towel and began patting David's back dry. Then she moved to his front, dropping lower, then lower still.

David sucked his stomach in harshly. He was desperately afraid he was falling in love with her and wildly unsure how he'd handle a fishbowl relationship. As Annie had pointed out, the children would be around another twenty years. And old Vic was stubborn enough to remain a thorn in his side for all eternity.

But with Annie here, now, none of that mattered. Not at all. "Annie?"

She grabbed his hand and tugged him back across the hall. "Please, David?" she said, making it sound a favor. "I really want this time with you."

Sensing her need—as well as his own wish—to make some memories to draw upon during the long winters to come, he went without protest.

They managed to drift through the day. Refusing to acknowledge tomorrow, they touched and played, half expecting a child to come around the nearest corner who would either be grossed out by their closeness, or tease them with a less than respectful "whooee."

But inevitably the light faded from the sky. The day had passed.

"Hello, Vic?"

"Yeah. That you, David?"

"Yes, it's me. Listen, Vic, I want Annie taking it easy tomorrow. I'm afraid she'll get overtired if she spends her time racing around preparing a Thanksgiving meal."

"You dumping Thanksgiving on me?"

"You're quick on the pickup, I'll give you that. I'll drive Annie down in her car tomorrow around noon. You can deal with the production of a meal."

"What's wrong with you? You can't help heave a turkey in the oven?"

"Sorry, I'm all baked out from that banana bread. And nursing Annie is hard work. I'm exhausted."

"All right, all right." Vic sighed. "I'll see if the Jewel is still taking orders for Thanksgiving meals. See you at noon."

David hung up, convinced it was for the best. He'd drop Annie off with Vic tomorrow and go back to sending care packages from a safe distance. But between then and now, he intended to create all the memories he could. This was a time he intended to always remember.

"You are bad," Annie informed him, having drifted into the room during David's phone conversation with her father. "There's no reason we couldn't have gotten a meal together."

"Did you want to be slaving all evening and morning in a hot steamy kitchen baking pies and sweet potatoes when we could be upstairs creating our own steam?"

"When you put it like that—"

"Exactly." David gave a satisfied nod of his head. "Now may I escort you up to the boudoir, madam?"

"Ah, I could be convinced."

Again they slept in each other's arms. David, feeling not quite as noble as the night before, still managed to limit himself to waking Annie only once during the night.

In the morning, they were quiet as David drove Annie's car into Northstream, both realizing their brief hiatus was over. He drove up Vic's wide brick drive and turned off the engine. He looked up over the steering wheel to the Glenn family home.

"Damn mansion," he muttered.

"It's even bigger than I remember," Annie fretted.

"Don't go getting cold feet now," David advised. "You're only here for a couple of days. It's not permanent."

He got out of the car, opened Annie's door and escorted her up the driveway. No, nothing was permanent.

The front doorbell went unanswered. David tested the nob. "It's locked." Frustrated, he touched the bell again. "I hope he's not on his way up to the campground with the kids. I was very specific that we were coming here and he vas in charge of the meal."

"Let's walk around. Maybe he's out back with the kids."

"Maybe." He grunted, but was not convinced. They'd robably crossed paths on the highway.

"I smell smoke," Annie commented when they were halfway around the house.

"What?" David took a breath. "You're right." He broke nto a trot. "I hope the kids are okay."

They burst into the yard.

"On your way to a fire?" Vic asked as he looked up from portable outdoor fireplace, obviously surprised by their ush.

"What the hell are you doing?" David asked in amazenent as he realized the smoky odor came from the small laze Vic was carefully tending. "You can't roast a turkey ver a wood fire like that."

Vic puffed out his chest and came at David like a bantam ooster. "Now see here, you're the one who's been telling ne I'm too rigid, too stubborn, that I lost Annie through my wn fault. You want me to lose my grandkids, too?"

"Of course not, but what the hell—"

"They decided they didn't want the same old turkey everybody else was having. Something called a hobo dinner vould be a lot more fun. I'm being flexible, damn it, flexile."

"I told you before to stop swearing. The kids might hear ou."

"Oh, so it's all right for you, but not me? And aren't you he one who told me I should learn to go with the flow so as 1ot to alienate everybody around me?"

David took a deep breath and fought to remain calm. Just once in his life, just once, he'd like a real Thanksgiving dinner. Not something reheated out of a doggie bag from the diner his mother had worked at, and not the TV dinner he'd eaten in front of the bowl games he'd watched in his den the past few years. "Although I ought to know better than to ask," he said through gritted teeth, "what exactly *is* a hobo dinner?"

"Beats me." Vic shrugged. "Ruth, my housekeeper, and the kids have been working on them. They're bringing them out now." He indicated the group of children on the patio at the back of the house hugging their mother. "Looked like meatloaf mix with a potato sliced on it and some cut-up carrot and celery sticks on top of that. The whole mess got wrapped up in several layers of tin foil from what I could see." Vic poked again at a burning log, shifting it a few inches. "Looked disgusting as hell, if you want to know the truth, but I'm going with the damn flow."

David knew he was being unreasonable, but he was feeling very, very sorry for himself just then. "The meat will be charred and the potatoes and vegetables will be hard," he predicted. His voice sounded dazed to his own ears as his vision of his first decent Thanksgiving went down the drain.

"Probably will be, at that," Vic agreed.

"You did this on purpose," David accused. "To get back at me for us coming here."

"I gotta eat it, too, don't I?"

David's arms rose in disbelief. "This is unbelievable. It's a perversion of Thanksgiving, it's—"

"It's fun, damn it," Vic roared. "It's memory making. When I'm dead and gone, those children over there will get together on Thanksgiving with their children and say, 'Remember the year Pop-pop let us make hobo dinners instead of turkey and they were all burnt and horrible?'"

Vic shook his poker at David. "They've gotta be burnt, by God, or the memories aren't half as good."

"You're sick, Vic, and I feel very, very sorry for you," David pronounced and walked away, heading for the patio and Vic's back door.

"Hi, David."

"Hi, David."

"David, hi."

"Hi, David."

"David, David, David! You awe heah!"

"Yes, I'm here, Amy. Did Mrs. Ruth give you Mexican jumping beans for breakfast? You're bouncing all over the place."

"That's 'cause I'm excited!"

"Oh, I didn't understand. And, hi, hi, hi and hi to the rest of you," he said to the children surrounding him. "Ruth," he acknowledged. "I'm David."

"Mr. Kennedy," Ruth responded. "It's a pleasure to meet you. The children do nothing but talk about you. You've obviously been very kind to them and I know Mr. Glenn is grateful, though he'd never admit to such a weakness. The truth is, he's been lonely. Spoiling a few grandchildren will be good for him, I think. Now if you'll excuse me, I've got to get these dinners out to him before he raises the rafters."

Not too many weeks ago, David had believed the same thing. Now he was petrified less spoiling those same children be what he needed, as well. "Thank you, Ruth. I wonder, would you point me to a phone? I need to check my messages."

"Certainly." She pointed to the back door. "Right through there. There's one on the kitchen wall."

"Thank you."

He wasn't feeling nearly as grateful when he hung up the phone a while later. Annie found him staring out the window over the kitchen sink, not having moved away from the wall phone.

"David, is anything wrong? You look sort of grim."

"Do I? Everything's just hunky-dory, Annie. Just hunky-dory."

He drummed his fingers on the countertop next to the sink. Everything was perfect, couldn't be better. Vic was already taking over helping Annie and her brood, just as he'd wanted him to for the past month and a half. No reason to be upset with the message on his phone mail. Only he was. Extremely upset. He slammed the counter. His promotion had come through. It would mean moving to Indianapolis. He'd known the next step up would involve a move. He'd known it all along.

"Damn it, anyway," he burst out. "What the hell's wrong with McKiernan, attempting to go into business for himself with the economy the way it is? Is he nuts? Is he crazy?"

"Uh, who's McKiernan?" Annie asked, not sure she really wanted to know.

"The branch manager in Indianapolis, that's who. The *former* branch manager, I should say. He quit. Bought himself a hardware store. Can you believe it? A hardware store!" David slapped the countertop once more. "It's my big chance, Annie. That branch is three times the size of the one here in Northstream. Its territory takes in most of the state of Indiana and it would be all mine. Almost double the salary, too."

Annie mulled that over, not liking the conclusion she reached. "You'll have to take it. Once you turn down a promotion, your career is dead in the water."

"I know that. I know."

"And what would you be turning it down for? A woman with five kids and a rundown campground in rural Wisconsin? You'd never be happy there and I wouldn't be happy anyplace else. We've only been fooling ourselves the past few days," Annie concluded unhappily.

Everything was falling perfectly into place for him. His career strategy was right on course, recession or no. He could go in peace. Annie would be taken care of by Vic. "Damn! Why now? I needed more time."

Annie shrugged helplessly, her eyes glittering with unshed tears. "Who knows why things happen the way they do? I'd have gone crazy long ago if I tried to figure out the why of everything."

David continued to stare out the window, glaring at Vic's attempts to remove the hot foil packets from the fire. "You know, when I was a kid, I wanted to go camping. I asked my aunt. She said the easiest thing to do would be to put up a pup tent in the backyard and she'd lock the door and not let me in to use the bathroom. Said it would be the same thing, only a lot less hassle. The older I get, the more I realize she was right."

Annie realized David needed to let off steam. She stayed quiet.

"The camper mentality is beyond me, you know, absolutely beyond me." David gestured toward the scene out the window. "Look at him. He's singeing his fingertips off. Explain it to me. How is this fun? You're eating burnt hamburger patties for Thanksgiving dinner when there's a beautiful stove with fifteen different types of electronic controls on it going to waste right here. I keep feeling I'm missing something, and then I think, no, it's them, not me. They're all crazy. I'm the sane one."

Annie cleared her throat, deciding the tirade had gone on long enough. While it was true she sometimes made two or three trips up or down the stairs before she'd remember what she'd gone up or down for, and she'd wait for the occasional red stop sign to turn green, she wasn't crazy. That did it. He'd run off enough steam. "Speaking of dinner, the reason I came in was to tell you yours was done."

"Oh, by all means, let us go out and dine on our charred Thanksgiving burgers."

"Actually, they're not always burnt. Timing can be tricky in outdoor cooking. Sometimes they're still raw."

David rolled his eyes as he shoved himself away from the sink. "Oh, terrific. Listen, Annie, I'm sorry. I'm behaving like a jerk. None of this is your fault. I think I'd better leave. Make my excuses to the family, will you? I need some time by myself right now."

He stopped at the door, looking back over his shoulder. "Amy's out without a jacket, Annie. She'll get chilled. And Billy's not zipped. Vic's not paying any attention to either one of them."

"I'll take care of it, David."

"Yes. You're very good with them. I'll—call you—or something," he finished lamely.

She looked as if she was trying not to cry, and rather than embarrass her he left. He heard her calling softly as he let himself out the side gate, feeling very much the outsider.

"Amy, come slip on your coat. Billy, zip up before you catch cold."

He'd found his car keys on the kitchen countertop. Now he unlocked the door to his precious green Mercedes and carefully backed down the driveway, looking for dashing children. He decided against stopping at the twenty-four-hour supermarket. For some reason, he'd find a TV turkey dinner particularly depressing this Thanksgiving. He had some hot dogs in the freezer back home. He'd make do with those.

He snorted to himself as the car purred almost noise-lessly away from the bedlam at Vic's. Imagine, he owned a beautiful home, not as large as Vic's, of course, but how many were? He could afford a Mercedes, and here he was, reduced to eating hot dogs on Thanksgiving. Well, one thing for sure, he was going to boil them in a pot on the range top *inside* his house. Maybe he'd go gourmet and put a colander on top of the boiling pot and steam the buns. That would show them all.

He swung the car around a corner and continued on a road that followed the train tracks for a while.

Let Vic take over. Let him deal with Annie's stubbornness. He could snap beans with her until the cows came home, for all David cared. Let *Vic* cope with naked children chasing each other through the house yelling "whooee" as they ran. It was nothing to him.

He turned and prepared to cross the tracks he'd been paralleling. "Look, you guys, there's a train com—"

He slumped behind the steering wheel as he waited at the flashing gates and turned red, although there'd been nobody to witness the fact that he was talking to himself.

He'd criticized them for being crazy and here he'd flipped out himself. He'd be ruined for the business world. Imagine a man of his age getting all excited over seeing a train, and then being disappointed because there'd been nobody with him in the car to show it to. Next thing he knew, he'd be calling them choo-choos and running around making whistling noises. He'd sue Mary Ellen for setting him up for ruination. He'd sue Annie. He'd sue Stevie for being so cute, and Vic for being such a pain. Hell, he'd haul them all into court.

He pulled into his driveway ten minutes later, determined to go in and enjoy some peace and serenity. In fact, he'd think of Vic shivering out in his backyard trying to scrape charred ground beef out of a tin foil packet while he ate his Thanksgiving hot dogs in the warmth of his own kitchen.

* * *

There was something wrong with Annie's hobo dinner. It didn't take a genius to figure out what, either.

Her dad's housekeeper had sprinkled every gourmet spice in her cabinet over the meat mixture. The potatoes were done perfectly, not even slightly crunchy, and neither were the carrot or celery sticks.

Her father had rotated and turned packets on a minute-by-minute basis for the entire forty-five minutes called for in the recipe, ensuring an even cooking. Nobody's meat was burnt. Nobody's was raw. It was a culinary miracle, but still she poked at it, unable to work up much of an appetite.

"Isn't this great, Mom?" Casey asked enthusiastically as she nibbled around a potato slice dangling from the end of her fork.

"It's wonderful. You and Mrs. Ruth did a terrific job with the seasonings." The whole thing needed a dash of David.

"Too bad David couldn't stay. Did he say why he had to leave so fast?" Casey queried.

"Well—" she said. Her father was listening and watching intently, as though any small motion she made might tell its own story.

"Eat your meal, Casey," he directed. "You, too, Anne. You've been ill and need your strength."

"Maybe she should go lie down." Ruth eyed her critically. "From the way you described how sick she was, being up so long might be too much for her just yet."

"I'm fine, Ruth," Annie insisted as she took a determined bite of her meat patty. "There's no reason to worry. David took perfect care of me and I'm totally recovered now."

Her father harrumphed at that. He looked at all the eager young faces around him, avidly taking in every adult word and commented only, "We'll discuss this later."

"Dad—"

"Count on it."

She probably could, too. She'd been out of touch for years, was a fully grown woman raising children of her own, but her father would never see her as an adult.

She took another bite of meat.

Truth be told, the fact that she was older and had children of her own made Vic's determined interference a whole lot more understandable. How did one turn off the parenting juices once they'd been turned on? Hadn't it been just last week that Casey had cried her eyes out because Tommy Marnett had taken her hat away at recess and played keep-away with it all during recess? It had taken every ounce of self-control she'd been able to dredge up to refrain from picking up the phone and giving Tommy's mother an earful.

Her newfound insight had her turning humorously to Ruth instead of getting angry. "You've been here for five years," she told her. "You learn how to handle him yet?"

"Don't look to her for help," her father interrupted. "She can't do anything with me. Nobody can. I'm incorrigible. Just ask your young man."

"He's not *my* young man." The temptation to pick up her father's potato and stuff it into his mouth was tough to resist.

"The hell, you say. That boy's hooked. He's just flapping around on the end of the line right now, waiting for you to reel him in."

"Dad," Annie admonished. "Don't swear in front of the children."

Vic rolled his eyes. "Don't you start in on my language, too. Anyway, you'll both see. I'm right. You're wrong."

"Well, it's going to be tough reeling him in long distance. He's moving to Indianapolis."

"What!"

It was the first time she could remember dropping a bomb on her father that left him speechless. He looked genuinely thunderstruck. As satisfying as it should have been, somehow her pain still won out. She turned to the housekeeper. "I guess that shut him up good and proper."

"Kids," her father all but thundered. "Run out to the kitchen and get the ice cream bars. But eat them out there. I don't want them dripping on the upholstery of the dining room chairs."

"Okay, Pop-pop." Casey spoke for the group. There was momentary chaos as the room emptied of children.

Her father leaned forward. "Now," he said.

Annie could almost picture him rolling up his shirt-sleeves as he prepared to get down to the business at hand.

"Perhaps you'd better tell me exactly what's going on between you and young Kennedy."

"That's just it, Dad." Annie shrugged helplessly. "Nothing."

"Damn it, don't tell me nothing," Vic shot back tersely. "That man's crazy over you."

"Maybe he's just plain crazy." She sat back in her chair, remembering David's parting shots.

Ruth stood and began collecting plates, obviously wanting to get out of the line of fire.

"All right, Anne," her father began when Ruth had safely retreated. "You tell me. If he's not in love with you, why would he stay up until two o'clock in the morning baking forty loaves of banana bread for your freezer—" Vic indicated the size of the mound of bread they'd baked that night. "Come on now, what sane individual would do that and then sleep on the floor all those nights he was up there if he didn't care?"

When Annie concentrated on the carrot at the end of her fork instead of a response, he continued, "I've done business with that man for two solid years, and I'm telling you, the past month he's metamorphosed into an idiot. You should have seen him rocket out of his seat when Casey called to tell him you were sick. Thought he had a bee up his—down his pants."

"Dad—"

"And you." He pointed a finger at her. "Sick as you were, barely able to lift your head off the pillow that first night, why you glowed whenever he was in the room. Fact is, you glow if I just mention his name. You're both in love, damn it, *in love*," he repeated as though Annie was so muddled she needed it pointed out. "And very conveniently with each other, I might add. What more can you ask?"

"You just don't get it, do you?" Annie flung up her arms in frustration. The carrot went flying. "We might as well back up the clock eight years. You're still not listening."

"Don't you say that, Anne. Don't you even think it," her father roared.

"Dad—"

"No! The only thing that's the same as eight years ago is your darn stubbornness. I'm flexible now, damn it. I'm more elastic than a rubber band!"

"Then let me talk without interrupting."

"You are talking. Look at your mouth move. The problem is you're not saying anything!"

Annie sighed. "Dad, your analysis is quite probably correct—as far as it goes. I mean, you're right. I—care a great deal for David."

"You *love* him," Vic corrected shortly.

It was past time to admit it out loud. "Okay, fine. I love him."

"And he loves you."

"Possibly."

"Oh, for God's sake—"

"Listen to me, Dad. It's not a lack of caring that's killed things, it's the geography of it all."

Her father sighed in his turn, as though burdened with spelling out simple explanations to an idiot child. "All right, Anne. May I assume he's moving to Indiana for a promotion?"

Annie played with her silverware. "A bigger branch."

"If you really can't live in normal surroundings and have some hidden need to be surrounded by khaki-colored canvas, I'm sure there are campgrounds dotting the Indiana countryside. Sell yours, buy one of those and move."

"It's not that easy. I've got two permanent RV couples who come up from Arizona every summer and stay with me. I can't run a campground during the season without help. During times of recession, campgrounds get busier, you know. People still want to take a vacation, but they economize."

"Indianapolis would only be another few hours travel time for them. They can follow you," her father explained, sounding overly patient and forbearing.

"The children need continuity. They've been traumatized enough."

"They adore him. And change is good for kids."

"Five children is too much to ask of a man. We'd be a burden."

Her father rolled his eyes. "And they accuse *me* of being inflexible. I'm a piece of putty compared to my own flesh and blood."

He pierced her with a look that insisted on seeing into her soul. "Why don't you just admit you're scared right down to the bone? And then why don't you step back and take a look at yourself? You're not the same person you were eight years ago. You could handle corporate life now—if you really wanted to. It all depends on how badly you want him."

Annie sat quietly, her dinner cold and forgotten. "All he's done is give, Dad. All I can do is take. First I'm depressed and he sits up with me all night, then I get sick and he waits on me some more. He runs the children ragged so they'll be tired for me. He boils applesauce, puts up beans, bakes banana bread—all for me. I don't think he's eaten an unbroken potato chip since the night we met. It's so one-sided! How can I let him do that to himself?"

Vic looked up to the heavens in amazement. "How the hell do I shake some sense into this woman? Tell me, please." Then he spoke directly to his daughter. "I haven't heard such a bunch of baloney since Attrison tried to have me ousted as CEO of my own company by spreading a bunch of lowdown, rotten lies about me." He stood at his place, spread his hands on the table and leaned over them. "He's getting *you*, isn't he? And those five wonderful kids out there? Doesn't he get his hands on them, as well? The man's a businessman. He'd be a fool to pass up a deal like that."

"Dad, even today I disappointed him, let him down. Did you know he's never had a home-cooked Thanksgiving dinner? I should never have let him call you yesterday. Look what happened. He gets served hamburger wrapped in foil for Thanksgiving."

"I was being flexible, damn it," Vic roared, obviously taking her criticism personally. "He could try it himself."

"It was my chance to reciprocate some of David's kindnesses and I blew it."

"All right, then," her father said too patiently. "If that's the way you feel, I will keep the children tomorrow. You go over there and make it up to him."

"What do you mean?"

"Anne," he father said impatiently. "Did none of my genetic matter get passed on to you at all? Figure it out!"

Vic stalked out of the room, muttering as he went. ''Go cook him a damn turkey, for God's sake. I'm taking the kids for a walk around the block. There's got to be a higher level of communication with them.''

Chapter Fifteen

At eleven o'clock in the morning on the day following Thanksgiving, Annie pulled into David's driveway. She got out of the car and circled to the trunk, staring up at the edifice David called home.

In her more logical moments, she'd known a branch manager for WCN could afford a nice house in a good neighborhood. But standing face-to-face with this two-story, all brick, center-entrance colonial burrowed into a nest of trees in a neighborhood of equally imposing structures made her flush with embarrassment.

She dragged the turkey out of the trunk and walked determinedly to the front door. She rang the bell. Faintly she heard the first several measures of the *1812 Overture* sound in the house. Sniffing, she decided it was ostentatious to have a doorbell that played Tchaikovsky.

What must David have thought of her turn-of-the-century, tumbledown farmhouse? No wonder he'd seemed taken aback at times by the antiquity of the kitchen she preferred to think of as quaint.

"David." She nodded self-consciously when he opened the door. "Were you working?" she asked, noticing he wore his glasses.

"Annie?" David inquired blankly as he stared at the apparition on his stoop. He took off his reading glasses and shoved them into his shirt pocket. Then he managed to get a grip and stepped forward to relieve her of her burden. He moved back to allow her to enter. "What are you doing here? Why am I holding a turkey? What's going on?"

Annie was unsure exactly how to explain her presence. What was she doing here? What was the point in dragging out the farewells? He was leaving. Period. End of story.

"I'm here to make you a home-cooked Thanksgiving dinner." She pointed to the turkey cradled in his arms. "That's the main course." Her eyes swept the two-story foyer with its magnificent chandelier hanging down from on high. A perfectly appointed living room done in cream, Wedgwood blue and burnt sienna opened off one side of the foyer. It was complete with an inviting sunken conversation area in front of the fireplace. Off to the right was a dining room with upholstered chairs and a wonderful glass-topped Ionic column based table. "David, this is beautiful. I can understand your not wanting to leave it for a listing tent or a rundown farmhouse."

Annie trailed through his home after him as he went back to the kitchen and put the bird on the counter. "Do you have anything else in the car to bring in?"

She nodded and he started back toward the front door.

"If you really want to compare houses, Annie, think about this. You've got a home filled with laughter and warmth." He shrugged. "I've got a professionally decorated shell."

Annie glanced around as they went back through the foyer. "Some shell." She was still doubtful.

He went outside and stood by her trunk. "You want all this stuff brought in? What army are we feeding?"

Annie looked at the groceries huddled in the trunk. Three more bags were filled with apples, sweet potatoes, marshmallows, regular potatoes, bags of stuffing, flour, cranberry sauce, green beans, celery, carrots, onions, whipped cream and a number of other items. She shook her head. "No. Not an army, David, just you. It's the only thing I can think of that I can give to you. This is twenty-eight years of missed or reheated diner Thanksgiving dinners."

She rubbed the back of her hand across her nose and shivered slightly in the November air. "I'm sorry about yesterday. Sorry I'm a day late meeting your needs when all you've done for the past month and a half is try and meet mine. But you know me by now. Sometimes a day late is as good as I can get it together."

David's eyes shifted from the bags in the trunk to Annie's face. "You don't have to apologize for yesterday, Annie," he said in a low voice. "And you don't have to cook me a dinner. I did a lot of thinking last night. I was out of line." He stuck his hands in his jeans pockets and wondered why he found it necessary to bare his soul out on the cold driveway. "The fact is, when I heard that message on my machine, I kind of flipped out."

Slowly Annie reached into the trunk and retrieved a bag. "But why? It's what you've been waiting for. You knew it was coming, you told me all about it. I know why I'm upset, but why are you?"

David hefted the other bag and slammed the lid. Side by side, they walked back to the house. "That's what I couldn't figure out. Everything was working out perfectly, on the surface. Vic was back in your life. I didn't have to feel like I was abandoning you as I took this next step. He would be there to take my place and help you out with the kids and the campground. I was off the hook.'' He kicked the front door shut with the toe of his shoe. They trailed back to the kitchen.

''But you know what? Everything Vic did, every time the kids turned to him for something or talked about Pop-pop taking them to the toy store, I got annoyed.''

Annie set the oven. She took the turkey over to the sink and slit open the plastic covering. ''How come?''

David shrugged as he opened a cabinet door in search of a pan big enough to hold the bird. ''Makes me sound pretty perverse, doesn't it? It was exactly what I was angling for and then it made me mad as hell. How's this pan?''

Annie was done rinsing the bird. ''That's fine. Can you find a bowl so I can mix up the stuffing?''

David ducked back down and began routing through the cabinet again. ''I suppose you want all those apples peeled?''

She pushed her hair back off her forehead after wrestling the turkey into the pan David had provided. ''I'll do it.''

''I can help.''

''I want to do this for you, David. I need to show you I can give, too.''

David placed a bowl on the counter and unwrapped a stick of butter to put in after glancing at the directions on the bag of corn stuffing. ''You think I don't know you can give?'' he asked as he opened the microwave door and set it long enough to melt the butter. ''That's all I saw you do. You were being drained dry. It was killing me to watch.''

''It was?''

''Of course it was. At first I think it was all mixed up with guilt over my mother dying from working three jobs and trying to support me.'' He removed the bowl from the microwave when it beeped and began adding the various other items the back of the bag called for. ''But I realized yesterday it had changed, and I don't know when. But thinking back, I realized the whole time I'd been complaining, I'd been enjoying the things we did together, even the beans from hell." He stirred the contents of his bowl. "It was fun working with you and the kids. Did you bring any of the applesauce we brought up for Vic?"

"Yes, there's a container in one of the bags. And the bag of beans is one we froze, too. It seemed appropriate for a Thanksgiving meal."

"Yes," David responded thoughtfully. "It does."

"We should have brought some banana bread, too."

David shuddered. "No thanks. That adventure is still too recent in my memory to be properly grateful for it."

Annie held the neck of the turkey open while David shoveled stuffing in. "Maybe once you've been in Indianapolis two or three months, you'll be able to look back and actually laugh."

David closed the oven door on the turkey and turned to a drawer to retrieve an apple peeler. "Maybe," he said without looking at her. Once he was in Indianapolis, he worried he'd never smile again. He started on the first apple, knowing it was from the small overaged orchard that guarded the entrance to the campground. "Annie?"

She'd rinsed out the stuffing bowl and was measuring flour and lard into it now for the piecrust. "Yes?"

"It would be hard to uproot six people, wouldn't it?"

The sadness she'd shaken rushed back in. "Yes, David, it would. Very."

He nodded in acknowledgment and kept his eyes on the length of thin peel he was removing from the apple in his hand. "A lot harder than one person making a change."

"I doubt moving to Indiana will be a snap for you, but you'll have the people in the office. That'll be adult conversation for you, at least during the day."

David picked up the next apple. "A mother staying home with young children wouldn't have even that much contact, I guess, but that isn't what I meant."

Annie dumped her mixture onto the counter, kneaded it a few times, then began rolling it out. "Then what did you mean?"

David was no longer used to being unsure of himself. His position at WCN demanded he be able to make decisions. Right now, he felt as though he were picking his way through a mine field. "I mean, for example, what if I came to you?" He refused to hold his breath. "What if I free-lanced for a while? Until the kids are gone?"

Alarmed, Annie looked up. "Oh, no."

But David hadn't been a salesman all those years for nothing. There'd been a glint of something in her eyes that had said yes, or at least maybe, while her mouth had been busy saying no. "Now, Annie, don't be hasty," he said. "I realize I'd never be able to write poetry like Craig. I've worked at it for over a month and the only style that seems to suit me is limericks. What do you think of:

"There once was a woman named Anne,
Who kept all her love in a pan.
She stirred it with care,
Leftovers to spare,
That lovely young woman named Anne."

Annie struggled desperately to control her eyes, and her voice wavered a bit. "That's awful," she said.

He'd known it was, of course. "My loving you wouldn't be enough, then? I realized quite a while back that I did, you know. Fought it like crazy, of course—because of the kids. Then last night as I was coming home, I sat at the railroad crossing and realized how attached I'd gotten to them, as well." He paused. "There'd be no poems, you know." He needed to be clear that all she'd be getting was a mundane, hard-working man who'd stay by her side and love her, not a romantic.

Annie met his eyes. Over the past year, she realized, she'd proven she could make it on her own. It was easier to share the burden, of course, but she could do it. She no longer wanted to. No, she wanted to go to sleep next to David and wake up with him at her side. She would have thrown her arms around him and hugged him, but her hands and shirt-front were well floured by then. "Oh, David," she whispered. "Your loving me is more than enough. But I can't ask it of you. You'd be giving up your career for me. And then there're the kids. Remember, it isn't just me, there are five of them, as well. They'd get to you after a while. Heck, they get to me sometimes, and I'm their mother."

"You don't think I'd make a good father for them?" How could she think that? "I admit I haven't much experience, but I'm a fast learner. There must be parenting classes someplace I could take."

She was shocked he'd interpret her noble rejection in that way. "David, you'd make a wonderful father! It isn't that at all. Why, just look how you've changed my own dad. You saw how hard he tried to bend yesterday. That was all your doing."

"Don't remind me," David growled.

Annie made a sound halfway between a laugh and a sob as she lifted the piecrust into the pan, wanting it done quickly so she could rinse her hands and go to him. "Come on, it was kind of sweet and funny to see."

David finished the last apple. "Maybe in ten or twenty years I'll see the humor in yesterday."

"In ten or twenty years, Casey will probably show up with her children and want to make hobo dinners for Thanksgiving like the kind she'd made as a kid with Pop-pop, you know that, don't you?" Annie sighed as David made a pained face. "I wish there was some way, David, because I love you, too. The Glenn stubbornness was insisting I stand on my own two feet, but I've got to tell you, those were the loneliest two feet in town. There was an emptiness inside me these past few weeks that nothing seemed to fill until you came back. It was almost worth getting the flu. It's just so much to ask, though..."

David heard the yearning in her voice and reveled in it even while he was torn. She was right. What he was offering to do scared him. He'd be giving up the job security that had meant so much to him and taking on quite a responsibility with the same stroke. But in the middle of a sleepless night, sometime just before dawn, David had recognized that path was where his happiness lay. "You're not asking, Annie, remember that. I'm offering. In fact, I'm pleading."

She looked at him with such wanting, her hand hovering motionless over the bowl she was slicing apples into, that he knew he had her. One more push. He came up behind her and ran his hands up her sides. "Please?" He nuzzled into her neck.

She quivered. He felt it and pressed his advantage. "Say yes," he growled into her ear. "I'll take a consulting position with WCN and communicate by modem out of your house. It'll all work out, you'll see."

"David, are you sure?"

"I'm positive."

"Well—then, yes," she breathed happily. "Let's do it."

"Amen to that. Let's throw that turkey into the oven and go do it!"

"David! I meant we'd get married."

"That, too. But first things first. Every good executive knows how to prioritize. And, Annie, I was a hell of a good executive in my time. Listen to this. I'm going to light the living room fireplace. This may be our only opportunity to make love on the living room rug for twenty years, so let's do it up right. I think I may even have some white wine in the back of the fridge. How's that for wild and crazy?''

"Pretty impressive."

"Damn right. When we're up all night with sick kids, we'll have this to think back on."

Things worked out just fine on the living room rug. David remembered to open the flue in the nick of time and the fire snapped, popped and cheerfully ignored their sounds of love. Finally, when they lay limp and spent before it, David watched its golden light flicker warmly over Annie's flushed body. The flames themselves were reflected in her eyes, he discovered and groaned. "God, Annie, if I'm old and gray by the end of next year, don't blame the kids. It'll be because of you. You're going to wear me out, I know it. I already want you again."

Annie laughed. "Now, David, I wouldn't want you wearing yourself out before your time. We'll develop a schedule," she teased, sure of her womanliness for the first time in years. "No more than once every three or four days, how about that? Maybe once a week when you hit thirty in a couple of years."

"No, no," David denied virtuously. "A man does what he must. I'm sure it's a matter of conditioning, like any other exercise," he explained. "We just have to get into shape, that's all." He let his hand fall to her breast. "See? This is a perfect example. Your breast is out of shape."

Annie looked down. "It is?"

David was amazed she couldn't see what was so clear to him. "Well, of course it is. Now when your arms are out of shape, you do push-ups. When your breasts are out of condition, you do this." He began kissing and nibbling the pink and white mounds, pleased when the mauve nipples began to peak. He leaned back to survey his handiwork. "Three, four times a day should probably do it."

"Three or four times *a day?*"

"Oh, yes."

Annie let out a wondering breath as his finger drew circles around one peak. "I'll have to rely on you to know what's best, of course."

"Just leave it all to me." David patted her shoulder reassuringly. "Now let me show you..."

That was when the doorbell rang. And rang. And rang some more.

David exhaled. It came out like the hiss of an angry radiator. "Who can that be?"

Annie had a feeling of foreboding and began scrambling into her clothing. "It doesn't sound like they're going away, does it?"

David pulled his jeans on. "No, it doesn't." Angrily he strode to the door and yanked it open. His mouth fell open. "Vic, what the hell are you doing here?"

"Don't swear in front of the children," Victor Glenn admonished. "Looks like you two have gotten things worked out. Kept telling myself neither one of you were totally stupid."

David leaned back against the lintel in resignation. "Vic, what are you doing here? What do you want?"

Vic nudged him back inside the door before turning to the children he had in tow. "You children can all go to the park we saw at the end of the block when we drove in. Casey, you and Mark are in charge. I'll come get you in twenty minutes." He watched them take off happily down the street before shutting the door and turning to David. "Need to get a shirt on, son. Man could catch his death running around like that."

The older man peered around David and looked pleased at the sight of his daughter hastily tucking her blouse in. "And where else would I be," he inquired, sounding gleeful, "for Thanksgiving Take Two, other than in the bosom of my family and those who love me?"

David did an exaggerated double take. "You mean there are people who do?"

"Don't be a smart aleck, son." Vic shrugged philosophically. "Besides, you've got the damn turkey."

"Don't swear."

"Then fork over some of the food. I gave Ruth the day off and I've got a hankering for some of Annie's apple pie."

David sighed. "All right, all right."

"For a man who's about to get a company as a wedding present, you're not terribly gracious."

"I beg your pardon?"

Annie just smiled. "Dad, he never mentioned the company. He's going to consult from the campground. He just wanted me. And the kids."

David turned to her, stunned. "Is that what you thought? That I'd come on to you to get my foot in Vic's door?"

Annie put her hands to her breast in a show of innocence. "Not me, David." She pointed at her father. "Him."

He turned back to Vic, jabbing a finger at him. "When pigs fly, Vic. That's when I'll go to work for you. When pigs fly."

Vic wheeled back toward the door. "I can see this isn't the time to discuss it. We'll talk about it after I finish arranging for the corporation's move to Kenosha. Easier for you to commute to Kenosha, I think. Now when I told the children you'd never had a decent home-cooked Thanksgiving meal, they worked in the kitchen all morning. We've got a few offerings of our own out in the car I need to go get."

As he passed his daughter, he stage-whispered, "Don't you worry, I'll work on him."

"Dad," she whispered back, "I honestly don't care what he does. He's there for me in ways nobody else ever has been. Whatever he chooses to do is fine with me."

Her father harrumphed, then beat a retreat. "We'll see about that," he muttered as he opened the front door. "We'll just see."

"When pigs fly, Vic," David called out the door. "Remember that. When pigs fly." He turned back to Annie. "The man is unbelievable. I ought to lock the door on him."

But she knew he wouldn't. "Come on. Let's go check on the things in the oven."

He came to her, looped his arms around her and looked down into her eyes. "Annie?"

Annie hugged him. "I know, I know, he's impossible. But it's something to think about. You could handle him."

"Would that make you happy, Annie? Is it what you want? To help your dad keep the company in the family?"

"I meant what I said. All I want is you. When I needed somebody, you were there. If this is something that might give you the best of both worlds, and it's in my power to give it to you, then so be it. David, I love you."

"I love you, too," he whispered into her hair. "I may never write you a poem worth the paper it's set down on, but I swear to you, I'll always be there for you."

They stood quietly, savoring the moment. Then Vic stomped in the front door, still muttering under his breath. He took one look at their single, melded form and stomped straight back to the kitchen, not even attempting to pass off his packages.

Annie smiled at his retreating back while David just shook his head in despair.

"How that man thinks we could work together for even two seconds without killing each other is beyond me. Is he nuts? Is he crazy?"

Annie kept her counsel on whom she thought would win this particular battle of wills. Instead, she teased, "Look at it this way, David. We can pawn the children for a weekend with Pop-pop every now and then while we work on our conditioning in front of the fireplace.''

David's eyes squinted as he mulled that over. ''Yeah. Good idea.'' He had no intention of telling her just what a perfectionist he was at certain things. It could take a long time to get into perfect shape. It might take a lot of practice weekends, indeed, before they had it down pat. Putting his arm around her, he directed her toward the kitchen and Thanksgiving Take Two.

There was a young man named Dave,
Who tried quite hard to behave.
He borrowed a family
While camping unhandily
And stayed with love, not poems, to misbehave!

* * * * *

For all those readers who've been looking for something a little bit different, a little bit spooky, let Silhouette Books take you on a journey to the dark side of love with

SILHOUETTE
Shadows™

If you like your romance mixed with a hint of danger, a taste of something eerie and wild, you'll love Shadows. This new line will send a shiver down your spine and make your heart beat faster. It's full of romance and more—and some of your favorite authors will be featured right from the start. Look for our four launch titles wherever books are sold, because you won't want to miss a single one.

THE LAST CAVALIER—Heather Graham Pozzessere
WHO IS DEBORAH?—Elise Title
STRANGER IN THE MIST—Lee Karr
SWAMP SECRETS—Carla Cassidy

After that, look for two books every month, and prepare to tremble with fear—and passion.

SILHOUETTE SHADOWS, coming your way in March.

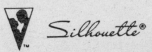

Silhouette®

SHAD1

Take 4 bestselling love stories FREE
Plus get a FREE surprise gift!

**Silhouette Books
is proud to present
our best authors,
their best books...
and the best in
your reading pleasure!**

Throughout 1993, look for exciting books
by these top names in contemporary
romance:

CATHERINE COULTER—
Aftershocks in February

FERN MICHAELS—
Whisper My Name in March

DIANA PALMER—
Heather's Song in March

ELIZABETH LOWELL—
Love Song for a Raven in April

SANDRA BROWN
(previously published under
the pseudonym Erin St. Claire)—
Led Astray in April

LINDA HOWARD—
All That Glitters in May

When it comes to passion,
we wrote the book.

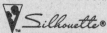

Silhouette

SPECIAL EDITION

It takes a very special man to win

That SPECIAL *Woman!*

She's friend, wife, mother—she's you! And beside each Special Woman stands a wonderfully *special* man. It's a celebration of our heroines—and the men who become part of their lives.

Look for these exciting titles from Silhouette Special Edition:

January **BUILDING DREAMS** by Ginna Gray

February **HASTY WEDDING** by Debbie Macomber

March **THE AWAKENING** by Patricia Coughlin

April **FALLING FOR RACHEL** by Nora Roberts

Dont miss THAT SPECIAL WOMAN! each month—from your special authors.

AND

For the most special woman of all—you, our loyal reader—we have a wonderful gift: a beautiful journal to record all of your special moments. See this month's THAT SPECIAL WOMAN! title for details.

TSW1